KINDRED SPIRITS

FRANCES PAIGE was born in Glasgow between the Wars, but has lived in the North of England for many years. She took up first painting and then writing with great success, and is the author of nearly thirty novels, including the popular 'Sholtie Burn' series.

FRANCES PAIGE

Kindred Spirits

This edition published by Grafton Books, 1999

Grafton Books is an Imprint of
HarperCollins*Publishers*
77–85 Fulham Palace Road,
Hammersmith, London W6 8JB

This paperback edition first published by HarperCollins*Publishers* 1997
1 3 5 7 9 8 6 4 2

The author asserts the moral right to
be identified as the author of this work

ISBN 0-26-167351-3

Set in Postscript Linotron Palatino by
Rowland Phototypesetting Ltd
Bury St Edmunds, Suffolk

Printed in Great Britain by
Caledonian International Book Manufacturing Ltd, Glasgow

For Anne, my kindly critic

BOOK 1

1970

One

'You must miss Van like hell, Hal,' Mish said. 'God, what a cryptic collection of abbreviations, Van for Vanessa, Hal for . . . ?'

'Harold. Bluff King Hal.' Hal Purvis, his brother-in-law, grinned. 'Mish for . . . ?'

'Hamish. Can't you hear the skirl of the bagpipes? I anglicized my name when we moved to Bucks. I was afraid my schoolmates would laugh at me.'

'As long as you didn't wear a kilt. Yes, I do miss Van like hell. We've only had that Easter weekend together since we got married, when I flew back to Glasgow. I miss Sam too. He's like a real son to me, not a stepson.'

'Shall you have any of your own?'

'Not until Van gets her Diploma. She's a real wee Scots lassie. First things first, she says.'

'She's an odd one, my sister. Living with black Ebenezer, having his child. It was pity, you know, not love.'

'She's a fount of pity.' Hal's heart swelled, he felt his eyes grow moist. He thought of her while Mish talked, her quiet exterior, her capacity for compassion. And especially just now, compassion and love for Bessie, that redoubtable woman who had looked after the family for so long and was dying of cancer.

The coming of spring made him miss her more. Even in New York you could feel it. Lovers sat or lay in

Central Park, skateboarders weaved between joggers, children clutched silver balloons bought at the gates, licked ice-cream cones. He found evenings in his apartment unbearably poignant without her. He hoped he wasn't making a nuisance of himself to her brother by dropping in.

Karin, Mish's wife, came into the room, beautiful in her early pregnancy, her skin dusky with health, her eyes full, luminous.

'Sit down, my love,' Mish said, patting the sofa beside him.

She smiled at Hal. 'What concern! It's for the content, not the container.' She sat, kissing Mish lightly on the cheek. 'Fusspot!'

'Do you know what you two remind me of?' Hal said. 'That painting in the Rijksmuseum, the Rembrandt. Have you noticed the tender way her hand rests on her tum?'

'"The Jewish Bride".' Mish knew. 'Better than the "Night Watch", even. Particularly apt in our case.'

'Are your family reconciled now to this Gentile you've married?' Hal asked Karin.

'Yes, at last. It's the prospect of a grandchild that's gentled them.' The look which passed between her and Mish drove Hal to his feet.

'Well, I'd better get back. I'm going to ring Van tonight. If I hear of any Rembrandts going cheap for your gallery, Mish, I'll let you know.'

Mish was on his feet too. 'Do that thing. Sometimes I get fed up with modern painting. It's so derivative, although they'd be the last to admit it. I'd give a lot for the old master's chiaroscuro, that warmth.'

'We could have given you supper,' Karin said. Hal shook his head smilingly.

'Drop in any time, old chap.' Mish saw him to the

4

door. 'But not next week, remember. We'll be busy getting settled down in Westchester, our Happy Valley.'

'You're not going to get rid of me, sad to say. I'll be scouting about that area for my project.' He was producing an art book on the Hudson Valley painters.

'That's why we chose the place,' Mish laughed. 'Hey, do you remember me saying to you the first time you came to New York that I'd be miserable living in the country? Famous last words!'

'But you can't beat it.'

'Living in the country?'

'No, the nesting instinct.' They laughed together.

Going down Madison towards his apartment on Forty-sixth Street, Hal felt obscurely envious, an unhealthy emotion, he told himself. And bereft. The Laidlaws' ungrudging hospitality in New York had been a great support to him. At least, he still had an excuse for dropping in on them when they moved out of the city. He smiled. It was comical to see the change in Mish, that hard-headed dealer in paintings, with the prospect of fatherhood. Karin wouldn't put such emphasis on her surroundings. Nor was she quite so starry-eyed as Mish. Being a mother would have to run in tandem with her career.

And yet, that exchanged glance ... Hal had a surge of desire for Van, a basic desire which must have been reflected in his eyes, because a smart, mini-skirted girl passing him smiled faintly, seemed to hesitate. Couples were strolling arm-in-arm, stopping to read menus, it would have been so easy ... he quickened his step, looking straight ahead. His philandering days were over, he told himself, the tally-ho, the chase, he was a respectable married man with an enigmatic girl in Glasgow who was his wife, whose shy exterior concealed such passion, for love, for the deprived and unfortunate, for her son, Sam, and luckily, for himself.

He had felt a crying need for her goodness when he had first met her, as well as for her body. And it had been two for the price of one, he had told her, because of the love-child she'd had to that 'black Ebenezer', that poor cripple who had died without ever having seen his son, or wanting to see him.

Now he was in midtown, and the roar of the traffic was in his ears, that peculiar New York sound so different from London's, which seemed more muted, more constant, and not punctuated to the same degree with the high yelps of sirens, of honking horns, over-excited sounds as if the city could not contain its exuberance.

Where Hal lived satisfied his love of urban life, with the Rockefeller Center nearby, the Central Station for any quick exoduses he wanted to make, the Algonquin Hotel bar for the occasional nostalgic drink, and most of all the New York Public Library which was private, not public, and where he went most days walking between Patience and Fortitude, the pink marble lions which flanked its steps.

He knew he was not a patient man, which was why New York pleased him with its febrile excitement, but the two lions gave him a feeling of subdued rectitude every time he went past them in search of information about the Hudson Valley painters.

He pushed through the crowds, reflecting that he wasn't ready for sitting back in some suburban heaven. When he finished this assignment they would live in London. He still had his Bayswater flat. Van would get a job as an almoner in a hospital nearby and they would find a school for Sam. He remembered passing one in Bishopstone Road. Van would like it. There would be visits to Hyde Park, to the Zoo, to Kew Gardens. It would be a good threesome. He liked being appealed to as a father by Sam. Those huge brown eyes with the faintly yellow whites, a beautiful child, like quicksilver, Puck, sometimes sly . . .

Painless fatherhood, preparation for children of his own, a childhood for them which he had never known with his own parents, who had shuffled him off throughout his younger days then shuffled themselves off fairly quickly, a few years after they had retired to Bournemouth.

He remembered the misery on their faces when he had visited them in the big hotel on Canford Cliffs. 'There's no one to know,' his mother had said, still with her yellow hair, her pale tended hands which had never known housework . . . Now his feet had taken him round the corner of his street, he had reached his apartment block, he went into the foyer and strode towards the elevator. His heart sank. Miss Kaplan, one of the occupants, was waiting there, and she turned to greet him, her face glowing with pleasure.

Ellie, she had insisted he should call her. She was a woman of indeterminate age, possibly over sixty, with the full-lipped downward-sloping mouth of a Bardot which gave her a clown look of sadness. It was a physiognomic fault. She was eternally, pitifully sprightly.

'Been out on the town, Hal?' she greeted him. She shook her hair backwards, like a film star, it was heavy, bobbed, and coloured dark red. He could see its black roots as it swung from her face.

'Yeah.' He had learned to say 'Yeah' pretty quickly. 'Visiting with friends on Upper East Side.'

'Upper East Side?' She nodded knowingly. 'I have friends there too. Never get round to seeing them.'

The elevator came and he bowed her into it. She skipped in girlishly. Her heels were high, her ankles

7

bulged over the tops of the shoes as if they were too tight. The backs of her knees, showing beneath a too-short skirt, looked unattractively knobbly.

'I'm glad I met you, Hal.' Her teeth were falsely white, emphasizing the yellow tint of her skin. 'I'm organizing a little drinks party on the roof on Sunday for the other residents. I feel since I've been longest here I ought to have a get-together. You and I, of course, are old buddies.' Her smile was flirtatious. Their acquaintance had begun when she had been tending her window-box and water had dripped on Hal's head as he'd been looking out. 'Since I baptized you.' She was arch.

'Blame that cat for its caterwauling.'

'Caterwauling! That's good. It's Mrs Keyser's. She puts it out when she has her gentleman friend. Perhaps he doesn't like it in the bed.' She giggled. 'Naughty Ellie! Casting aspersions. You'll meet her on Sunday, if you'll grace our humble gathering with your presence. Mrs Keyser asked me if you were an English lord.'

Hal laughed. 'Some hope!' He tried to look enthusiastic. 'I'll be glad to come, thanks.' Sometimes he wished he had gone back to the hotel nearby where he had stayed before, but he needed space for the books and papers he was accumulating on his present project.

'That's dandy. Twelve o'clock? There will be a collection to buy pots and tubs and plants. Bring your cheque book? I'm planning a garden up there. Maybe you can give me some advice. You English are great gardeners.'

'Not me. Sorry, Miss Kaplan.' He'd slipped up. She pouted.

'Now, we agreed on Ellie and Hal, didn't we? At one of our little coffee mornings?' He regretted having accepted those invitations. One had led to the other, had led him to tell her about Van because she was usually uppermost in his mind.

8

'No, I've always lived in flats – apartments – since I left university. Except when I was a schoolboy.' He thought of his parents' garden in Singapore, and how when he came home from school the Malaysian gardener had let him help, pushing a barrow, making a bonfire.

'Ah, but when you get back to England and set up house, your lovely wife, Van, is bound to insist on a garden. Englishwomen always . . .'

'She's Scottish.' He thought of Clevedon Crescent in Glasgow's West End, where Van lived with her parents, Anna and Ritchie, and how of all the subjects he had heard discussed round their table, gardens had never been one of them.

Ellie looked disappointed. 'I saw her in a big straw hat with a trug over her arm. Oh, dear!' But, brightening, 'She bakes oatcakes? A tartan shawl round her shoulders, in a big farm kitchen, stone-flagged . . .'

'Sorry, no. But she's very good at the Highland Fling.' The downward curves of the sad mouth turned upwards, clown-like. She giggled.

'You're pulling my leg again! I can see that gleam in your eyes. Well, all I can say is she's a lucky girl to have such a handsome guy as you for her own.'

'I'll tell her when I call her tonight. This is me,' he said thankfully as the elevator stopped at his floor. He got out.

'Midday on the roof, don't forget, Hal honey.' She waved her painted finger-nails as she was borne upwards. He laughed ruefully as he opened his door and went into the lounge to pour himself a drink.

Two

'I'm worried about Bessie today, Mum. She's weaker.'
Van and Anna, her mother, were drinking their coffee
in the kitchen. 'I don't think I'll go to College today.'

'I don't like you missing it.' Anna looked drawn. They
had been sharing sitting up with Bessie at nights
because she seemed when they had washed her and
combed her hair as if she would hardly last till morning.
But her cocky half-smile was still there as she watched
their ministration. 'Now, whit has a puir old soul like
me done to deserve this attention?'

'Do you know what she said to me?'

'Tell me.'

' "It's me for the high jump." ' Van's voice wavered.
'She hadn't the strength to smile. Her eyes were pitiful.'

Anna put down her half-finished cup of coffee. 'We'll
go in and have a look at her and then you'll decide.'

'All right.' Van got up and emptied her coffee into
the sink. Neither of them had the taste for it.

Bessie looked very small in her bed in the room off
the kitchen. Smaller, younger-looking, as if her seventy-
nine years had fallen away from her and she had
reverted to the spry young girl who had tended Rose
Mackintosh, Anna's mother, and Rose's own mother
also, over six decades of service.

They both stood silently looking down on her. The

10

hands at her sides on the counterpane were purple-stained with bruises, mystery bruises. She hadn't been out of her bed for the past month. And there was a bruise under one eye. Who was the hidden enemy, Van wondered, afraid to think. The rest of her skin was parchment white, but smooth now, like marble. She lay, narrow and still, as if in a sarcophagus.

Van bent down and kissed her cheek. 'Are you awake, Bessie?' The old woman stirred. Her eyes remained closed.

'Aye, I'm wakened,' she said. 'There's nae point in sleepin' noo.' Her chest rose, fell. 'I'll get plenty o' that soon enough.'

'I thought you looked much better, Bessie.' Anna's voice shook. She was afraid of death. Van had seen plenty of it in hospitals.

'Did ye, noo?' There was a note of sarcasm in the faint voice. 'If ye want to know, Anna, I'm lyin' here wondrin' hoo ye'll manage.'

'Don't bother your head about us . . .' and then, quickly, 'What's this rubbish you're saying?' Bessie turned her head away as if tired of the subterfuge.

Van and Anna exchanged glances, Van's eyes holding the question. Anna said, casually, 'Van has her classes today, Bessie. I'm trying to persuade her to go.' She won't face up to it, Van thought.

Bessie turned. Her eyes for a moment had an unnatural brightness. 'You go to they classes. You don't want to become like yin o' these pouffes in the drawing-room upstairs, saft. I've worked aw ma life and never depended on any man. They're good at lovin' you and leavin' you, although you always think it would never happen to you.' Had there been a brief affair, Van wondered, maybe one of the tradesmen who came about the place? She didn't think it likely. Invitations to take

11

a cup of tea in Bessie's kitchen were not given lightly, whatever the blandishments.

'Right,' Van said. 'I'll go. I can see you wouldn't like me to be begging in Argyle Street if the worst came to the worst.' She bent and kissed Bessie's cheek. 'You be good while I'm away. And no getting round Mother to let you get up.'

'That stove's no' getting its usual shine. Maybe I'll . . .' her voice tailed away. Anna nodded to Van.

She got the bus in Great Western Road which took her through Charing Cross to Pitt Street where her college was. She was more worried about Anna in one way than Bessie. Her days were numbered. It made her heart ache, but she didn't have the fear of death which Anna had. And yet she knew that when the crisis came her mother would be level-headed, as she had been on that day when she had telephoned from London having to swallow to find her voice, 'Mum, I'm pregnant.' She thought Anna's fear stemmed from her terror at the thought of losing Ritchie.

She enjoyed the morning's lecture. Her mind was receptive. She told herself she must use her time wisely, absorb what she was being taught, even Bessie realized the value of independence.

Nevertheless, at a break in her classes she went to the corridor where the telephone was and rang home. After a time Anna answered. Her voice was shaking.

'How is she, Mum?' she asked.

'I don't think you should have gone. I can't get her to talk to me. The doctor's been, but he said there was nothing he could do. He'll call back tonight. There's no one here. Ritchie had an appointment.' Ritchie would, Van thought. It wasn't because he didn't dearly love

12

Bessie. His commitments couldn't be broken at a moment's notice. Or could they?

'I'll come home right away, Mother,' she said, and hung up.

Her tutor was sympathetic. 'Is it your mother?' she asked.

'No,' Van said, 'it's our housekeeper. She's been with us for so long that she's more a friend.' The tutor, a young woman who lived in a bed-sit in Carntyne, looked vague.

'Oh . . . well, on you go, Miss Laidlaw. Remember, if you're more than three days off we'll need a doctor's certificate.'

She half-ran up Clevedon Drive when she got off the bus and turned into Clevedon Crescent. How tranquil it looked in the April sunshine, the daffodils blowing in the lawns, the almond blossom already faintly pink. 'West End', the terrace breathed, that combination of respectability, Scottishness, segregation. The Laidlaws, Anna and Ritchie, were like exotic flowers in its primness. Was there a Bohemian quarter in Glasgow where they might have been better suited? Not in their opinion. They needed the solid background, the tradition of the Mackintoshes, and the house had to be maintained in the standard Anna's grandmother had set.

She ran up the steps and opened the front door, ran along the hall and into the kitchen behind the dining-room, through the kitchen to Bessie's bedroom. Her mother was bent over the bed. 'No, Bessie, no,' she was saying, her hands on the woman's shoulders, 'you aren't fit. I told you.'

'It's that stove, Anna.' Bessie's eyes were wild. 'I canny leave it in that state.' The stove in question had once been in the kitchen but had been replaced by an

13

Aga. Ritchie had known a man who would take it away but he had never materialized. Van went swiftly to the bedside.

'Let me, Mother.' She felt competent. It was one thing she could do well, to minister. 'Bessie,' she said sternly, 'I'm surprised at you making such a fuss over an old stove. I'll do it for you. Where's the . . . don't bother. I know.' She pulled out a drawer in a dresser and found the blacklead tin, the brushes for burnishing, the emery paper for the steel rim. The dresser should have been removed along with the stove, but there was another man Ritchie knew . . . she set to with a will. After some minutes spent brushing and rubbing hard with a duster, she stood up, cheeks flushed with the effort.

'There you are now. Does that please Your Highness?' Her heart lurched.

Bessie was lying where Van had gently laid her, her head askew on the pillow. Her eyes were closed. There was spittle at the corner of her mouth. She was breathing, rasping difficult breaths. 'Phone for the doctor, Mother,' she said in a whisper.

When Anna came back they stood together silently looking down. Van could feel her mother's arm trembling against hers. They scanned Bessie's face, peaceful now. Her lips moved. Once a faint smile, like a shadow, passed over her face. She's thinking of her stove, Van thought. Bessie's religion was founded on practicality. Cleanliness was next to godliness.

A change came slowly over Bessie's features, wavered, changed again, as if frames were being substituted, one for the other. Then there was a cessation, a long fearful stillness when Van felt obliged to put her ear to Bessie's chest. Straightening again, she saw a subtle looseness, a readiness. Her arms lay limp on the

14

coverlet, her whole body was relaxed. There was no mistaking it, the stealthy advance of death.

All those years, Van thought, part of our lives, interwoven with them, sharing in all their joys and sorrows, changing from a young girl to a woman, and now to this. One of her favourite songs (Mish had given her his gramophone when he left), was Harry Lauder's 'Keep Right On to the End of the Road'. She had done that. She had arrived.

The silence in the room was like the stillness before a storm, the same hush, the same expectation, only broken by Anna's quick indrawn sobbing breath, immediately stifled.

They stood while time passed. Outside the spring leaves were pale green burgeoning, and inside, death. Van put her hand in her mother's, whether for support or to give support she hardly knew, mostly for contact. Anna's hand responded, shaking, a fearful hand. 'Doctor . . .' she whispered, 'wasn't in. I left a message.' Van met her mother's anguished eyes.

Jean, Anna's twin, always maintained that her sister had it easy. No grand tragedy. Happiness most of the way, except when Ritchie had that flutter many years ago. Sometimes Jean was quite proud of the difference between them. If Ritchie were here, he would take Anna in his arms as he always did to comfort her. Only two people mattered in Mother's life, Van thought, Jean and Ritchie. The others were also-rans.

Bessie sighed, a long warning sigh, and they both turned their eyes on her. It was a sigh of seeming acceptance, of resignation. A certain smugness, even. She had given them all she had, not by gallivanting or by having followers in the kitchen, oh, dear, no, but by minding her folks, and minding her own business.

Now it was over. Her body moved slightly, as did

15

her lips. They bent to listen to the faint whisper. 'Aye,' they had to strain their ears, 'all ma life tae the Mackintoshes.'

They murmured words of agreement, of appreciation, of love. Van's eyes, more trained than Anna's, saw again the subtle changes in Bessie's face. She had always liked ironing. Now it seemed that someone was busy on her, smoothing out the creases, the lines, making everything smooth, neat, ready. Van felt a movement beside her and saw that her mother was swaying. She settled her on a chair and took one on the opposite side of the bed. She tried to smile reassuringly at her mother. Was it because she was so beautiful that she couldn't bear to watch disintegration, imagining herself at that stage?

Bessie's face was settling slowly into death. The bruises were fading into the parchment of her skin, there was the sense of blood being slowly drained from her body. Her face from being merely immobile became fixed, stiffening into its final set, as it were, that of giving up the ghost. It was a favourite phrase of Bessie's, sometimes said with a certain degree of satisfaction.

Van gently smoothed and straightened the cover. Habit was a prop. She looked at her mother, saw the stricken face. 'She's gone, Mother. We were both here, that's the good part of it.' The doctor couldn't have done a thing. She wished Ritchie had turned up for her mother's sake, but she might have known he was never there at the critical moment, missing trains, appointments, now, death. Perhaps he would have been too full of life for a death bed, and in any case Bessie wouldn't mind. There had been long talks between the two of them. Sometimes he had emerged from her little room, his eyes streaming. There had been plenty of love there.

'Maybe . . .' Anna's eyes were on the still figure. 'Are

you sure, Van?' She appealed like a child, her mouth quivering.

'No, Mum, she's gone. Remember the doctor warned us. Do you want to sit here for a little, or would you rather phone . . . everybody?'

'I'll sit. Get used . . . to it.' Anna put her hand to her mouth. 'Oh, I'll never get used to it, but I'll *realize* it, every day of my life.' The tears came, and Van put her arms round her, rocking her. *She* hadn't cried yet. That would be later.

'I'll go and telephone the doctor again, then Mish, then Hal. Then you could phone your sisters.' She kissed the wet cheek, patted her shoulder, a stand-in for Ritchie.

In the hall she looked at her watch. It would be eleven-thirty in New York. Karin would be in their apartment and perhaps Mish. He had been in the habit of coming home for lunch recently, Karin had told her, a smile in her voice. What a doting father he would make! Unlike Sam's.

And when Van had spoken to Mish, and they had consoled each other, and she had agreed with him that it would be better if Hal stayed behind with Karin, she rang Hal. His voice in her ear brought her first tears.

'Yes, darling. Mish has been on, this minute. He's really cut up, but anxious not to leave Karin alone. She's been warned not to move around much by her doctor.'

'Perhaps a threatened miscarriage. No, she shouldn't travel.'

'It's so sad for you, for all of you.'

'We loved her, you see.' She was weeping openly now. 'For so long there's been Bessie, our mainstay. None of us . . . can think of the house without her.'

'I'll call Mish again. I want to be with you in this,

hold you close. Perhaps someone else could stay with Karin.'

'No, don't do that. Mish would feel happier with you around. And I'll be busy. Mother needs me.'

He was reluctant. 'Well, okay. I suppose it's a family affair, after all.'

'*You*'re family.'

'The Mackintosh family, I meant.'

Her tears had dried now. 'Your bit will be to look after Karin. I think Mish is taking this pregnancy more seriously than she is.'

He sounded convinced. 'Go and comfort your mother. I'll take care of Karin, although I imagine she's better at that than I am. But I'll be with you in spirit. I love you. On you go.'

'After all,' she said, 'Bessie didn't die so that we could have a quick leap into bed. And you were home at Easter.'

There was a hint of laughter in his voice. 'Yes, I know. Awful. I'm only talking to keep you with me. Hang up and I will.' Van replaced the receiver slowly, braced her shoulders and went to find Anna.

But Ritchie was with her, and there had been a metamorphosis. Her smile was there now, but watery, there was grief in her eyes, but she was partially restored, the planner, the organizer *par excellence*.

'I think we should drive down to Wylie and Lochhead's, Van, and make the funeral arrangements. Ritchie has to go and see the minister. Bessie liked him. And while we're in Buchanan Street I'll have to buy myself a black hat. I want one with a wide brim. That cloche kind of thing I have is quite dated.' Even in grief Anna would always think of her appearance. Van remembered her grandmother's funeral. It had been perfect. So indeed would be Bessie's.

18

Three

There they were, the three sisters: Nancy, the youngest, now fifty-four, Jean and Anna, two years older, the twins.

What a sensation they must have made all those years ago when they had gone as students to the Art School! The apocryphal story was that one of the tutors had called them 'Our Own Glasgow Girls', likening them to that talented band of women who had made such a mark on the artistic life of the city at the beginning of the century. Hadn't it been that former lover of Jean's, Frederick Kleiber?

There was Nancy, her black outfit showing the still fairness of her skin, teetering as usual on too-high heels, attended by Uncle James who whenever Van saw him seemed to be more desiccated than the last, and there was Gordon, their son and one-time Adonis, whom she had been infatuated with when she was fourteen.

How could I, she thought now, seeing his portliness, his smugness, the smile that went off and on like electric light, without warmth. Wendy, his wife, was beside him, perhaps less plump nowadays, but still not suited for flying through windows. Mothers should think well before they named their daughters.

And how about her own name, Vanessa? Had that been wishful thinking on Anna's part, a pious hope that she had produced some exotic butterfly instead of a dun-coloured myopic moth? Apt that she had blundered about like one until it was discovered she needed glasses.

Then how clear, how utterly beautiful the world had seemed, everything in focus, seeing the expression in people's eyes, the Look, as Sartre had it, the detail of a flower, the petals, the sepals, the stamens. Hal had said to her once that a serious beautiful girl wearing glasses was even more beautiful. Anyone would be serious who had lived in a fog for most of their life.

And Wendy, she remembered as they exchanged glances, had confided in her a few years ago that she was secretly dissatisfied with her role as wife and mother. She must ask her sometime if she had given up her dream of becoming a lady explorer. She remembered her surprise when Wendy admitted that she had got herself pregnant to Gordon for the sake of excitement. A Wendy with knapsack would not look well at the Grosvenor and Malmaison dinner parties they gave or frequented, nor even at Arran, that island of quality for Glasgow's upper crust.

And Aunt Jean, the tragedy queen as she liked to think of herself with more than a hint of humour. Now married to Uncle John, after all her vicissitudes, a love affair with a married man who had drowned the day he had impregnated her, a baby which had died at birth, then a born-in-wedlock Downs Syndrome child who had died in early manhood.

It was all in Jean's painting, the wildness, the strength, the boldness of colour, a female Matthew Smith, that devotee of Matisse who could even make apples on a dish look voluptuous. She would never reach Ritchie's superior talent, hers was too undisciplined, too dashing, only one painting in four came off. And John, dear John, a very present help in time of Jean's troubles, always loving, always disadvantaged because her passion had already been given to someone else.

And there was Mish, talking to Sam, listening to him the way Hal did, an older Mish, touched with the tenderness and awe of approaching fatherhood. Would he be disappointed if Karin didn't take motherhood quite as seriously? American women had been work-oriented before the British.

The solemnity of the occasion seemed suddenly to descend on the family gathered in the long drawing-room with its wide windows on to the quiet crescent. Thoughts turned to Bessie, lying now in her coffin, never to be seen again, never to make her acerbic remarks, no sentimentality, only sentiment, and love. All her life she had given so much and asked so little. A silence seemed to come upon the room, as if they were each in their own way trying to face the gap she had left. It was broken by Anna's clear voice summoning them to the table where she was serving coffee, elegant in her large-brimmed black hat, slim black dress, black court shoes, impeccable, she had perfected perfection. And as if to counteract this impeccability, there was Ritchie, in his seemingly badly-fitting suit although it had come from the best bespoke tailors – but that was the effect he had on everything he wore – with his slightly raffish handsomeness, his too-long, too-bushy head of curls. The trip to the barbers had as usual been a failure because he always stopped the scissors when they were warming to the task. Van went over to Mish.

'Is Sam telling you all about school?' she said.

'Yes. And about Bunsen burners blowing up in the science lab and all kinds of exciting things.' She thought

21

of saying that he was too young to be in the science lab.

'I told you about it, Mummy. Rab told me. How Stinks lit this burner and there was a loud pop! It didn't really blow up anything, though . . .' He looked at Van. She thought of saying that Rab, his current chum, was too young also, but you didn't deflate, especially at a funeral. She put an arm round his shoulders.

'Sam keeps on hoping something will blow up,' she said, 'the whole school, preferably.'

'I'm going to be a doctor when I grow up, Uncle Mish. Grandpa's given me a science set with a little book of experiments inside and glass saucers and things.'

'I thought he would have liked you to be a painter?'

'No, he says one in the house is enough. Besides, he shuts himself up all day. I want to be like Mummy, going round hospitals and seeing people in bed.'

Ritchie joined them. 'Great to see you, Mish, even on such a sad occasion. We appreciate you coming so far.'

'Well, Bessie, Dad . . . she was special. I wanted to come. So did Karin, but I felt the journey would have been too much for her.'

'Did Hal not want to come?' Sam asked.

'Very much.' Mish answered him. 'But he's looking after Aunt Karin for me while I'm away.' The boy shrugged, as if suddenly bored with this family talk. He pushed against Van.

'I wish I could have had Rab here. We could have gone to the Park to look for newts in the pond.'

'It isn't a party, Sam,' she said, thinking that like most funeral gatherings it was beginning to resemble one. 'It's Bessie's funeral.' His eyes widened, his thin brown face became sad.

'I know that. Last night in bed I couldn't sleep, thinking I'd never see awld Bessie again . . .' his lip trembled.

22

'She was tired, son,' Ritchie said. 'Come with Grandpa and we'll get a drink of lemonade.' And to Van, 'We should be leaving now.'

'Yes.' She heard Anna's clear voice.

'I think we'd better start for the church. You're all welcome to come back here for lunch after ... we've been to the cemetery.' They talked together quietly as they filed out.

Bessie had wanted to be buried, not cremated. 'Nae shovin' me in a furnace, thank you very much,' she had said. They stood in bright cold sunlight in the bleak city cemetery on the north side of Glasgow. Here Bessie had been born eighty years ago and spent fourteen years of her life before she had gone into service and shut the gate on Maryhill. No one had been interested in her once she was working with 'the toffs'. It was one less mouth to feed.

They watched her coffin being lowered into the grave. Sam wept. Van, her arm round him, wept too, for her loss, for regret at subjecting Sam to a burial ceremony, yet knowing it had been the right thing to do. Bessie had loved him from the first, had never turned away from him because of his colour. He must pay his respects to that love.

Bessie had no friends, no family. Nancy's former housekeeper had wanted her to share a retiral cottage in Helensburgh but she had turned that down. 'I'm no' gonna be ordered aboot the place by that Mary Pollock. At least I'm boss in ma ain kitchen.' Her life was with the Mackintoshes. She gave her devotion to them, the last of her kind, the last of an era.

Van thought of the time when she had wept on Bessie's shoulder at the death of Eb. She had been stoical when she had told Anna because her mother had only tolerated Eb and in her secret heart might be glad that

23

he was no longer in her daughter's life. But Bessie had understood the sorrow, and the pity. She looked around the group gathered at the graveside. They would have their own thoughts, their own memories. She felt for a moment omniscient, as if she could read their minds.

Her father, eyes swimming with tears, was taking in the scene with that painter's gaze of his, missing nothing. He's thinking what a handsome bunch the Mackintoshes are, Van thought, and how lucky he was to have chosen the best of the bunch in Anna.

And Uncle James, that anxious man who had been so subdued by marriage, and yet so fearful that his wee Nancy shouldn't be too upset. Uncle John, who had the drawn face of suffering – it would be his angina – was looking at Jean, his bonny Jean, standing straight and tall, tearless. His passion for her would only be dimmed by death.

And Gordon, with Wendy, who seemed to have more character showing in her face than her husband. Wendy might surprise them all yet. Gordon's expression was ever so slightly resentful, the pouting face of a small boy who had been spoiled by a doting mother. Was he thinking that sometimes Bessie hadn't really liked him? If he is, Van thought, he'll be wondering why.

Four

The Sunday drinks party on the roof of Hal's apartments was boring after a while. The residents whom he met were amiable enough, mostly middle-aged or older, pleasant to talk to, and their interest in him seemed sincere. New Yorkers, he had thought at first, seemed to be excessively interested in anything he said, but he had come to the conclusion that they asked questions simply to hear him *talk*. They marvelled at his accent. He felt sure their idea of England was rooted in an Agatha Christie-type of world which no longer existed, of thatched-roofed houses, cricket on the green and vicarage strawberry teas. He suspected it was partly gleaned from films.

Ellie Kaplan was lavish with drinks and appeared to be imbibing pretty freely herself. She became flirtatiously tight, hanging on to Hal as if he were her own private property. He got the impression that the others thought he *was*.

At two o'clock the party showed no signs of breaking up. People were now lounging in the deck chairs she had provided, the laughter was becoming ribald, some of the men were telling jokes which sent the women into gales of laughter.

Mrs Keyser, a large lady with large teeth, large earrings dangling from outsize ears – everything seemed

25

to be oversize about her – was particularly friendly. 'I'll be making Ellie jealous. I understand you two are the best of friends?' Her perfume, close to, was overpowering.

'Well . . .' he deprecated, 'she's been very kind.'

'She talks about you a lot.' She leant nearer to him, and he saw down her cliff-like bosom to a valley of what looked like powdered snow between her breasts. 'I think I ought to warn you, Mr Purvis, she's got a *thing* about you.'

'Oh, she's friendly with everyone.'

'That's only her pose.' Her face loomed large, so did the pores of her skin. 'Poor Ellie. You know, she's subject to . . . well, mood swings, up one minute, down the next. I've seen her low, *very* low . . .' She looked at Hal meaningfully, thick black eyebrows pulled together, and he muttered something about being sorry to hear it.

'I'm afraid I'll have to go.' He looked at his watch. Mrs Keyser put a jewel-decked restraining hand on his arm.

'This idea about a roof garden, for instance. She's been mad keen about it for ages, but the owners aren't. It's an old building. They don't want any more rubbish up here than they can help.'

'Oh, a few tubs of flowers shouldn't make much difference!' He felt he had to defend Ellie.

'But you don't know her, Mr Purvis! She always goes to excess. It won't just be a few tubs. She'll have flower beds, and bushes and pergolas and God knows what. She's obsessive. An obsessive compulsive neurosis, I think it's called. Well, she should know. She visits her shrink often enough . . .' Ellie Kaplan was there, swaying slightly before them, a bottle in her hand.

'Don't listen to a word Hattie tells you, Hal. Freshen your drink, dear?' She waved the bottle.

'No, thanks. I have to be going.' He noticed Mrs Keyser had melted away.

'But it's early yet! I told you, we're going to have a ball. Sunday afternoons ... they've got to be filled in somehow. So dreary. Know that song, "Suicide Sunday"?'

He shook his head. 'As a matter of fact, I've arranged to see a friend this afternoon.' He would ring Karin when he got back to his apartment.

'Oh, you shouldn't have done that!' Her full mouth was a half-circle of gloom. 'I was counting on you. We might have finished up in my place. I could have rustled up ...'

He interrupted her flow by drawing out his notecase from his breast pocket. 'Let me give you my contribution now.'

'No, don't bother.' She waved her hand. 'I'll get it any time. It's no use anyhow. Everything I try to do ... that bitch, Hattie, says the owners will object anyhow.' He thought she was going to burst into tears, and he remembered what Mrs Keyser had told him. Maybe there was a grain of truth in it. He made another apology and escaped downstairs to his apartment. He lifted the receiver immediately.

'Karin,' he said when he heard her voice, 'I hope you weren't resting. It's Hal.'

'Goodness, no. I'm not an invalid! Has Mish been alarming you? I'm off work for a month on doctor's orders, but I'm going back again, maybe before that.'

'Good for you. Has Mish been on the phone?'

'Yes, he called me. He's glad he was able to be with the family. He should be back Wednesday or Thursday. I told him not to hurry.'

'Yes, they're close-knit. I wondered if you'd like me to call for you in the car? Perhaps drive up the Hudson Valley? Have a meal somewhere? It's a nice day.'

'Great idea. I was going to do some pretty boring household tasks but I'm always willing to escape.'

'So am I. I'm running away from a predatory female.' He told her briefly about Ellie Kaplan.

'Lonely New York ladies of a certain age get pretty desperate.' She was amused.

'Well, you're the psychologist. Half an hour's time?'

The streets were less busy as he walked to his car park, a Sunday quietness. Some of the cars were open tourers probably heading out for Long Island or upstate New York. Pedestrians walked purposefully, not many loitered at shop windows. He could understand Ellie Kaplan's feeling of alienation. The streets were a place for couples, for families, the lone figures could be distinguished by their slower pace, their aimlessness. Gloomy Sunday. Suicide Sunday, she had said.

Karin was waiting for him in her apartment, bright-eyed, dressed in a cool-looking linen dress of navy blue with a white collar, and blue-and-white spotted floppy bow. As yet there was little sign of her pregnancy. She had a squarish compact figure, broad-hipped, unlike Van, who had grown thinner since their marriage. Van had always been conscious of what she called her 'lumpy figure'. It would take him years of telling her how beautiful she was to make her believe it – the penalty of having a mother whom she thought of as perfect.

'What a good idea,' Karin said as they kissed. 'At least I'm a substitute for Van. You must miss her.'

'Going back at Easter made it worse,' he agreed, 'but I'm glad she was with Bessie when she died, and there for Anna.'

28

'Van's always there when needed. Would you like some tea before we start off?'

'No, thanks. Let's stop on our way. The sooner we get on the road the better.'

'Okay.' She went about the apartment efficiently, closing windows, adjusting curtains, lifting a navy linen jacket and her handbag, her 'purse', he remembered they called it. How eminently sane and sensible she was compared with poor Ellie Kaplan with her unsuitable dress and all her insecurities.

He was cheerful as he drove out of New York and on to Route Nine. The trees were a haze of early green and the air from the open window seemed fresher once they had left Yonkers behind and were running alongside the river.

'I should think you're going to like living out here,' he said. 'I've been reading all about those rich families who used to sail out of the city in their sloops.'

She laughed. 'We haven't a sloop and our new house is far from stately, but it's fairly handy for Mish and me for travelling. Winter may be a different thing. Mish thinks we shouldn't bring up a family in the city. He's already quite involved in the whole idea. That's how he's been brought up, I guess.'

'Do you have the same in yours?'

'Show me the Jewish family that isn't close. I'm the one that got away. But they're all crazy about him, and he's become a kind of icon for my cousins. He's so polite and charming, and he's a wow with my mother. I believe he'd even wear a skull cap if she asked him.'

'Having that background would prepare you for Biafra, I suppose. Didn't your family object to you going to such a troubled place?'

'No, they didn't. Indeed, some of the older members have known the same tragedies. They thoroughly approved of my going. It was a concept they could deal with.'

'You were at Umalia?'

'Yes. It was Colonel Ojuku's capital after Port Harcourt. The children there ... well, what can I say? You've seen the pictures.'

'Heartbreaking.'

'The terrible thing is you get inured. Day after day. Any medical student could pass his anatomy exam after being there a week. The starvation, the skull-faces, the matchstick legs. For the first week I couldn't eat, couldn't sleep, then you're in a time warp dealing daily with broken bodies, death. I did a nursing training. There seemed to be more call for my nursing skills than my psychology. That's for the sophisticated, the well-nourished people I see in New York. I still dream of those children.'

'What made you decide to give it up?'

'Well, I had to think of Mish eventually, and the effect my experience might have on him. I was beginning to think of myself as Mrs Fixit. Dangerous. Pity drove me to Biafra, but what distressed me after a while was how cynicism had taken over, no, that's too strong, detachment, which you have to acquire if you are to function at all. I thought if I stayed too long I might kill my capacity for emotion, and then I shouldn't be able to function either in my job back home or as a wife.'

'I see that.'

'You see, I worked in Biafra not looking for a reward, then I thought I owed something to Mish, that he deserved to be considered too and I knew he wanted to start a family. But you don't *deserve* anything. No one does. Life isn't a balance, two pounds here, two pounds there. It's random ... although with patients

30

I'm generally objective and I can deal with their problems. Of course, there's a danger there too, it tends to make you feel, well, omnipotent, that you're for a second touching His hem. Gosh, will you listen to me!' She put her hand to her mouth. 'I'm getting carried away.'

'So you came home and got pregnant?'

'Will you listen to the man! A typical male. It wasn't as easy as that. As well as a lot of other things you have to feel right with the idea.' She laughed. 'I'll be psychoanalysing myself next! Well, it all came right in the end, and here I am, fair, fat and fertile and that's enough about me. What about that cup of tea we promised ourselves?'

They had their tea and sugary doughnuts in a roadside café, and then because Hal hadn't seen the Chagall and Matisse windows in the church in the Rockefeller estate, they paid it a visit. He was charmed by the polite and knowledgeable enthusiasm of the Daughters of the Revolution, as he called the ladies who showed them round.

'Are we near your new house?' he asked Karin.

'It's not far. Oskanawa direction. The area's called Furnace Point. Would you like to see it from the outside? The owners are still there.'

'I'd love to have a look. You know you aren't going to get rid of me when you move in,' he smiled at her, 'I'll have to go to Yonkers to the museum to study my painters from time to time.'

'I guess we can stand that since it's only for a short while.' She laughed at him, her brown eyes shining.

She's quite something, this girl, he thought, diamond bright. And as hard? Single-minded certainly, about her career, about her place in life. She would never be only a mother. But then, neither would Van. She would want to have her own thing as well, as her mother had, as her experience with a man who couldn't provide for her had taught her. But there was an essential malleability in Van's character, a winsomeness, a sweetness. Was it the difference between a New Yorker and a Glaswegian? Glasgow had a cosiness, perhaps a parochialism. You couldn't say that about New York where every man was for himself.

Their mood was light-hearted as Hal drove through the suburban countryside of Westchester. The dense wooded areas which often still existed between the houses made him think of the Indians whose home it had once been. Now it was occupied by comfortably-off commuters who had taken the same trail as the rich Dutch settlers who had built a railway running along the Hudson so that they could head off quickly to their country homes.

When he was finished with his painters he might think of a book about the indigenous natives who had been ousted, leaving only their Indian names to remember them by. But, on the other hand, once back in London the publishers might have other ideas for him.

'"The world is so full of a number of things, I'm sure we should all be as happy as kings . . ." Do you know that quotation? I'm glad you let me take you out.'

'I'm glad I came. You live in the present, Hal,' Karin said. 'You'll always enjoy yourself. Like Mish's father, I think. Don't you ever get a feeling of . . . premonition?'

'If I do it doesn't last. Do you?'

'Not often, but I do when I think of a patient I'm seeing just now. He wears a camouflage especially for me, but I know he's smart, and deceitful, and I can't get him to trust me. We're like water and oil. We don't mix.'

32

'That must be difficult. The thing is your problems are psychological, mine are factual, which are easier to solve. But yours are people, more fluid, there aren't any rules.'

She looked at him. 'You should be doing my job.' They drove in silence for a few minutes, then she put a light hand on his arm. 'Go more slowly now, Hal. We're getting near.'

They turned to go home when he had duly admired the new house, a clapboard structure set on a hill above the Hudson. It was adequate, Karin said, if not beautiful, and the view was marvellous. It would be nice to come home to. He agreed. Soon he and Van would be living in Bayswater together, and perhaps they too would start looking around for a house of their own. The nesting instinct must be catching.

They were thoroughly at ease with each other as they eventually settled on an Italian restaurant near Croton. He looked smilingly across the table at her and thought how strange it was that he could admire and like a woman so much and yet not desire her.

'You seem so wise, Karin,' he said, when they were sipping their Chianti.

'Only Jewish.'

'What do you mean by that?'

'Matriarchal perhaps. I don't know. Methuselah. Everyone seems younger than me, even you and Mish. What age are you, Hal?'

'Twenty-nine.'

'I'm thirty-two. I *feel* older than you. When I first met you I thought, there's a young man with a great potential.'

'Cheeky sod.' He laughed at her.

'Thank God, I thought, he's had the good sense to choose Van.'

'Van should hear you. I spend my life trying to build up her self-esteem.'

'Van is sophisticated in the truest sense. She's profited by experience, she hasn't just let it happen. Oh, you'll be all right with Van. Treasure her. You'd go a long way before you found anyone so good to live with. It isn't low self-esteem. It's true humility.'

'You're so right. I tell her I'm going to look after her, but it's she who's going to look after me.'

It had been a lovely Sunday, he told Karin when he dropped her off at East Sixty-third Street. She assured him it had done her a lot of good, although she looked tired with dark circles under her eyes.

'I was told to take good care of you by Mish,' he said.

'That old fusspot! It's just because I'm quite elderly to be having a first baby. He thinks I should be wrapped in cotton wool.'

'Are you working tomorrow?' he asked her.

'Yes, I'll go in. This patient I was telling you about. The receptionist rang me and said he had been bothering her, wanted to know when I was coming back, he wanted to see me, had to see me, and so on.'

'Weren't you supposed to be resting?'

'Oh, I get enough of that. I'll go in. It's easier. Maybe if I dig some more . . . the trouble is that guys like him fight against the probing by taking a personal interest in the one who *does*. I must warn the receptionist not to give away any information away about me, especially our new address. I've a feeling he's got a contact somewhere, maybe an office cleaner. They can be garrulous.'

'That must be upsetting.'

'Yeah; but my professors warned me about it. It's what's called a transference situation. They didn't warn me it might work two ways, an obsession.' There was a hint of something in her eyes, an uncertainty, a fear?

Could she possibly be attracted by this man, Hal wondered. He keeps cropping up in her conversation, but he dismissed the idea. Not Karin. She was eminently sensible. 'It's a good thing,' she was saying, 'that this patient – I'm avoiding mentioning his name because it's most unprofessional to go on about him – it's a good thing he hasn't rung our apartment when Mish was there. He'd tear into him.'

'I can't imagine Mish tearing into anyone.'

'No?' She smiled at him. 'There are two sides to everyone. Never go by appearances. Once a guy let a glass door swing against me in the foyer right here,' she waved a hand, 'and you should have heard Mish! Tore into him! Gave him the fright of his life. You'd have thought I'd been injured for life.' Hal shook his head unbelievingly. 'Look, Hal, the meekest mildest man I ever treated was a rapist and a murderer. Fortunately the cops caught up with him. Would you like to come in for a night-cap?'

He laughed. 'How do you know I'm not a rapist and a murderer?'

'Because there are some people I'm quite sure about and you're one of them.'

'All the same I shan't come in, thanks, but I'll see you to the elevator. Make sure there are no weirdos lurking about.'

'Okay.' She looked tired now.

'You should lie down for a bit,' he said.

'So who's the doctor?' They kissed and he waved as she was taken upwards. She looked composed. She was smiling.

When he went out into the quiet street it was deserted, but across the street, facing him, he could see a man standing in a doorway. He turned his head away as if aware that Hal was looking at him.

He drove down Madison Avenue, his mind pleasantly playing on the day he had spent with Karin. He had got to know her better, to see in her the practical New Yorker with all the sharpness of their kind, but still someone who could be disturbed and worried by one of her patients.

And Mish, seemingly, was not always cool, calm and collected. He had a temper, and could be fiercely protective of Karin, even to the extent of rowing with someone who had let a glass door slip out of his grasp. Was it a typical atavistic reaction, that of the man guarding his mate who was carrying their offspring in her womb? Fanciful, Hal, he told himself.

And yet, Mish came from a close-knit family, a thing he himself had never known but was now joined to by marrying Van. And that led him to think of her, which occupied his mind exclusively until he had parked the car, walked to his apartment and opened his door. As he turned to shut it he noticed a scrap of paper lying on the carpet, and he sat down to read it. The writing was a scrawl, on a piece of paper evidently torn from a diary: 'Called to see you around eight but just my luck, the bird had flown. I was feeling low and I thought we might have had a drinkie together. Your sad little Ellie.'

He threw it into the wastepaper basket, thinking, poor old thing, and that she had the same nuisance value as Karin's patient. Van, his lovely Van, wouldn't approve of that thought. Well, she had enough charity for two of them, and perhaps after they'd been living together for a few more years, he would grow a halo. He fell asleep thinking of her.

Five

Jean and John Whitbread were driving home to Kirk-cudbright. It was a route Jean always liked and which had first endeared the little town to her ever since father had driven them to see great-aunt Jessie. It was Jessie who had sheltered her when she was pregnant with Frederick Kleiber's child, and who had subsequently left her the house in old High Street when she died.

She thought of those family jaunts from Clevedon Crescent through Abington, Crawford, Elvanfoot – lovely name – Moffat where Rose, her mother, liked to stop for lunch or tea ... 'Mind how you sit on your pleats, *gerls*!' Her mother's Kelvinside vowels would start them giggling behind her in the back seat of the roomy Vauxhall. Then Beattock, where their ears popped, Dumfries, bustling Dumfries redolent of Rab-bie Burns, and the last tranquil seagirt miles to Kirkcud-bright, her home with John for the last thirty years.

Here, inspired by the work of those women who had come from Glasgow to paint each summer in Green Gate Close, she had begun to paint in earnest herself, at first for therapeutic reasons, and for a long time now as the principal motivation in her life.

John respected that, didn't expect her to perform the usual duties of a doctor's wife, was proud of her accom-plishment, my staff and comforter, she thought now, against the trials and tribulations which seemed to gather round her as if she were a magnet. She lit a cigarette to clear her throat which had thickened with emotion as she thought.

'It wasn't just any funeral, that, eh?'

'You're right.' He smiled. 'The Mackintoshes have a capacity, almost a monopoly on feeling.'

'Ah, but Bessie . . .' But then, only a Mackintosh would understand.

'Shall we go in and tell Alastair and Sarah about it?'

'No, tomorrow will do.' She made her voice casual. 'Denis Carter. It's his evening.'

'You should have put him off. You'll be tired.'

'It'll get my mind off the sadness.'

'I was surprised at you agreeing to give him tuition. You always said you hated teaching.' There was a slight note of criticism.

'I do. But Alan McAlpine caught me on the wrong foot. And then, knowing Alan quite well when he was courting Van . . .'

'She's much better off with Hal Purvis! They're suited. Alan McAlpine would never have understood Van, her . . . tenderness. He's got the right wife in Cissie Crichton, busy with town affairs, entertaining, improving the house, oh, she's having a fine time, her and her mother. Van would have been wasted on him. Anyhow, why was Alan sponsoring Carter?' He came back to it.

'Didn't you realize? He helped Denis with his divorce. They're old friends. Denis was born here.'

'But he lived in London.'

'They've always had a house here, a holiday place. He didn't come up much, but I think his wife used it occasionally. And after they split up he decided to live in it for a bit and look around. It's partly business. He's a partner in a posh London estate agency and they're interested in property in Galloway for the fishing and shooting set.' John didn't reply. When he disapproved, or wasn't interested, he was silent. He rarely said anything he would regret.

Denis Carter had made an impression on her that evening at the McAlpines'. He was darkly handsome, but it hadn't been that. She was impervious, usually. But there had been something about his bearing which had reminded her of Frederick, his assurance, the way he smiled, the worldliness. Londoners in Kirkcudbright were as scarce as the Viennese might have been. She had responded to the strangeness in him. She rarely if ever found it in men, nor looked for it now.

He had surprised her with his knowledge of modern painting. He'd had easy access to galleries and museums, living in London, and had taken any opportunity he found to keep abreast. He had surprised her even more when he had said, 'I'm in Kirkcudbright for a bit – you know my marriage is over. I've been pulled through the whins lately.' He had smiled, with bleak eyes. 'To keep me from climbing the walls I've been trying my hand at painting. Always wanted to.'

'Well, it's better than hitting the bottle.'

'So you don't think I'll be any good?'

'Adults who "take it up" as they say, are generally quite good but not good enough. It's the difference between a hobby and hard work. Children are better. They aren't inhibited.'

'Can I show you some of my daubs?' He was direct. His bleak eyes held hers, belying his smile, and she thought, he's lonely. And when she had hesitated, 'Like tomorrow, when I'm passing?'

'I can see why you're a success at selling houses,' she remarked, and she whose time was sacrosanct had said,

'Yes', and she who was intensely critical had actually seen some talent in his work – at least they weren't merely pretty daubs of the Galloway countryside – and she who'd said she would never teach had agreed to have a look at his work occasionally while he was in Kirkcudbright. But, redeeming herself slightly in her own eyes, she had said it must be in the evening, as earlier than that she didn't want to be interrupted.

'You strike a hard bargain,' he had laughed at her. 'I wonder if I'll be able to afford your fees.'

'I don't take money.' She hadn't smiled. 'There must be no commitment.'

So why hadn't she cancelled his appointment for this evening? She said to John, breaking the silence, 'I'll probably tell him tonight to stop coming. He's a bit of a nuisance, really.' She stubbed out her cigarette. John didn't like her smoking in the car. She wished he would say so.

That might be the difference which interested her, the feeling of latent aggression in Denis Carter compared with the always-considerate John. He was too good. She wanted to be shaken by that hardness, that difference, be stirred by it, before it was too late.

At nine o'clock Denis Carter hadn't come. She had made a meal for John, had been careful not to hurry him over it, had been relieved when Alastair had telephoned and said one of John's patients with terminal cancer was going through a bad patch. If he could just see Dr John for five minutes ... John's father had been the one and only Dr *Whitbread* in Kirkcudbright with the older patients.

She was cleaning her brushes which she had scarcely used when there was a tap at the door and Denis Carter came in. 'So you're back,' he said. 'How did the funeral go?'

'Funerals don't *go*.' She disliked the lightness in his voice. 'They aren't board meetings. It was deeply moving.'

'Ah, well, they are. Full stop. It's the space they leave. How to fill it. You don't have to have a death to leave a space.'

'Some can't be filled.'

'They close over eventually.'

'I admire your pragmatism.'

'Oh, if I weren't a pragmatist I should have cut my throat long ago. I don't miss my wife but I do miss my daughter. She's got custody. Fathers have a special feeling for daughters, especially when they're just two and a half. They're . . .' He opened the portfolio he was carrying. 'This is my latest. I did it while you were away.'

The picture he showed her was of a darkening sky, dark blobs of trees, moonlight. 'You obviously didn't paint this *in situ*,' she said. It had atmosphere.

'No. I saw it on the way home from you. There's a piece of open ground at the tail end of the town with those hills unrolling in front of you like fabric. You know? Satisfying in the moonlight. It was the tree patterns silhouetted against the skyline, and so artfully placed, you had to admire the design. I found it easy to recall, as if I'd had some heightened perception when I saw it. Why do you think that was?' His unsmiling eyes were on her.

'Perhaps you were thinking of someone you love.' And then, daring the bleak eyes, 'Your little daughter. What's her name?'

'Katie. "K-K-K-Katie . . ." I used to tease her by singing that old song. It made her laugh. Those little milk teeth . . .'

'There you are, then.'

41

'It could have been someone else.' The direct gaze, then lowered to the painting. 'Well, what do you think of it?'

'It's better than it ought to be considering your technique can't keep pace with your emotion, but,' she scrutinized it, 'oh, yes, the feeling's there.' She handed it back to him. 'Perhaps you *need* to paint.'

'Don't give me that old crap,' he said, putting the painting back in his portfolio. 'You'll be telling me I'm sexually deprived next.'

'Well, perhaps you are.' She took out a brush from the jar of turps and began to wipe it vigorously with a rag. Oh, stupid, stupid remark, she thought. A married woman of fifty-six ought to know better. The silence in the old stone studio at the bottom of the long garden reminded her of its lonely situation above the estuary.

'Any tips?' His voice came out of the silence. His gaze was direct, but she thought his mouth lifted at the corner.

For years she had been unable to blush, had outgrown it, which had been a relief. 'See your doctor,' she said.

'Oh, I don't mean *that*. I was referring to my painting.' Yes, his mouth had definitely lifted at the corner. She subdued the long-dormant blush, but as a protest, it seemed, she felt wetness in her armpits. Surely a late-menopausal symptom only?

'Did you walk here tonight?' she asked. Reply with another question.

'Yes, I had to fill in the time until I was sure you would be back from Glasgow.'

'Well, look at your scene for an even longer time on your way home. It's woolly in parts, imperfectly observed, imperfectly recollected. You want to feel it *intensely*, get it into your bloodstream, then carry that

42

feeling and the image in your head, carefully, like an over-full . . . jug. Good painters might do the same subject a dozen times before they're satisfied.'

'Right!' He saluted. He was making a fool of her.

'It helps to give it a title.'

'Oh, I've already got that. It's called "Longing".' The direct, bleak gaze, but behind the bleakness she saw the hurt.

'Do you mind if I shoo you away now?' she said. 'I'm suddenly tired. I've had a long day.'

'Of course. But I have to come back.'

'Why?'

'Because you have given me a further commission. I may have to come back a dozen times.' The closed smile. She had fallen into another verbal trap.

John was back from his call when she went back into the house. 'I thought you might have been longer,' she said.

'I thought the same about you.'

'No, I can't be bothered with him tonight. Tired. You were right. It was a mistake not to cancel it. Let's go to bed, darling.'

In bed she asked him if he were too tired to make love, feeling obscurely that she had to make up for something. And during the lovemaking, because he relished the invitation and took his time over it, her mind wandered, to Bessie, who had left a space, to a little girl called Katie. The similarity between Frederick Kleiber and Denis struck her again. Denis longed for his child, Frederick could never have borne to leave his little Hilde.

She didn't believe in reincarnation, she told herself, nor coincidences. There was always a flaw in them. But you couldn't deny that absent ones left a space which was never filled. She heard John's quickening breath.

43

Like the tide, there was an eventuality about him. She helped him to touch the shore, joining him in his pleasure.

Six

'I've brought you another one, Miss Gottleib,' Paul Laskins said.

'Thank you.' Karin was in her consulting room in Park Avenue on a sunny morning in June. She was in her sixth month of pregnancy and the early worries of losing the baby had gone. She felt fine. She had walked downtown feeling light-footed although she had given a rueful glance at her bulky silhouette in the occasional shop window, not helped by the minuscule bikinis displayed on long-legged, narrow-hipped, flat-bellied models. Definitely a prospective mum, she had thought. Mish, however, caressed her bump nightly with proprietorial glee. 'Our house is going to look like the Guggenheim soon,' she said, after scrutinizing the picture, then, thinking she was being churlish, 'You're too kind, Paul.'

'I want you to have it.' His eyes were on her. 'It's for you.'

She looked at it again, her mind working fast as it usually did when he was there. What was it about his presence that alarmed her? She was used to disturbed people – that went with the job. She had always prided herself on her detachment. The painting was composed of three broad layers of colour, white, blue and yellow, obviously a landscape, perhaps a seascape. In one corner of the yellow layer there was an embryonic figure, a smaller circle on top of a larger one. Bone white. It might be rocks. He had talent, but then most patients to whom she suggested art therapy showed some kind of talent, it was their way of communicating.

'Interesting,' she said coolly, laying it aside. 'Would you lie on the couch, Paul, and we'll get started.'

'Okay.' He got up, a lanky figure, more youthful than his age suggested, which was thirty-three. He was prematurely bald, what hair he had grew mostly round his crown, he had a fine baby-like skin, large round eyes, a small rosebud mouth. He looked immature, his wrist bones were prominent, his neck too long.

'What did your husband think of the last one?' he asked. 'He's an authority, isn't he?' Here it was again, his apparent knowledge of her background, now of Mish. He was clever, she never doubted that, his IQ was above average and he would have the obsessional's infinite capacity for taking pains. He didn't work. He would have plenty of time at his disposal. She had a mental picture of him standing at the plate glass window of Mish's gallery, looking in, watching . . .

'Can't remember,' she said. 'Let's get on. You were telling me about your schooldays last time. In Maryland, wasn't it?' She referred to her notes.

'Yeah, a dump. Miles from Baltimore, the original Hicksville. There was a lot of bullying at that school. Now, here's a problem for you to solve, Miss Gottleib,' his voice was free of innuendo, 'I was as big as anyone else there, I was cleverer than most of them, so why would they want to bully me?'

'Maybe you were too clever.' He ignored that.

'Ross Clancy was the worst, a dummy. Swanking about how he laid half the girls, he had a great fat ass, excuse me, Miss Gottleib, but I get mad just thinking

46

about him even now. Accused me of not being able to
. . . But there were good times too. There was a young
teacher I liked, he taught me a lot, praised my essays.
That dummy, Clancy, couldn't write to save his
hide . . .'

She listened with one attentive ear. He was going
over the old ground again, how he was bullied and
persecuted at school, how his father had advised him
to go back and knock the living daylights out of them,
but how he never got the chance. His parents seemed
to have been understanding about his problems, and
they were indulgent. His father was a rich farmer, and
Paul had wanted for nothing, fishing tackle, books.
Reading and fishing were what he liked best.

It was when he began to talk about his sister that his
voice changed from its whining note to malice, how his
parents had always preferred Kathleen.

'Your sister is married now?' Karin asked. She had
listened to him picking the scab off this wound before.

'Yeah, God, what a relief when she moved out! But
she was always there when I was home on vacation,
and then after I got my degree and moved to New York,
every time I went back.' He spoke in falsetto. ' "Why
don't you get married, Paul, and have kids?" She had
two. Everything they did was right, right, right! It was
like when we were kids together, spying on me, reading
my notebooks. She once stole a very private notebook
and showed it to Mom and Dad and I got belted.'

'Maybe you *should* have got married to be upsides
with her.' Karin spoke lightly, hearing the rising hys-
teria in his voice.

'Me!' He spluttered with laughter which sounded
false. 'No, thank you! I'm fancy free . . . but, honest,
Miss Gottleib, if you'd seen those two brats of hers, like
twin Shirley Temples, Natalie and Mary Jo, for

47

godssake, twisting Mom and Dad round their little fingers just as Kathleen had done, turning them against me ... I never got a chance. She's back home altogether now. Her husband couldn't stand her. Keeps *me* from going home, her there.' He moved restlessly. Karin waited. Sometimes she felt like a Sphinx. She straightened her back, listened.

'Sometimes in my apartment when it was hot and New York was full of stink I'd think how good it would be to see the Bay again, feel that fresh wind on my face, go fishing in my little boat. I'd catch lobster for Mom and Dad – they liked that – make it up with them, it would be just like the old days. Then I'd think, but *she'd* be there, her and her damned kids.'

His voice droned on, a kaleidoscope of memories, of loneliness, of grudges, but always drifting back to Chesapeake Bay, how there were girls who had liked going with him on his boat until they had been put off by his sister. 'Every time!' His voice rose hysterically, and she felt momentary pity for him. There's another kind of deprivation than what I saw in Biafra, she thought. She interrupted him, looking at her watch.

'Your half-hour's up, Paul. We're getting along fine. You feel better?'

He was grudging. 'Just talking about that bitch doesn't make me feel better ...'

'Better out than in. You're following the regime I gave you? No lying late in bed, exercise, good food, keeping off drugs?'

'I was never on them, much.' He swung his legs off the couch and stood up. 'Just cannabis at school. No, that's a mug's game. Spoils the physique.' He clenched his fist towards his chest, posing. 'Do you think the painting will look okay in your new house?' He was deliberately casual, his eyes sliding away from her in

48

that peculiar way of his. Karin felt the familiar apprehension which always came, sooner or later, like watching an animal in a cage which was not quite secure. How did he know they had moved? 'I like the thought of something of mine in your place,' he said, eyes limpid now. 'So that you won't forget me . . .'

He was standing in front of her and he stopped speaking suddenly. She followed the direction of his eyes. He was looking, not just looking, observing, scrutinizing her body, her swollen stomach, in an almost clinical fashion. She willed herself to keep her hands on the arms of her chair, not to move them, as a shield. She spoke calmly.

'We're not at the picture-hanging stage yet. Too busy. Why don't you get yourself a job, Paul, since you're interested in art? One of those bookshops near the Met, for instance. Coffee-table stuff. They like men with degrees. They might take you on.'

He shrugged. 'I don't need the money when Dad is paying me to stay away.'

'It could have been interesting, filled your day. You could make friends.'

'I don't need friends. I get enough of that where I live. There's a nosy old cat there dying to make friends, dying to sniff out any information about me she can.'

She looked down at her notes. She had noticed before he lived in the same street as Hal. She must ask Hal if they had met. Could the 'nosy old cat' be the woman *he* had talked about, Ellie Kaplan? She had a good memory for names. It could be interesting to talk with her. As Hal had described her, she would take an excessive interest in other people's lives.

'Well, it's up to you,' she said. She made herself smile at him. 'Anyhow, you seem to be more at ease with yourself. That's progress.'

49

'Progress to what? I don't know why that doc sent me to you in the first place.' Probably because he felt the same unease as I do and wanted to get rid of you, she thought.

'You went to *him*, remember?'

'Maybe I did. It was because I couldn't sleep, that was all. Tossing and turning all night. Worn out with not sleeping.'

'We'll talk about that next time.'

His eyes had shifted to her stomach again. She felt exposed to his gaze. She didn't make a practice of sitting behind her desk. It constituted a barrier. She could have done with it now. She felt slightly agitated, she who prided herself on never getting agitated. She stood up.

'Session's over. I have another patient waiting.' She moved to her filing cabinet, opened it, riffled through its contents, and spoke with her back to him. 'On you go.' She listened to his footsteps slowly crossing the room towards the door, heard him open it, shut it with a slight peevish bang. She found she was trembling.

They were in their new garden after their day in the city. 'Lie back, darling,' Mish said, 'and I'll psychoanalyse *you*.' He lifted her legs on to the lounger he had made ready for her. He had been first home.

'No, thanks.' She smiled up at him. 'You might discover some dreadful secrets.'

'Okay.' He bent down and kissed her. Occasionally he would be overcome by a feeling of unreality, that he, Hamish Laidlaw, son of Scottish parents, was married and living in harmony with Karin Gottleib of Brooklyn Heights, in their own home in Westchester, New York, above the Hudson river. Sometimes he felt ever so slightly in awe of her capability. Such capability had an edge to it. She could seem unapproachable at first when she came home from the city. It could be tiredness. 'When's Hal coming?'

'Not till after eight. He has an appointment with someone in Tarrytown who has some information about his painters.'

'Good. You've time for a drink. What would you like?'

'A large gin and tonic, no, make it a small gin and tonic. I've to remember my lodger.' She patted her stomach, and with the action her pleasure in being home disappeared. She remembered that scrutinizing look of Paul Laskins. 'I always thought I was good at leaving my worries behind me.'

'Awful day? I don't know how you do it, listening to all those crackpots.'

'They aren't all crackpots. They haven't all got it together as well as you.'

'Okay.' He handed the drink to her, looking rueful.

'Thanks, honey.' She knew she was edgy. It would be the baby, of course. Pregnant women were supposed to be edgy. Perhaps it would have been better if she had decided to have a year's sabbatical, or two, or three, got the family bit over, maybe have another one. There was no money problem. Mish's gallery was doing well.

'Was there someone who annoyed you?' He sat down again with his drink.

'No, not annoyed me. It's become a kind of . . . personal thing. Or rather, this particular patient wants it to be that. I feel I'm fending him off . . .'

'Has he made a pass?'

She laughed. 'Don't look so fierce. No, he hasn't, but he asks personal questions, knows more about me than I care and today, he seemed to be . . . staring at my stomach . . .'

'Staring at your stomach! For God's sake!'

51

'It's not done in polite society, I know. I suppose I'm used to being a cipher, and then, this personal thing.'

'He's fallen in love with you. That's it. You wouldn't reconsider taking a year or two off, Karin? Really enjoy this phase in your life?' It was a mistake. He saw it in her eyes.

'We've been over all this, Mish. We agreed. Don't go back on your word. I'm not houseproud, nor do I think my whole life should be given to rearing children. My work is important to me. I'd miss it.'

'Don't protest too much.'

'Hey! Are we quarrelling? We agreed it wouldn't do a child any good to have a resentful mother.'

'It's seeing you tired . . .' He had noticed her swollen ankles. 'I'm sorry.'

'Maybe it's you being Scottish. A woman's place is in the home and all that. But, don't forget, your mother always worked but fortunately she could do it at home, whereas I don't want to fill ours with what you call "crackpots".'

He knew when he was on dangerous ground. 'No, two's enough.' He smiled at her, thinking, we *are* different, her whole culture is different from mine.

'Did you have a busy day, honey?' But she was his mate, 'trusty, dusky, vivid, true . . .' A Scotsman had said that.

'No, quiet, strangely enough, as regards clients.' The little spat was over. 'The good weather makes them head for the Hamptons or whatever. It gave me a chance to go down to the basement to see what I had stashed away.'

'That reminds me.' She lifted the flat parcel which was propped against her briefcase. 'This is Paul Laskins's latest offering – the patient I was telling you about. Where did we put the first one?'

'It's stashed away in the gallery somewhere. I put all our pictures there when we were moving. Don't worry. I shan't sell it by mistake. Let's look.' He untied the string, took off the brown paper wrapping and propped the picture against the garden table.

'You, Anna and Ritchie have a way of *looking*,' Karin said. 'No wonder Van felt left out.'

Mish nodded. 'Anna would suss this out in no time. Ritchie would too, but he'd take longer. My vision is tainted by the god Mammon. I can tell you it wouldn't sell. It's a mess technically, but there's something there.'

'It's his way of getting back to the past. It's quite usual therapy.'

'Everybody paints to find out.'

'I thought it was a beach, a bay somewhere. What are the two circles? Stones?'

'Or an embryonic body. Where are the legs?'

'Maybe they haven't grown yet.' She felt something like morning sickness in her throat although it was evening. 'It's strange. He lives at the same address as Hal. Which reminds me,' she struggled to rise, 'I must go in and rustle up some food.'

'There's no need. It's all taken care of. I went to the village and bought some ready-made stuff, and fruit and cheese and some of that good ice-cream from Bertorelli's.'

'You'll make me fatter than ever.' She turned as she heard footsteps. 'Here he is. Hi, Hal!'

Hal came towards them across the flagged terrace. He was carrying a large brown paper bag. 'Hi, Karin! Hi, Mish!'

'You look like a packhorse.'

'I saw this Polish shop on the way here. And I've got some wine. Would you like me to put it in the fridge for you?'

53

'I'll do it.' Mish was on his feet. 'Sit down beside Karin. What's your poison?'

'Mother's ruin. Hey, less gin! Thanks.' He took his glass and sat down. 'Bliss. Were the roads bad for you, Karin?'

'No, not once I cleared Yonkers. I like the run home. It gives me a chance to unwind. It's pretty. Bosky.'

'You're glad you came here?'

'Oh, yes, glad.' Mish had gone inside. 'Mish would like me to settle here and raise a family.'

'And give up work?'

'Would you expect it of Van?'

'Whatever she wants. I'm no patriarch.' She looked at him, his easiness, his essential cheerfulness, but it could be a coat he'd worn for a long time to cover a hurt.

'No, I don't see you with a long white beard. Between you and me, Hal, I'm not overly maternal. I'll be quite happy to get a good nanny.'

'And no guilt?'

'No. I've worked it out. Maybe it's an English disease.'

'As long as you both think the same.'

'That's it. As long as we both think the same.' She could feel his eyes on her. He was astute. All sensitive people were.

'Shall you have a pool here?' He had taken his eyes off her and was looking round appreciatively.

'No, Mish is paranoid about pools. Small children drown in them.' Their eyes met again. His were smiling. She decided to change the subject, and Paul Laskins came into her mind as if the thought of him hadn't been far away. 'By the way, have you run across a man called Paul Laskins who lives in your apartment block?'

His brows were drawn together. 'Can't say I have. Name isn't familiar. Why?'

'I . . . met him the other day.' She decided not to say he was a patient. 'His address is the same as yours.'

'I'll keep a look out. I really only see people on the elevator, and then there's this woman I told you about, Ellie Kaplan, who gives roof parties. People drift in and out. What does he look like?'

'Tall, gangly, prematurely bald. His limbs give him trouble. He looks . . . alien. You get to know that look. It's commonplace in clinics.'

'Ellie will know him. Would you like me to ask her?'

'Heavens, no! I just wondered. From what you told me, I'm sure you don't want to get more involved with Miss Kaplan than necessary.'

He grimaced.

'Men are heartless.' She teased him. 'You should be kind to her. She's lonely.'

'Even so, I don't want her climbing into my bed . . .'

'What's this I hear?' Mish was beside them with a laden trolley. 'Have you struck lucky, Hal?'

'Not if you saw the lady in question.'

'Don't budge, Karin,' Mish said. 'It's all here.' He gave her a napkin wrapped round a fork. 'Would you pour the wine, Hal, while I tend to my darling wife?'

'See how he makes an invalid out of me, Hal?' And then, regretting her tone, 'My goodness, honey, you have done us proud. Pastrami, bagels, salad. What are those?'

'Hal's contribution. Tell her.'

'Now that I look, not very Polish. Salmon mousse, blueberry tart, butterscotch peach pie . . .'

'State your preference, madam.' Mish had a napkin over his shoulder and a plate in his hand.

'Okay,' Karin said. 'I'll start with pastrami and bagels, being a true Jewish girl, and don't tell me, are those prawns?'

55

'King-size. Some olive bread as well?'

'Please.'

They sat eating and talking until the sun went down. Hal said Anna had found a responsible woman to run the house for them, a middle-aged widow called Mrs Fairbairn recommended by their doctor, and although she would never be Bessie, they were getting along fine.

'Van's up to the eyes. Her examinations are next week. I'll fly home at the end of the month, in three weeks' time. I'll have to get my skates on too with my Hudson Valley painters.'

'What do you think of them?' Mish asked.

'Fascinating. They don't come into the "great" category, Titian and that lot, but I am a fact-finder, not a connoisseur like you. I've been charmed by them. It's been the greatest pleasure. They were explorers as well as painters. They made thousands of sketches on the trail. It's an interesting combination when you think how easy it is for painters nowadays, well, perhaps not so easy.'

'All my father's struggles take place when he's stretched out on his old sofa.'

'I suppose that's no less valid. It's a different style of painting but the aim is the same, a search for nature, or themselves. Thomas Cole, one of the earlier painters, once urged his listeners – he was given to dissertations – to nurture the oasis in us as a retreat from the world. At that time America was plunging headlong into economic development.'

'I like that. "The oasis in us." That would certainly apply to most of us in New York or any big city. We should pause . . .'

He's a romantic, Karin thought, not of the New World although it attracted him enough to come and live here. He wants an Eldorado here, the laughter of children, a wife to cherish.

'I've covered most of them,' Hal was saying, 'the early stuff, Inness, Marin and Wyant in the Met, but it's the later work which has more charm, for me at any rate.'

'Less anecdotal, more . . . mood?'

'That's it. And the technique's looser, more French influence, less of the Germanic. I'd like to have some long talks with your father, I've got prints to show him, and get his reactions. That would be really interesting for me. My creativity is used up on trying not to make the book sound like a fact-finding mission.'

'Call on me if I can help in any way,' Mish said. 'Pity you aren't staying longer.'

'Ah, but think of the attractions in the Dear Green Place,' and seeing Karin's puzzled look, 'Glasgow.'

'Ah. We'll miss you, Hal. But remember, now that we have this house there's room for you all at any time.'

'Thanks. I appreciate that.' He lifted his glass to them. 'You two have been marvellous.'

'It's scarcely goodbye. We'll be in Scotland soon, won't we, Mish? I have to get to know all my Scottish relatives. There's a lot to be said for families, most of the time . . .' Paul Laskins. He was back again. Could she perhaps see his sister, the one he had such a grudge against, get her point of view?

'It's amazing how optimistic the human race is,' Mish said. 'Despite wars and famine we keep on creating more of us, building family trees . . . what are you two laughing at? Am I being smug? Knowing about pestilence, fear, want. You saw that in Biafra, Karin.' She nodded. That she still found difficult to talk about. 'It's fear of loneliness,' Mish was saying. 'We can't bear to be alone.'

'So what about old Cole's theory about nurturing the oasis within us?' Hal said.

'This is the last piece of olive bread,' Karin said. 'If no one wants it I'm going to have it.'

'In your condition,' Hal laughed at her, 'you have prior claim.'

The three of them sat talking desultorily as they looked over the darkening garden and beyond it to the broad silver-grey expanse of the Hudson. That at least would remain, Karin thought. What about us?

'This is a Brahms night,' Hal said.

'Musical, as well as all your other talents?' She thought, looking at him, how attractive he was, and that look of his, his 'sexual beam' she called it. Maybe it was as well Mish didn't have it. It would worry her sick. She saw he was rubbing his arm. He had a tender skin. 'Are you getting bitten, honey?'

'It's the blue blood they like. Maybe we should go in before the bugs bite.' He laughed. 'We had a password when Mother was tucking us in. "Goodnight, goodnight," she would say, and we'd reply, "Don't let the bugs bite!" They're the most sentimental of people, the Scots, and yet they scorn sentiment. "Ach, don't be daft!" they say.' Karin looked at him and saw the little boy.

'I envy you people with families,' Hal said. 'Mine wasn't like that.' He got up.

'Well, you've got us now.' Karin smiled at him.

He bent down and kissed her. 'Thanks. Do you want a hand up?'

'No, I'm going to sit for a little. I've got a hide like a rhinoceros.'

'Come on, then, Mish.' He turned to him, 'I'll help you clear up before I go. It'll be my apology for staying so late.'

They'll be talking about London and painters and all the traditional things that men talk about, Karin thought, watching them loading the trolley and pushing it through the patio doors. Neither of them, with all their sophistication, understand this urgent city which bred me. It was poles apart from their background, brittle, nervy, exciting. London to her was gracious but ponderous, slow-moving, the difference between a skittish pony and an old mare.

Her eyes were on the river, its dulling gleam, and there it was again, Paul Laskins's presence and its concomitant mixture of fear and pity. Perhaps it was her pregnancy that was making her so introspective, so unlike her usual cool detachment. She sat until she began to feel cold, lacking the energy to get up.

'Dreaming?' Mish was standing beside her. 'Come on in. Hal's gone. What were you thinking of?'

'I was wondering if you ever had a boat? "Feel that fresh wind on my face, go fishing in my little boat . . ."'

'A boat? Do you mean here? To sail up Park Avenue?' He laughed.

She got up. 'No, it wouldn't do. Yes, honey, let's go in.'

Seven

It was the day of Van's finals. Sam was manly. 'Don't worry, Mummy. Exams are easy, easy as pie.'

'Maybe to you. I'm an old lady. It's ages since I was at proper school.'

'You don't have to get a job, do you, now that you're married to Hal? He'll keep us.' She laughed at him.

'Of course he will. But I've studied for this for a long time and I want to work in a hospital. Grandma works and *she's* married.'

'But hammering and things isn't work!' He looked up at her and she saw Eb for a second in the dark skin, the tinge of yellow in the whites of his eyes and a liquidity which wasn't an Anglo-Saxon thing.

'You've got egg on your face. Wipe it off. Oh, yes, it's work, hard work. But you can enjoy your work. She does. She's an artist, like Aunt Jean. They both earn money from it.'

'But not as much as Grandpa.'

'No, not as much as him but then he's special.'

'Is he special in Spain as well?' Anna and Ritchie were at their house in Arenys de Mar. Ritchie had a big show on in Barcelona and Anna had gone with him. She had apologized to Van.

'I'm sorry I shan't be at home to spur you on to victory, but I daren't let that man out of my sight.'

'Oh, he's past the dangerous age, Mum,' she had said.

'Believe me, men are never past the dangerous age. It's a good thing that handsome man of yours is coming back from New York. There are some very smart cookies there.'

Van left in plenty of time, telling Mrs Fairbairn she wouldn't be back all day and that she would eat in the College canteen. Sam would come home from school as usual, but she was to be sure to check that he wasn't late.

'He'll be all right with me,' Mrs Fairbairn said. 'I've promised him a strawberry tart from the City Bakeries, two if he's on time, and a fizzy drink.'

'You know the way to his heart.' Mrs Fairbairn would never be Bessie, she was too ladylike for a start, but she was no fool, and she had got the measure of Sam. She had a son who was a cadet in the Merchant Navy, and she could enthral him with tales of Jack's exploits on the high seas. She was already Ritchie's willing slave.

Van walked down Sauchiehall Street, having got off the bus at Charing Cross. Her stomach was turning. The motion of the bus had made her feel slightly sick. '"Now's the day and now's the hour,"' she muttered in time to her steps, '"See the front o' battle lour . . ."' She mustn't make a mess of things with nerves. She thought of Hal, and the bouquet of pink roses which he had organized to arrive early this morning.

'Go to it, babe!' the message had read, 'Love and luck, Hal.'

She stopped and looked across Sauchiehall Street, to the steep hill of Scott Street which led to the Art School, and which the three Mackintosh sisters, and Ritchie, had climbed so often when they were students there.

But you, she told herself, are on the point of sitting the most important examination in your life! It's sheer terror which is making your mind shy away from it. She drew in a deep breath and turned right into Pitt Street, seeing the College looming ahead of her, square, unyielding. '"Now's the time and now's the hour ... On to victory!"'

She met the Principal as she went through the swing doors. 'Well, Miss Laidlaw,' he greeted her, 'it's a long time since I saw you. That time when your son had an accident, wasn't it? Is he all right now?'

'Yes, thank you,' she said, 'fighting fit. I'm married now. My name's Purvis. Perhaps you haven't seen the change in the register?'

'Congratulations! But you won't throw away your Diploma in spite of that, I hope?' I like your confidence, she almost said, as she thanked him and followed the arrows to the Temple of Doom.

In the examination hall she meekly accepted the first sheaf of papers handed out by the adjudicator. She was stiff with fright. 'Go to it, babe!' Hal had written. Well, this was it.

For some reason she thought of the Glasgow Girls as she lifted her pen. These were adult women, she had realized when she looked at their work. Maybe she too was moving into a new area of self-awareness, of greater confidence in herself. She read the first question.

'Describe the benefits a widower of seventy-five could expect who had been removed from his home to hospital with suspected malnutrition and anaemia, and who had no other means of support.' She started to write, her mind cleared for action, 'on to victory'. She laughed at herself, which was certainly mature.

Her mood of confidence, but not over-confidence, remained with her. She wrote steadily all morning and, after a short break, well into the afternoon, experiencing that most prized feeling desired of all examinees, that the questions had been designed especially for her. When she sat back, having finished the last paper, her mood was one of quiet elation. Hal, she thought, would be quite pleased with her.

She waited impatiently that evening for Hal to telephone her. Mrs Fairbairn had gone out to visit her married daughter, unlike Bessie who had had to be persuaded to take time off. Sam had been tucked in to bed. The big house was silent, the Crescent from the drawing-room window looked a picture of subdued gentility. In Maryhill, she thought, the children would still be playing out on the street, the women gossiping at doorways, the men making their nightly trek to the corner pub.

She was restless. Her mood was flat after the tenseness of the day when adrenaline had seemed to pour through her veins. She felt she had done good papers, but was suffering now from the usual remorse that she hadn't answered the questions more accurately, too precisely, more fully, less fully, and hadn't divided her time between the questions more sensibly.

She climbed the flight of stairs to the attic rooms where Anna's and Ritchie's studios were. They had asked her to air them from time to time, but had insisted that she kept them locked, safe from the mischievous fingers of Sam and the prying eyes of Mrs Fairbairn. Ritchie thought the housekeeper's delicate susceptibilities might receive several shocks if she 'took a dekko', his words, at his paintings.

Anna's studio, which Van went into first, was as neat as a new pin, indeed as Anna herself. The pieces she had finished were on display blocks – her usual practice so that they could 'settle into themselves'. No one, even herself, Van thought, could fail to admire them, the exquisite photograph frames, hammered into designs and motifs very similar to the arabesques so beloved of the Glasgow Girls, jewel boxes and clock faces which were particularly Spanish in influence.

Anna was not prolific, but each year her prices increased, and according to Ritchie she was close to earning as much as he did. The whole room was a work of art which could have been transported as it stood to a display window in any exclusive shop window in Glasgow or London. If you looked closer you could see her signature, a Gothic letter 'A' buried amongst the convoluted shapes. Van closed the door quietly in case she disturbed any of the displays, and locked it.

Ritchie's room, larger and with huge windows set in the roof, was the opposite. Chaos. Huge canvases stacked end-to-end against the walls, others displayed on the floor, some on easels, murals covering most of the wall space. Lately he had developed the habit of working on several paintings at once.

'What mood am I in today?' he would ask himself, and anyone else, at the breakfast table. 'What do you think, Anna?'

'Do you want me to feel your pulse?'

'What do you say, Sam, should I let Grandma feel my pulse?'

'I'll do it, I'll do it! I'm good at pulses!' He was in his element with this kind of play-acting.

'Right, Doctor.' Ritchie would extend his strong arm across the table, the hand like a workman's, no dainty drawing-room painter he. Sam would grasp it, put his finger on Ritchie's wrist, put on an attentive air, his lips pursed.

'He would make a good doctor,' Anna would say. 'Well, what do you think, Doctor? Perhaps the Spanish mural today?'

'I would say the Spanish mural,' Sam would repeat, nodding his head solemnly.

'Okay.' Ritchie would withdraw his hand. 'Good thing you called in a specialist. First-class wumman that.' His smile was for Anna alone. 'Ye'll no meet anybody better in a month o' Sundays.'

'Isn't Grandpa daft, Mummy?' Sam would be in fits of laughter, often interrupted by the entry of Mrs Fairbairn.

'I don't want to hurry you, but it's time the lad was setting off for school.'

Now Van studied the biggest mural, the Spanish one. There was always a Spanish one on the stocks. As usual it was non-figurative, a jazzy jumble of colour at close quarters, but when she retreated to the other end of the room she saw something which looked like a townscape with a church-like building emerging from it, a Grimms' fairytale kind of church with lopsided walls, a crooked tower and a bell which seemed to be tumbling through the air. 'I've become an art critic.' She preened herself. 'I've suffered an artistic conversion on the road to ... Bayswater.' Now she saw or thought she saw a ladder resting against the tower of the church, with a jingle-jangle of black lines scored through it which might be arms or legs ... or maybe she didn't. She looked at the title Ritchie had written on a scrap of paper and tacked on the wall. 'The bell'.

Why the bell? 'Ding dong dell, pussy's in the well ...' 'Rings on her fingers and bells on her toes ...' And that lovely poem about ringing the bells of heaven. There was a ring of black lines round the foot of the church which might be figures dancing the Sardana ... Her speculations dried up and she saw only a mural which didn't make sense.

She raised the windows to let the warm summer air

stream in, and heard the muted roar of traffic from Great Western Road. For seven years or more that sound had been in her ears if she opened her window at night, seven years since she came here pregnant with Sam and was given a home. Glasgow would always be dear to her. She knew intimately the West End, the city, and the housing estates on the outskirts, like Easterhouse and Castlemilk. Although they had supplanted the slums of the inner city by their remoteness, they had created a new kind of deprivation, that of the soul.

She had grown to love the Glasgow people, best typified by Bessie with her inherent kindness and wry common sense. And her ability to cock a snook at life. No one Van had ever known had had such a strong sense of their own identity. She would always be one of them, even when she, Sam and Hal were living in London. Her ties were too strong, not only to her parents but to the city itself. It would draw her back, because part of her heart would be there.

She closed the windows, locked the door, and was halfway downstairs when she heard the ring of the telephone. She tripped on the last two steps in her hurry.

It was Hal. 'How did it go? Was it a walk-over?' She was shy with emotion at the sound of his voice.

'Oh, all right, I think.'

'Were you confident, or screwed up with nervousness?'

'A little of both, but I thought of your roses, and the message, and I went to it, babe!' She laughed. 'Oh, I've been dying to hear you, Hal. How are you?'

'Clearing up. Only two weeks to go, and I can hardly wait. I've seen quite a lot of Karin and Mish even now when they've moved out of the city. I'm doing research

66

in the same area. They love being there. They want us to visit them whenever we can.'

'And we'll have them wherever *we* are.'

'We'll buy a house. Choose it to suit your work, and Sam's school, and incidentally, me. I've never had a house since I was at school, and even then . . .' She knew he didn't like to talk of his schooldays.

'We'll have a house, don't worry. Anna has offered to come home and see us off to London but I've told her not to dream of it. We'll slip away from Glasgow, fold up our tents. That way no one will see my tears.'

'You'll be sad, darling.'

'Oh, I'll be sad. They gave me shelter, gave me a home. I was thinking of it tonight. But I'm happy too. Sam's happy. He thinks it's all a great adventure, but he'll cry too.'

'Don't make me feel like a marauder.'

'Oh, no, Hal. He loves you. Do you think he should call you Daddy, now that we're married?'

'If he comes to it naturally. Go to bed, darling. You must be tired. And think of me.'

'That's no recipe for sleep. Let me know your times of arrival and I'll meet you. Mother has left her car.'

'Okay.'

She did sleep, even thinking of Hal.

Eight

Hal was fully occupied for the last two weeks of his stay in New York. His happiness at the thought of living with Van and Sam filled him with a creative energy which flowed into his work, and he spent most of the day and a good part of his evening working on the book about the Hudson Valley painters.

Art led to history. The Civil War fascinated him, and when he looked at the broad sweeping vision of Cole's paintings, they seemed to be an expression of faith in the painter's country, of his intense pride, perhaps heightened when it was being fought over.

There was a painting by Worthington Whittredge, what grand-sounding names they had, called 'The Old Hunting Grounds', which was so poetic in its vision that he could see there the country as it had been in the time of the Indian, feel the mystery and the close link with nature, the pantheism. The slender trunks of the birches, the abandoned boat, drew him again and again to look at the painting, to enter into it, until it became almost a mystical experience. He had to prevent himself straying too far into such realms, and remind himself it was a book he was writing, not a testament of faith.

The broad sweep, the sureness and mastery of Winslow Homer's works had to be admired, but he preferred

68

the 'mood indigo' school of Ryder, the painter of dreams, the poet. He learned, in writing the book, to keep his prejudices out of the way, not completely for that would have been dull, but not to be opinionative. It became a substitute for Van. He flew to it like a lover.

He learned a good deal about himself also in those last weeks, about his butterfly mind, which in turn made him think of Van, his Butterfly Girl, *Vanessa cardui*, the name he sometimes teased her with, and then his thoughts would become intimate and he would have to get up and have a drink. 'A cold shower for you,' he'd mutter.

One evening when he was working around midnight he heard an unexpected knock on his door. No one, he thought, could arrive outside the apartments and gain entry without first ringing him on the intercom. He thought it must be Ellie Kaplan, as he rose reluctantly and went to the door. And then, as he opened it, he remembered with dismay that she had invited him to drinks that evening. There she was, and he saw by her flushed face that she had been drinking.

'Ellie! My God, I'm sorry! I was working away and I quite forgot! Come in! What on earth must you think of me?'

'Come in!' She repeated his words, giggling stupidly. 'Come in, he says, after keeping me, *and* my guest, waiting, till he couldn't wait any longer.' She staggered against him and he guided her to a seat which she spilled into like a laundry bag. He stood in front of her, hiding his irritation, partly at himself.

'I'm so sorry. I'm working to a deadline. I thought if you were having a few residents that I wouldn't be missed, then I got engrossed ... Would you like a drink?'

'That's more like it,' she said. 'Bourbon, please.' And

that was stupid, stupid, he thought, pouring the drink for her at the cabinet. She's more than half-seas over already.

'Thanks, Hal, honey.' She leered at him as she took the glass. 'Yes, you're naughty, very naughty, and I ought to be very angry with you!' She shook her finger at him, slopping the liquid down the front of her bright green cocktail suit.

'Did you have many guests?' he asked, sitting down opposite her.

'No, only one. People are very discourteous. When I think of all the trouble I've gone to, organizing those roof parties, and then when I buy my own drink and made those damned canapés and dips, the only one who turns up is that weirdo, Paul Laskins!'

Hal was instantly alerted. 'Paul Laskins?' That was the name Karin had mentioned, surely. He got up and poured a drink for himself, and this time sat down on the sofa beside her. He must get this straight.

'I don't know what you must think of me,' he said, 'it was the height of rudeness . . .' She went into gales of laughter.

' "I don't know what you must think of me, it was the height of rudeness." La-de-da! My God, you English slay me! You'd think you'd stepped straight out of a history book, with a long, dangling sword . . . Oh, excuse me, that was a bit near the bone.' She spluttered into her glass.

'I'm good at ignoring innuendo. Have I met Paul Laskins? The name rings a bell.'

'Rings a bell, does it? Ting-a-ling-a-ling?' She slurped and giggled alternately. 'Yeah, you've met him. At one of my roof parties. If it's any consolation to you he doesn't remember you either. But he's a weirdo anyhow. Lives on his father's money, won't work. He used to confide in me a lot after his girl left him. I gave him really nice little dinners, no takeaway stuff, made it real homey for him, but I got fed up eventually. I'd be offering him some good advice, about how girls like to be treated, and then when I looked at him he'd be just staring across the room like a zombie. "Look," I said, "Paul, is it worth my while talking?" That's what everyone does with me. Takes my hospitality and then throws it in my face.' She was suddenly weeping, the tears streaking her cheeks with mascara.

Hal put his arm round her. 'Don't distress yourself, Ellie. You're tired.' Karin had said he should be kind to her. He was so lucky, so happy. Her head fell on his shoulder.

'Yeah, I'm tired, tired. I sometimes think I should give up trying. That's what Paul Laskins said tonight. Sometimes he feels he should give up trying. We drank to cheer ourselves up.'

'I'm trying to remember him,' Hal said. 'What does he look like?'

'Like a lamp-post. Long neck. This bald head with a fringe of hair. Bobbie, that's his girl, *was*, used to see to his clothes, but now he just wears tee-shirts all the time. He says they're easier to wash. Goes for long walks on his own, cooks for himself. He could eat out, he could take *me* out, considering all the hospitality he's had from me. And now you give me the go-by too . . .'

'It was an oversight. I'm so sorry.' And, thinking, what the hell, I'm going away, 'I really like you a lot, Ellie. You've shown me such kindness . . . here, use this.' He surrendered his handkerchief. 'What do you say if I make a pot of coffee and we have a good chat?'

'Are you telling me that you like me?' She sat up, and he saw her flushed face streaked with black, the trembling, full-lipped mouth, the hair which stood out

71

in glued spikes from her head. 'Me, an old hag? A bloody bag lady?'

'Nonsense! Of course I do.' He laughed, and the laugh in his throat was suddenly throttled by her darting forward and planting a fierce kiss on his mouth, nearly knocking in his teeth. 'Hey, hey!' he protested ineffectually.

'That's just a sample, honey.' She lay back as if exhausted by her effort. 'Now, I want you to be a good boy and help me to the ladies' boudoir because I suddenly have to go, and then we'll have a nice long chat over that coffee and maybe a drink, and then, who knows?' Her provocative glance from under the stiff black eyelashes put the fear of God into him.

'Great!' he said, and helped her to her feet, guiding her with one arm round her waist towards his bathroom, where he thankfully shut the door on her. He had the coffee ready when she eventually came out.

'I didn't bring my purse. I feel naked without my purse. Well, maybe that's a step in the right direction, eh?' Her glance was arch. She fell rather than sat on the sofa, taking up most of it which gave Hal the chance to sit down on a chair opposite her this time. He turned to the side-table where he had put the coffee and filled a mug for her.

'Here you are, Ellie. Hot and strong. Would you like an aspirin?'

'No, thanks, looking at you's as good as taking a pill. Gee, I bet you get up to some tricks in bed with that English princess of yours!'

'Sugar? Tell me about your friend, Paul Laskins. Did you know his girlfriend well?'

'Bobbie? In a way. She was gone all day, she worked in some office, but she stuck to him for a long time, two or three years. More than I would have done. If

72

my man wasn't working to keep me I'd say "Bugger off!"' She took a slurp of her coffee and then another one. It seemed to clear her head. 'A nice girl, trim, all of a piece. Latterly they had some rows, I think, although I never heard anything. Sometimes she looked as if she had been crying when I met her on the elevator, but she was proud. She'd smile and say, "Hi!" and ask me how I was doing. Proud, didn't want to share her troubles, I guess.'

'Where did she come from?'

'God knows! Where does anyone in New York come from? Out of the woodwork, mostly. No, I shouldn't say that about Bobbie. She was a nice girl, smart, but not overly smart. Nice to people. She spoke to Mrs Wallechinsky in the basement, I think. Baby-sat for her. Wouldn't take payment, Mrs Wallechinsky told me. Then one day Paul knocked at my door in a state and asked me if I had seen her. I asked him in and after that he used to drop by to talk about her.'

'What did he tell you?'

'Come to think of it, nothing much. That she felt lonely for her folks. About the good times they'd had. How he couldn't understand why she left. He had even promised to get a steady job if she would stay. Buy her a house in Long Island. But she had wanted to go back home. I never got to understand it. I had thought they were going to be married. *Three* years she was there, now I remember. Bobbie . . . Bobbie . . . can't remember her other name . . . yeah, that was one unhappy girl. But Paul, he's too deep for me. Something there. Could I have another drink? Talk about me for a change? Or you?' Her face was pitiful, sad. Hal was full of compassion, something he might have learned from Van.

He got up. 'No more drinks, Ellie. You're tired, and

73

I'm going to get you to your apartment. Come on.' He helped her to her feet and she didn't resist.

'Throwing me out, are you? That's the story of my life. Thrown out of all the best places.'

'Far from it. I told you, I like you a lot. Now, I'm going to call you tomorrow and we'll fix up an evening when you'll allow me to take you out to dinner. You can choose where we'll go. Promise?'

He got her, thankfully, to her door, where she seemed too tired, too dejected, to argue. Her look as she shut it on him would remain with him for a long time. Karin was right. She was one of the many. It was a pity that instead of living in a city she wasn't in a small town where she might be accepted for her eccentricities. Her desire to make a roof garden might have been transferred to a garden outside her front door. Next time he saw Karin he would tell her what he had found out about Paul Laskins.

Van was waiting for him at Renfrew airport when his plane arrived. Sam was at her side. Hal couldn't believe how beautiful she looked. It wasn't only that she was slimmer, that the pale skin and black hair, the intensely blue eyes were arresting, but over and above, there was a characterful quality, a quality of outgoing love which included everyone. He swept her into his arms and said, 'It's been so long.' Then after a time, aware of his jacket being pulled, said, 'Okay Sam!' released Van and pretended to lift the boy, groaning exaggeratedly. 'Hey, what weight are you for goodness' sake? Have you been fed on grow-big pills or something?' Sam was giggling as he put him down.

'Aunt Nancy measures me with wee Gordon. I'm the biggest although he's the oldest.'

'Bully for you. Come on, folks, we're holding up the

traffic.' He lifted his case. Their joy, his and Van's, was so intense that they kept stealing covert glances at each other. 'I caught you,' he said, smiling at her.

'Well, you were looking at *me*. You're different, but the same. Americanized in some special way.'

'New York leaves its mark. I suspect you don't get it anywhere else. They all bend forward from the hips, they're in such a hurry. But it's a heady city. I can see its attraction for Mish.'

'How are they?'

'Blooming. Karin's fine now. They love their house. The guest suite is being kept specially for us, she says, when we visit them.'

'Does that mean me too?' Sam asked, hurrying along beside them.

'Whither we goest, thou shall go. Have no fear,' Hal said. 'In other words, yes. We'll go next year sometime and see the new baby.'

'Ach, babies! I'm fed up with babies.' He kicked at an empty carton at his feet.

'We'll have to watch our step,' Hal said, looking at Van. She raised her eyebrows and nodded.

'This way.' She pointed to an arrow indicating the car park.

'I have to rent a car first. I can dump it in London when we arrive.'

'We've got our very own car,' Sam said. 'Grandma gave it to us.'

'Don't steal my thunder, Sam!' Van laughed at him.

'Is this true?' Hal asked.

'Yes. It's mine. Mother telephoned me a few days ago. She says she never gave me a proper wedding present and she wants me to have it. She'll buy a new one for herself when she gets back from Spain.'

'That was generous.'

'She's got loads of cash.' Sam swaggered along.

Van looked at him. 'Sam! Where are you learning to speak like that?'

'Well, Grandpa said he'd sold another picture and he didn't know what to do with the money he was making. He'll have given Grandma a pile.'

'He was only joking.' She glanced meaningfully at Hal. 'Anyhow, it's very generous. Mother reckons that I'll need one when I get a job in London. I reminded her that I hadn't had my results yet.'

'Oh, you'll pass with flying colours!' Hal put his arm round her waist and squeezed it as they went into the car park. 'So what's the drill? Back to Clevedon Crescent?'

'No. I've packed the car with all our clothes, books, possessions, the lot. And said goodbye to Mrs Fairbairn.'

'Mummy was crying,' Sam said.

'So were you. Here we are.' She stopped at the red Vauxhall. 'Would you like to drive, Hal?'

'No, thanks, you're far more competent than I am in Glasgow traffic. What a great thing to do, I mean, your mother. Did I ever tell you how lucky I feel to be part of such a family?' He wiped his eyes, making Sam laugh. 'I'll be crying next.'

Hal decided to sit in the back, not to oust Sam. Maybe that was what being part of a family meant, consideration for others. He was a newcomer. He had to learn new ways. 'What about your school, Sam?' he said, leaning forward and putting his elbows on the front seat. 'Did they give you a farewell party?'

'I don't want to talk about it.' He wriggled in his seat. Hal shut up for a second, then to the back of Van's head, 'So we don't call in at Clevedon Crescent?'

'No, not again.' She didn't want to talk about it either.

He sat back, realizing fully for the first time that he was taking this girl and her son away from a stable background to the unknown. They'd had to cut a lot of ties.

'Okay,' he said, 'what do you say if we stop when we're well out of Glasgow, choose a hotel and stay overnight? I know a good one which has a swimming pool and water chutes for kids. Does that appeal, Sam?'

'I suppose that'll be all right. Will it, Mummy?' Hal saw how he nestled into his mother's side.

The hotel they stopped at in the Midlands was part of a chain with all the requisites for children which Hal had promised. He asked for a large room with a double and a single bed. He saw by the look in Van's eyes he had done the right thing.

Hal went into the pool with Sam, and the thin body he held in his arms when they were frolicking seemed precious. The brown face, in spite of the laughter, had sad eyes. There will be no children of our own until we get this one settled in, he thought.

He bathed him afterwards in the bath with its fake gold faucets, as Hal told them they were called in America, then he and Van tucked him up in bed, laughing and teasing, but both aware of the boy's vulnerability. Because of his skin he must often feel different. It was important that he should feel part of a family.

'My turn now,' Van said. She lifted her case and went back to the bathroom where she undressed and put on her nightdress. The room was quiet, the top light off.

'Hal's in already, Mummy.' It was Sam's sleepy voice.

'So I see.' She made a sudden dive in beside Hal, and when he felt her close to him his heart nearly left him with delight.

'Night night, Sam,' he said.

77

'Don't let the bugs bite.' The boy's voice was loaded with sleep.

Hal put off the side light and took Van his arms. It was enough for tonight.

BOOK 2

1971

Nine

'Where have you been for so long?' She moaned against him, listening to the moaning with the fifty-six-year-old Jean's critical mind while her body pressed into his shamelessly. 'Two weeks, then three weeks! I thought you were on the moon!'

'In my moon buggy?' He laughed, kissing her. 'Kept you on the boil, have I?'

She hated these remarks of his. They cheapened her. Frederick had never spoken like that, but then there had been no colloquialisms in his always formal speech. He'd never blasphemed. Looking back over the period of thirty years, she realized it had been an old-fashioned seduction, not like this one where it had been as much her fault as his, as well as deceiving her husband who had brought her to life after the death of Frederick's baby.

But he was pushing her as he teased, his arms round her, pushing and guiding her with his body towards the old couch in the corner of the room where sometimes she had to lie down when she had exhausted herself by painting half the night. Once John had found her there in the morning and had helped her back to the house, made her some coffee, insisted she should go upstairs and sleep while he was at the surgery.

Her heart filled with shame and regret and dislike of

herself, at the same time as she fell on to the couch with
him, helping him to unloosen his clothes, undoing hers,
utterly shameless, and yet when he entered her, when
she saw that handsome face above her and the same
strangeness in it which had been in Frederick's face,
she gave herself again and again to the overwhelming
waves of desire which came like the waves on Glenluce
Bay in winter, crashing and dashing and hurtling
against the rocks.

'You needed that,' Denis said when it was over, when
they lay still.

'I needed it. Shame goes out of the window.'

'That's as it should be. Live for the moment.'

'But you were away a long time,' she said.

'Katie was with her grandparents while my wife, I
suppose I should say my ex-wife, was in Spain. They
asked me to come and see Katie.'

'That was nice for you.' She lay in his arms, spent.
Why do I do this, she thought, a woman happy with
her husband, blessed with a talent, everything anyone
could want. She hadn't told Anna. She would have
laughed her to scorn, Anna, the faithful one, whose
faithfulness had been rewarded, who had in Ritchie a
husband who had strayed once but never again. 'I can't
believe this is me,' she said. 'When you're away I get
time to think and I haven't found the answer to my
question, "Why do I do this?"'

'Because you aren't ordinary, Jean. You could never
be ordinary. Not anyone who paints like you. The
yearning is always there.'

'Yearning? Yes, it could be that. A seaside village, a
dark wood, an attempt to recreate, forget the tragedy
which followed.' Something clutched at her heart, so
physical that she moved with the pain. Did tragedy
always follow ecstasy? Was it one of the quid pro quos

of life? 'I've never known happiness like that. Maybe only youth can feel it.'

'Maybe that's why you're trying to find it again.'

'Maybe.' Her voice was bleak. 'Fifty-six to twenty-six. Thirty years' difference. No future in it.' There were sudden voices at the door, and before she could think properly, even sit up, it was pushed open by Sandy, her grandchild. Sarah was behind him, talking as she came into the room.

'Mother, I came to the house to borrow your jelly pan . . .' She was looking around, was suddenly transfixed. Sandy, unperturbed, came running towards Jean. 'Grandma! I'm up late! It's a special . . .' He too stopped, seeing Denis, and, suddenly shy, hung his head.

Jean was somehow on her feet, Denis beside her. She knew her hair which he had clutched would be all over, her clothes in disarray. They had been too needy to get undressed. She tucked her blouse into her skirt, ran her hands over her hair, said, 'We were looking at some paintings . . .' It was feeble beyond words. She gave up and bent down to kiss Sandy. The child would smell her, she thought, her after-coital smell. 'You know Mr Carter, Sandy. We were looking at some paintings. Aren't you lucky to be up so late? Isn't he, Denis, lucky?' She was raving. She made herself look towards her daughter. 'Did you find the pan? You know where it's kept.'

'Oh, I know where it's *kept*.' The scorn in her voice was withering. 'But I wouldn't take it without asking.'

'Oh, Sarah!' She could have wept.

'Dad's doing the evening surgery with Alastair. This was just a little treat for Sandy.' Her brown eyes, her sandy hair were John's, it was John accusing her, John with the same scorn in *his* brown eyes.

'You know Denis Carter, of course.' It's laughable, she thought in her despair, laughable if it weren't so awful.

'Yes.'

'He has a little girl,' she went on with this foolishness, 'about Sandy's age. He was just telling me about her.' Why didn't Denis help her? 'Katie . . .'

'I daresay.' Sarah had become over the years what Jean would never be, a capable doctor's wife, able to handle a situation with a difficult patient or finding her mother *in flagrante delicto* or very nearly.

'I'll go with you and get the pan . . .'

'No, don't bother. You're busy.' Oh, the scorn, the disgust, in her eyes. 'When you weren't in the house I naturally thought you'd be . . .'

'Well, will you take it yourself?' This ridiculous harping on about a jelly pan.

'No, thanks. It was just a wee run for Sandy, a ploy . . .' The boy, hearing his name, burst into speech.

'I got a medal at school today, Grandma! It's on a blue ribbon. I wear it in my class for a whole week! Dux, it's called, it makes me Dux.' He laughed with pride, showing white milk teeth with a gap at the front.

'Well done!' Denis joined in. His voice was false, over-hearty.

'We'll go now, Sandy.' Sarah grasped him firmly by the hand.

'I'll come with you,' Jean said.

'No, don't!' Sarah turned and walked towards the door, the boy almost running at her side, shepherded him through, and shut it firmly behind them.

'Oh, God, oh, God,' Jean cried, '*because* you came in so unexpectedly, *because* I was so surprised, so glad, so bloody glad to see you, I didn't lock the door. But she never comes in the evening, three children, and I knew

John was at the surgery. What in God's name possessed her to come here at this time of night?'

'She wanted the jelly pan,' Denis said.

She looked at him, mouth open, then fell against him, laughing and weeping.

'It isn't the end of the world, you know,' he said.

'There speaks a man of the world. To me it is. But Sarah, of all people! She's so *upright*. She's caught it from Alastair. He's Highland, Wee Frees. Oh, I could die, die, die . . .'

'Will she tell John?'

'Never in a thousand years. She adores him. She knows it would break his heart. So do I!' She wailed the words. 'So do I . . . I'll go and see her tomorrow morning, try to explain. But there's no explanation! Why am I weeping? Because I've been caught out? Or shame? Or a combination of both?'

Denis was straightening his hair. It was short and black and never needed much straightening, unlike Jean's. He settled his jacket on his shoulders. 'It isn't the end of the world,' he repeated.

'It is in Kirkcudbright.'

'Kirkcudbright isn't the world. Tell her it was me who got a bit out of hand.'

'In Sarah's world men *never* get out of hand.'

'She has to get around. Put the blame on me. Tell her I'm wicked. I'll go now, Jean.' He kissed her lightly, tidily.

'Is that it over?'

'It's up to you. What you do is your own affair, not Sarah's. You say she won't tell John. That's the main thing.'

She put her arms round his neck. 'I can't do without you, Denis. I need you in my life.' She met his eyes and saw an unhappy man in spite of his casual demeanour.

85

'I feel the same.' He spoke softly. 'At first it was merely a sexual adventure. Now I need you. When I'm in London I think of you, my *raison d'être*. But I respect your husband too much to break up his marriage, break his heart. I'd go away before I'd do that.'

'You're right, of course. Words are useless. I can't think straight. Go home.'

'Unlike you I have no home, but I'll go back to where I live.'

'You'll be there for a bit?'

'Yes, I'm in the middle of a transaction. Combining business with pleasure.' He was trying to make her smile.

'I'll want to see you after I see Sarah.'

'I'll drop in tomorrow. What would be the best time?'

'Come to the house around six. John will be at evening surgery. But not here . . .'

'Okay. We'll be circumspect for a day or so. And I haven't shown you my latest painting, by the way.' He kissed her lightly on the nose.

When he had gone she took up her brushes and painted like a mad thing until John came into the studio, looking tired as he always did now in the evenings. His freckles stood out in the paleness.

'Cocoa's up. Come and join me.' He came and kissed her then stood with his arm round her, looking at the painting. 'What's that supposed to be?'

'It's called "Turmoil."' She swirled her brushes. 'Sometimes I think I'll give it all up.'

'No, don't, darling. You know you need it.' And in the same breath, 'Did Carter come tonight?'

She scarcely slept that night. John wakened about three as if he knew and asked her what was wrong. His tone was so tender that she contemplated for a second telling him what had happened to give herself relief but stopped in time. What about *his* relief?

'It must have been that Hawaiian pork dish I made. Anna gave me the recipe. She got it from Karin.' It had been especially rich, and tedious to cook, an effort to make up to John in some way. She had also drunk too much wine. 'Go to sleep. You need your rest.' She was fearful that he might take her in his arms and want to make love to her.

And yet, in spite of her misery she knew she couldn't give Denis up. It was as if all her passion which had been in cold storage for so long had been brought to life again when she was with him.

Life was too bleak to contemplate without him. At least, for the time being. But how could she explain that to Sarah who since a small girl had been practical, unimaginative, as straight as a die and, like many unimaginative people, convinced that her way was right.

Next morning she telephoned her to break the ice. 'Are you in this morning, Sarah? I'd like to come round.'

'I was going shopping.' Her voice was cold. Was she now bolstered in her uprightness by Alastair? She would surely have told him what had happened. And what about Sandy? You couldn't tell a boy of six to keep a secret about Grandma rolling on a couch with a man without making him feel guilty, which would be a bigger sin.

She dressed carefully, no flamboyant colours, hair flattened as far as it would allow, determined not to bear any resemblance to a *femme fatale*. She left off eye-makeup and lipstick and thought she looked terrible. She had always felt it was necessary to highlight her face the way she highlighted her paintings. The intense blue of her eyes demanded the kohl outline, her mouth had to have its fullness accented. Her pale complexion was the background, her black hair the frame.

Sarah was in the kitchen, her hands in a flour bowl. 'Hello,' she said, not taking her hands out of the bowl.

'Where are the children?' Jean asked, sitting down although Sarah hadn't invited her to do so.

'The girl's taken them for a walk and Sandy's at school.' Jean felt relieved. She didn't want too many signs of domestic bliss. It would make her feel more guilty than ever.

'Would you like some coffee?' Sarah took her hands out of the bowl, it seemed reluctantly. She was proud of her pastry-making abilities.

'No, thank you. It would make me sick. I didn't sleep ... I just wanted to speak to you. Do you think you could stop doing things and just sit down?' Sarah looked at her, went to the sink where she rinsed her hands, then came back and sat on a stool.

'You should have some coffee ...'

Jean waved her hand. 'I'm so sorry about last night, Sarah. So sorry. You know I wouldn't have had it happen for the world.'

'Sorry I came in, or just sorry about – what was going on?' Sarah's mouth was tight.

'Both. This ... situation with Denis. There's no excuse. We fell in love. He came for advice about his paintings and, well, it just happened. It's difficult to explain. Have *you* ever, in spite of Alastair, felt attracted to any other man?'

Her brown eyes were shocked. 'No, never! I can say that honestly. I *love* Alastair. He's the father of my children. I've never known another man, as you know. He was the first ... and last.'

'Yes, I know that. Perhaps you're exceptional, admir-

88

able but exceptional. I can't say the same. I had a love affair when I was young, and then your father was so good and kind to me and I loved him for that and we got married. Oh, I love him, don't doubt that, but there's always been an element of *gratitude* in my loving. You won't ever have known that, with Alastair.'

'No, honestly, I haven't, but then I'm humdrum compared with you, content with my role, my husband, my children.'

'Oh, Sarah!' She took the girl's hands across the table. 'I know that, and I don't know what I did to deserve such a wonderful daughter. I never forget how wonderful you were with Roderick. "Wee Chinky", you called him.'

'I loved Roderick. I grieved deeply when he died. I know you did too, but you were bothered by your guilt, that you shouldn't have put him in that home . . . I just grieved. I don't think you realized that. He was my brother.'

'I did, Sarah. I knew.' But she hadn't, or not as fully as she did at this moment. The tragedy queen, Anna called her. Did she in fact enjoy the role, make a meal out of it, to the exclusion of everyone else?

'Then there's the other side of it,' Sarah said. 'Van and I were so sad for Roderick because he *knew* he was different, how he looked to other people. I don't think you ever realized that. I once found him in his bedroom, looking at himself in the mirror, crying.'

'Oh, no!'

'It's true. I sometimes wondered if his appearance bothered you. Remember when he was born? At first you wouldn't push him out in his pram and left it to Jane and me.'

Jean was filled with shame. 'That passed. I grew to love him, I *more* than loved him, he was my especial care. Ask your Aunt Anna. I was *desolated* when he died. You know that.'

'Yes, I know that, Mum. I'm sorry I ever mentioned Roderick. He's dead. If you've come to ask me if I'll tell Daddy about Denis Carter, you know I never would. Dad's happy with you. He adores you, always will. How could I ruin his life?'

'You make me ashamed.' She wanted to say, 'But that wasn't my only reason for coming. I wanted to know if you were shocked, if you hate me.' Sarah spoke while she was forming the words.

'Well, there's a simple way to cure that.' She was the upright doctor's wife. 'Give Denis Carter up. Unless you mean to break Daddy's heart and ask for a divorce.'

'Denis doesn't want to marry me.' She looked at her daughter, the sandy hair tied back, the clear eyes, the unlined skin. 'He and I are adults, Sarah. We're finding in each other something that was missing from our lives. He's been through a hurtful experience with a divorce. I'm worse, much worse. I'm deceiving my husband. I don't have to be told where my duties lie. Believe me, I know only too well.'

'Oh, Mum!' Sarah's eyes filled with tears. 'You're not *like* a mum. You're so beautiful, and so gifted, and so different, and I know that people like you are bound to live a different kind of life from a mousy creature like me. I've always felt like a mouse beside you. But I'm lucky, don't you see? I don't have any doubts. I don't lie awake at nights and torture myself. I get on with things, running the house, helping Alastair, being a good mother to my children. You see, I want to be *respected*.'

'And you know what you would do in my place? You've no doubts? Tell Denis to go to hell?'

Sarah got up, came round the table and put her arm

90

round Jean's shoulders. 'But you're not me. I realize that. You have all sorts of things going on inside you that I can't begin to understand. I know you feel things more deeply, I even understand about the painting, how you feel so much that it's got to come out.' She straightened. 'I can't tell you what to do. I'm going to make some coffee ... or, would you like a sherry instead?'

Jean looked at her. 'In the morning? Don't tell me I'm having a bad influence on you?' She knew her eyes were full.

Sarah smiled. It was a charming, wide smile. It lit up her whole face. 'Oh, Mum,' she said. She shook her head as if her mother were a hopeless case. 'I have to learn to live dangerously. Just a minute.' She went out of the room and was soon back with two small glasses of sherry. 'Alastair keeps it locked up.' She giggled as she handed Jean a glass.

'Does he think you're going to become a toper?'

'Oh, no. It's charwomen, and workmen, and so on. He doesn't want to put temptation in their way.'

'I see.' Jean sipped her sherry, chastened. 'I'll try to give up Denis,' she said, 'I really will. I'll have a long talk with him. It's ridiculous, of course. He's twenty years younger than me.' Sarah's eyes on her were round with wonderment.

'Twenty years! I never thought ...' She can't believe it of her own mother, Jean thought, baby-snatching. She couldn't believe it of herself.

'Don't worry about Sandy, Mother,' she said. 'I told him it was just a game.'

Some game, Jean thought. Sarah didn't know, and probably never would, the delights of what she called a game, the heights, nor the depths. How by playing it the twenty years' difference disappeared and she was back in the past.

91

Ten

Van, Hal and Sam had moved to Richmond about six months after arriving in Bayswater. Van had been appointed as almoner to several hospitals on the west side of London, only one of which could be called salubrious, and they had chosen their house because it was accessible to all of them. It suited Hal, whose office was in W8, and there was a school nearby for Sam.

They loved the house immediately. Its unprepossessing front hid the fact that there was a rambling back garden whose original landscaping was all but obliterated by overgrown bushes and trees, but it was a delight to Sam who selected his site for a tree-house at once. 'You'll be lucky, mate,' Hal said, 'if you're expecting me to build you a tree-house,' but he promised to look around for a carpenter who wasn't afraid to risk life and limb.

It was a tall Victorian edifice with a basement, the price being reasonable because the basement was occupied by an old man who had right of tenure. Most people regarded this as a disadvantage, the house agent had hinted, but Van was used to old men. She went to see Mr Elder, and found him testy but independent.

'I lived here with my wife,' he said. 'Brought up a family too. They're scattered, my wife died five years ago.'

Van knew better than to wallow in sympathy. 'I see you have plenty of books,' she said, looking around. And catching sight of a title, '*The American War of Independence*? My husband's just back from New York. He'd be interested.'

Mr Elder looked cagey. 'I need peace and quiet. That's all. Promised myself all my life I'd get into this. Sight's good, just the legs occasionally. Post Office's a bit far.'

'Sam, my son, could run errands for you. Save your legs.' She saw the gleam in his eye.

'Might take advantage of that,' he said. His moustache pursed up. 'But it would have to be a strictly business arrangement. I don't want him cluttering up the place. I need peace and quiet.'

'I'll tell Sam that. He'll understand.' Privately she decided she'd look in occasionally to see that Mr Elder was all right. And she'd go carefully with offerings from her kitchen. She'd been brought up in a household where the family had to respect the parents' privacy.

She thought she had never been happier. The house was roomy with a good attic where all Hal's books could be stored, and from where there was a splendid view of the river. It was as good as living in the real country, they told each other, although neither had ever been a country-dweller.

Each was surprised in the other which completed their happiness. Hal secretly marvelled at the change in Van from a rather shy awkward girl to a young married woman of confidence and energy who drove around London every day; she secretly marvelled at the metamorphosis in him from a man-about-town to someone who even tackled putting up shelves – practising for the tree-house, he told Sam – even in mowing the lumpy lawn. And he won Mr Elder's confidence by lending him some books and even more so by quoting from Jefferson's Declaration of Independence.

Van found that old people were the same in London as in Glasgow. They complained or they were stoical. She wondered sometimes how she would face her own mortality looming as closely as it did for many of her patients. The thought was unbearable in her present happiness. The doctors too were the same in London as in Glasgow. Young ones and older ones. Cheerful ones and gloomy ones. Self-important ones and efficient ones.

And the problems never varied, especially the inevitable one of blocked beds and the necessity to see that her patient didn't get pushed out too quickly. Sisters said she had a way with patients and relatives, especially the troublesome ones. But prestige was a foreign word to her. What was important was protecting the rights of her patients.

'Can you imagine, Hal,' she said, 'people who can't face the outside world and who find their only refuge in a hospital bed?'

'Does it have to be a hospital one?' he teased, tumbling her on to their own bed and imprisoning her by lying on top of her. She loved him.

'Shoosh!' she said, 'you'll waken Sam.'

One Sunday in late September Anna and Ritchie came to see them en route from Spain. They had flown in at Heathrow. Anna enthused about the house. 'How sensible of you not to go in for a modern semi-detached or whatever. Just look at the cornices in this room, Ritchie. Almost as good as Clevedon Crescent. And the windows! A real French window suitable for a Noel Coward play, not those dreadful sliding doors. And you said you had someone in the basement?'

'Yes, Mr Elder, a widower. He used to own the house

years ago, and there's still some of his stuff in one of the attics. I told him it was all right to leave it.'

'You would. I hope you don't end up looking after him.'

'You looked after Bessie.' She smiled at her mother. 'But he's hale and hearty and just seventy. He has a mind as keen as a knife blade. He talks more to Sam than he does to me.'

'He makes me do my sums when I buy stamps. And work out my commission.' Sam had been listening. 'Oh, he's all there, Mr Elder, although he's elderly!' He doubled up laughing. 'That's good, isn't it, Grandma, elderly Mr Elder!'

'Not bad, but don't laugh too hard at your own jokes.'

Ritchie said the house was fine. He wasn't a good connoisseur of houses except from a painterly angle. He liked the attics and said they would make good studios. Perhaps Sam would use them when he was older.

'Who knows?' Van said. 'But considering his parents, there isn't much chance.' She had never seen in Eb any interest in what Ritchie did, only to ask if he made a lot of money at it.

'Well, maybe the next one will.' Ritchie gave Hal a wicked glance.

Sam was telling Ritchie about the elderly Mr Elder and Ritchie was listening attentively then laughing uncritically when Sam prodded him. Perhaps he's ready for a brother or sister, Van thought, watching his happy face. Am I? She was enjoying her work and needed the experience, but truth to tell, when she and Hal discussed it they both agreed that they were loving life so much that they hardly wanted circumstances to change.

In the evening they were in the habit of strolling down their road arm-in-arm, greeting any neighbours

95

who might be working in their gardens, and keeping in sight of the house in case Sam wakened. She sometimes wondered how long such a quiet and uneventful life would satisfy Hal, but then remembered he had never known a happy home life. For the time being life was good.

Anna confessed she was worried about Jean. 'She's being secretive. I can tell by her voice she's hiding something. We used to tell each other everything when we were girls.'

'The sad fact is, Mum,' Van said, smiling, 'you're no longer girls.'

'She's my girl,' Ritchie said, putting an arm round his wife.

'Maybe she has a lover?' Hal suggested.

'A lover!' Anna was horrified. 'No, no, not now. She's happily married. All she has to do is just rest in the shallows. Like us. Eh, Ritchie?' She appealed to him.

'Go on. Calm her suspicions.' Hal laughed.

'No, Anna's right.' Ritchie was smug. 'It's a good time, this, most of the striving over, treading water for a few years before we start going down the slippery slope.' Hal caught Van's eye and they burst into laughter.

'And the band played "Believe it if you like",' Van sang. She looked at her parents, Ritchie still handsome, sexy – there was no other word for it – Anna, still beautiful, dressed in her usual expensive simplicity – she had evidently found a couturier in Barcelona who suited her. Her style was so different from Jean's, who dressed like her paintings, sometimes stunningly, other times like a rag bag. 'Are you really worried about Jean, Mother?' she asked.

'I am. I went to Kirkcudbright before we left for Spain and I *know* there's something wrong. Her painting was

96

all to hell for one thing. And she's thin, but not as thin as John. I insisted they come out to Arenys de Mar – you know how Jean dislikes leaving Kirkcudbright ever since Roderick died – well, they came, to my surprise. We fed John up, and Jean varied between being madly gay and flirting with every man in sight – she even tried it on with old Manuel till I told her she was wasting her time – and being unnaturally solicitous about John. Oh, there's something up there. But they went away looking much better, didn't they, Ritchie?'

'Yes . . .' He looked doubtful.

'I told her I had been worried about her, but she says it's John, really. He has this bad heart and he works harder than ever. The practice is growing.'

'You haven't had a holiday this year?' Ritchie changed the subject by addressing Van.

'No, we've both been too busy. But we're planning to go to visit Karin and Mish quite soon.'

'That's great,' Anna said. 'Why don't we take Sam back with us? It would give you much more freedom, and he always enjoys staying in Glasgow.'

'Well, it's a good idea, but why don't we ask Sam tomorrow morning?'

'You do that. Ritchie and I can't go until next year, unfortunately, although I'm dying to see Mish's baby. We've too much work to do. Benjamin's a year old now, isn't he? I wish they'd call him Ben. Benjamin is so . . . biblical.'

'You were going to say Jewish,' Ritchie said.

'I was not! Honestly, Van, your father trips me up wherever I go.'

'Children, children.' Van laughed at them. 'Yes, a year old this month. He's not walking, but Karin has a good nanny. She went back to her clinics quite soon. I think she likes her work too much to give it up.'

'Sometimes I envy people who go *out* to work.' Anna had calmed down. 'The trouble is that if you work at home people call it a hobby.'

'Ritchie, you have the best of both worlds,' Hal said. 'Your wife working *and* at home beside you. Think of poor Mish and me.'

'You don't mind that?' Van asked.

'No, I think it's great. I'm not so sure about Mish.'

Anna looked at him. 'Oh, I'm sure you're wrong there. He's so up-to-date!' She turned to Ritchie. 'Isn't he?'

'He should be, working in New York.' He laughed. 'When we lived at Renton the men I met on the train when I occasionally went up to London were convinced I was a wealthy dilettante.' And you're an adept at changing the subject, Van thought.

Ritchie went upstairs with Hal to see his collection of prints of the Hudson Valley painters, and Anna and Van washed up the dishes companionably.

'I think he's the right one at last,' Anna said, casting her eyes ceilingwards.

'As long as he doesn't go off the rails the way Father did!'

'You young folks. You're so critical!' She smiled at Van, as one woman to the other. 'Besides, he came back!'

Sam said, 'Ach, babies!' when it was put to him that he might go with Van and Hal to America. 'I'd much rather go back with Grandpa and Grandma to Glasgow. They've promised me roller skates.'

Eleven

Karin looked at the young woman sitting opposite her, late thirties, competent, well-dressed, dark-haired, totally different in appearance and demeanour from her brother. 'It's good of you to drop by,' she said.

'Oh, I was coming to New York in any case when I got your letter. I have an old schoolfriend who lives here, and we get together occasionally. She married late and she's still bogged down by kids. Fortunately mine are able to be left. They're at high school, and my husband'll look after them.'

Karin looked at her. 'I understood from Paul that you were living with your parents, that ... you had split up with your husband?'

Kathleen Kovac raised her eyebrows in surprise. 'Did Paul tell you that!'

'Yes, he did. He said you were always there when he went home.'

'Of course I visit with the girls. Not so much now, but more when they were little. Mom and Dad like to see them. It's Paul who's hardly ever at home now. It worries my folks.'

'Your father supports him financially?'

'Oh, yes. I tell you, Miss Gottleib, Dad always fell over backwards trying to make up to Paul.'

'Make up?'

99

'Yes, didn't he tell you? They adopted him. His parents were old friends and they were both killed in a car crash. Mom couldn't have any more children after I was born, and I think Dad kind of hankered after a son. Well, they took him to live with us after his parents were killed, and then they adopted him.'

'He never told me that. Did he know?'

'Oh, yes. They were straight with him. Besides he was three when he came to us, a lovely little kid, fair-haired, fair skin. He would remember them.'

'What age were you?'

'Nearly six.'

'I think he feels you were . . . preferred.'

'No,' she shook her head, 'that's not the case. They made no difference between us, and there was no one prouder than Dad to have a son. He hoped he would follow in his footsteps eventually, run the farm. He was proud of his farm, Dad. His reputation as a breeder was widespread. No, they treated us equally, and they backed him up, even when they began to realize they were being . . . taken for a ride.' She laughed ruefully, but not vindictively.

'I see.' Karin looked at the young woman. She seemed honest enough. It was easier to believe her than someone who had been sent to her for treatment. 'And you haven't left your husband?'

'Left Al? My goodness, why should I? We get on well, and in any case my two girls, Natalie and Mary Jo, *need* a father. You hear such terrible things nowadays about young girls going off the rails. We're an average, happy family, or so I like to think.' Her smile was wide and disarming. She didn't look deceitful.

'Would you tell me what Paul was like when you were both at home? I mean as children. He talks a lot about his schooldays.'

100

'Well, to be truthful, I hadn't much time for him after he grew up, but as a little boy he was kind of cute, and wistful. But once he went to school he changed. He became difficult, secretive. He didn't make friends easily and he was always complaining about the other boys. My folks tried really hard, giving parties, sending him to summer camp, but he just wasn't happy with kids of his own age. At home there was nothing about the farm that really interested him. He spent most of the time in his room. Well, of course, Mom and Dad were disappointed, but they made excuses, that he'd been orphaned and if they gave him a good home he'd change.'

'Some children are loners. Was he clever at school?'

'Oh, yes, he was clever, and that made us all really proud when we went to see him get his prizes.'

'Have you ever wondered why he was … difficult, Mrs Kovac?'

She looked at Karin for a second. 'I can say this to you. I used to think he was gay, that he was having difficulty coming to terms with it, but I didn't say anything like that at home. My folks are old-fashioned. Even although it was all coming out in the Sixties and that. I once spoke to him and said if there was anything worrying him he could tell me, or our doctor. He blew up, got really mad with me and that made me think I was right.'

'But you were proved wrong?'

'Maybe. Anyhow, he started dating. He brought home some really nice girls from University, and for a time it looked as everything was okay with him …' She paused.

'Something happened?'

'Yes, he flunked University. He was at Baltimore. Wrote to Dad that he couldn't stand it and he was going

101

to take time out. Dad was older, losing some of his patience, and he went to see the University authorities and they said Paul had done nothing wrong, had got good grades, but just wasn't a mixer and suggested Dad should go along with it for a bit.'

'They didn't advise your father to seek medical opinion?'

'No, if they did Dad didn't say. To tell you the truth I think he was out of his depth. Mom said they had a long talk together and Paul said he would work on the farm for a bit and try to learn the ropes but it was no use. He spent most of his time on his boat on the creek. He always liked fishing. Suited him.' She smiled at Karin. 'I kind of lost interest in it all. I was engaged and planning to get married, and you know what you're like when you fall in love?'

'Yes. I know.' It was difficult not to like Kathleen Kovac. 'So did he stay down on the farm?'

'Did he heck? I was married by this time and I heard from Mom that he had got a job on Wall Street and left for New York. He had a great math flair, you know. I think they were both relieved. They were getting old, couldn't take it so easily. Then he met this girl . . .'

'Do you know her name?'

'Yeah. Bobbie. Can't recall the rest, but we were all pleased. He said she was right for him, and I guess we all sat back with relief then got on with our lives. Trouble was he threw in his job, or they threw *him* in, but Dad, for peace and quiet, gave him an allowance, still gives it as far as I know. He's been out and in various jobs. Never sticks in them. But I guess we thought at least he had this girl, Bobbie, and maybe she'll knock some sense into him. And then one day when Dad called him and asked how he and Bobbie were getting on he said she had gone. They lived together for three years and suddenly she walked out on him! That was all we knew. Dad continued to give him an allowance – I thought he was nuts and so did Al – but by this time we were busy with our girls and we decided to forget about Paul and concentrate on bringing them up.'

Karin nodded. 'Perhaps that was for the best. At least he wasn't on drugs.'

'Dad always said that, "at least he isn't on drugs." The way he looks at it is that Paul is using up his inheritance with getting the allowance. Fair shares for all, Dad always said, and if that's the way he likes it, well, that's his outlook. I should think Dad's pretty comfortable. He was a prize breeder in his time, travelled all over. We think he's been real forgiving, and maybe it's being a farmer that does it. They know it's the luck of the draw. Al says they should have kicked Paul out long ago, disinherited him, but then Dad says you don't throw out a sick animal, or one that hasn't bred true.'

'He sounds very wise. In spite of your husband's forthright views you get on well together?' Karin smiled at her.

'Yeah. There's no one quite like my Al. Does that sound soppy?'

'I feel pretty much the same about mine. How about a cup of coffee? This inquisition must be tiring you, but it's invaluable to me.'

'A cup of coffee would be very welcome. Have *you* any children, Miss Gottleib?'

'A little boy. He's just had his first birthday.'

'We don't have a son, but Al says he's quite content with our two girls. Men like to have women around the house. We've had our troubles with them, hot pants, boys, pop music blaring from morning to night, but they're fun. Keeps us young.'

'What did Paul think of them?'

'Not much. He couldn't stand them if we were staying at the farm. I once said, when he was downright rude, just to annoy him, "Why don't you and Bobbie have some of your own?" And he flew into a rage, face like a turkey-cock's, eyes wild, I thought he was going to strike me. Shook his fist in my face, called me a bitch, said he would be glad if he never set eyes on me again. Simpering brats, he called my girls. Al was furious. I think he would have punched him on the nose if it hadn't been in my folks' house. The girls were scared of him. They wouldn't go back to the farm unless I promised them their uncle wouldn't be there.'

'That was upsetting,' Karin said. 'What did you think of it afterwards?'

'That he hated kids! Wouldn't you, Miss Gottleib?'

'Or that he was jealous of yours?'

'Yeah.' Kathleen Kovac nodded. 'I thought that too.'

Paul Laskins had an appointment the following morning. Karin sat at her desk turning over in her mind the interview she'd had with his sister. It had been useful. She thought the woman had been honest. She believed what she'd told her of her brother's attitude to her daughters, substantiated by her memory of his sly looks at her own stomach when she had been pregnant with Benjy.

Jealousy? Envy? Generally you only felt jealousy or envy for something you wanted for yourself. Or in his case, something he had wanted for his girlfriend, Bobbie. And that he had been unable to give to her. Kathleen Kovac had thought he might be gay, but on the other hand Bobbie had lived with him for three years and presumably they'd had sexual relations in that time.

He was due for a session in half an hour and she was seriously thinking of telling him not to come back. In her work she didn't look for quick results, but there was a lack of trust on his part and a feeling in herself which was unusual, of fear, or at least apprehension, which she was unable to shake off.

She recognized that he was a pathological liar. Whether he was a psychopath or merely psychotic she had still to decide. Would she ever know, since she was unable to trust him or what he told her? Every case was a crossword puzzle and therein lay her pleasure in her work, but in this instance something personal between them had established itself which made it impossible for her to remain detached.

Karin didn't think he was homosexual. She had studied him carefully, questioned him closely about how he spent his time, which bars he went to. There was nothing there to make her suspicious. Nor had he any need to be in shady company, take part in shady deals. He got an adequate allowance from a father who was generous enough to pay out for an adopted son who had been a disappointment.

Paul came in with his usual gangling gait, the expressionless face. How well she knew those expressionless faces which hid so much.

'I asked your sister to come and see me yesterday, Paul,' she said. 'Did you know she was in town?'

'We don't communicate.' Suddenly, the aggression was there. His voice, which had been flat, rose in anger. 'Why the hell did you ask *her* to come here? Don't you know you'll get nothing but lies from her? I've told you what she's like!' His eyes were darting fire at her. He got up and walked about the room.

'Sit down.' She tried to be calm, cool. 'You didn't tell

me you were adopted.' She watched him stop in his tracks, saw the tremor in his mouth, how his eyes slid under his half-closed eyelids.

'So what?' The half-smile. 'It's of no importance.'

'Well, why did you keep it back? If you aren't honest with me, Paul, I don't think I can go on treating you. There must be trust between us.'

He shrugged, sat down, seemed to speak with great earnestness. 'She's been poisoning your mind, that bitch. Excuse my language. She does it with all my friends, now you. There was something going between us, now you're believing *her*.' Karin would have preferred him to be angry. 'She's like the rest of them. Believe me, Miss Gottleib, I know what women are like.'

'Is that so?' She looked at her notes. 'You told me more than once that her husband had chucked her out.'

'So he should have done. Oh, she went crawling back to him with her two brats, real preppy they are now, noses in the air, no time for Uncle Paul.'

'Maybe you hadn't any time for *them*. You've certainly got it in for the female sex.' She met his eyes. His upper lids hid the gleam in them, like a watchful animal.

'Because they're all the same. Even you. You believe what that bitch tells you, not me.' Now his eyes were making her afraid. She had her foot on the bell push under her desk. It made her feel safer.

'There are two sides to everything. It depends where you stand.' She straightened her back, clasped her hands on his notes. 'I have to tell you, Paul. I'm considering bringing our sessions to an end. It's not fair to you or myself. Or your doctor.'

'There's no problem.' He was bland. 'I can pay. I can afford it.' He lifted his chin, looked about the room as if he was assessing the worth of its contents. 'I've told you before. The old man shells out the dollars to keep me away. Cheap at the price, he thinks. Oh, I can see through him, see through everybody.' His eyes were laughing at her.

'He's certainly been very generous.'

His face softened in one of his quick changes of mood. 'Yeah, he's always been open-handed with me, I can't deny that, even at school. I got really decent clothes, anything I asked for, I had just to say it was school's orders and he forked out. Mom followed his lead. They loved me, you see. I was their son.' His eyes were moist. 'Now that Ross Clancy, he could never get a bean out of his folks. He used to steal money from his mom's purse. Once when they were at the country club with my folks he went up to their bedroom. Just for a lark, he said, easy as pie.'

'Have you noticed,' Karin said, 'how often you harp back to your childhood? But, don't forget. You grew up. You went to University. You dated. And then you lived with a girl. What was her name?'

'I don't remember.' He turned away impatiently. 'I don't remember anything about her.'

'You don't want to remember.' Karin sat back, suddenly determined. 'You have half an hour to remember. Go and lie on the couch and tell me about this girl who hadn't a name.'

'She *had* a name.' He got up from his chair. 'Time for beddy-byes, Paul.' His voice was mocking. He said as he lay down, 'It's just ... this girl ... that girl, they come and go. It's difficult to know the difference.'

'This one lived with you for three years.'

'How do you know that?' His voice was sharp.

'It's common knowledge. Don't waste my time. If you don't remember her name, tell me what she looked like. Was she dark, or fair?'

'Dark. The fair ones are cheats.'

'So she didn't cheat. She was faithful to you. She lived with you in your apartment in East Forty-sixth Street. What did *she* think of you not working?'

'She didn't know. She went out every day to her work. She thought I was going out to mine. I said we could save up her money and we'd live on what I made.' He laughed. 'From Pop! She was quiet. I told her not to talk to neighbours or anything. She did what I said. There's an old hag in the block who waylays you if you step out of the door.'

'So you lived a nice, cosy little life, you doing the shopping . . .'

'Yeah, I liked to shop. And sometimes I cooked supper for us both. Italian. She liked Italian.'

'What about your mythical job?'

'I just said my hours were less than hers. Of course, sometimes I took a temporary one if there was something big we needed, like a new dishwasher or something. I broke ours. You see, the damned door wouldn't shut and I got fed up and kicked it. Broke it.' He giggled.

'Anyhow, here you both were, living together. Did you go out, to the cinema, or the theatre?'

'No, we had plenty to do inside. Sometimes we took a walk, or went to the Park, but mostly we just stayed home and went to bed early.'

'Were you planning to get married?'

'That would be telling, wouldn't it?' He screwed his head round to meet her eyes. 'Let's just say there were certain contingencies. You'll know all about that, Miss Gottleib. How is your baby, by the way? Must be about a year old now?' He lay back on his pillow.

Karin decided to ignore his remark. 'Since you were so happy, why did she walk out on you?' There was silence for a second and then he was standing over her, shaking with anger. His fist was raised, threatening her.

She went rigid. She had never been attacked, yet. 'Calm down, Paul.' She hoped she sounded cool.

'It's that bitch, Kathleen. I know it! You shouldn't have seen her. She spoils everything, always did. You were my friend. I was interested in you, in your nice life with your nice home. It was a little paradise, like the one I could have had, with . . . Bobbie.' His fist had dropped.

'Sit down again, Paul.'

'No, I don't want to.' He was sullen, one foot moving over the carpet, head down. 'I don't want to talk about Bobbie. It's over, the whole thing's over. She got tired . . . waiting. Nothing goes right.' He raised his head. 'Now if it had been someone like you, Miss Gottleib, someone who . . .'

'Your time's up, Paul. There's another patient waiting. Next week?' She took up her pen, looked at him enquiringly.

'Who the hell cares?' He turned and stumbled to the door, wrenched it open and was gone. Karin blew out her breath. She was sitting straight-backed at her desk, her hands on it, when Denise, the receptionist, put her head round the door.

'That was a quick exit, Miss Gottleib. Anything wrong?'

'No, just a little tantrum. Book him for next week at the same time. He'll be back.'

Twelve

She was like a child, Hal thought as he watched Van's bright eyes following the movements of the other passengers in the plane before it took off, the nervous ones, the nonchalant ones, the smiling insouciance of the hostesses.

'Aren't they competent, but kind?' she said.

'It's their job, honey.' She lifted an eyebrow at that. 'I'm getting into practice for the States.'

'Okay. But that dark-haired one helping that old lady with putting up her holdall – that's more kind than competent.'

'Sure, sure. Are you scared?' It was her first long flight.

'Scared? Not me. Sam doesn't know what he's missing.'

'I was surprised at him turning down the chance to come with us.'

'In a way, yes, but he has a lot of hidden insecurities. He knows Glasgow, knows his cousins. He worries about his colour. The only place where he was really confident was in Spain. He *merged* there. And I think he's afraid of the long flight but would never admit it. Ever since he fell through the ceiling at Miss Clewes' school, he's easily made sick. I think it knocked his sense of balance a little. It'll sort itself out.'

'We're off!' How often that violent revving reminded him of flying to and from Singapore as a boy. He had been terrified the first time, then proud, but never blasé. The first experience of flying above the clouds had been a thrill he'd never forgotten. So clean, so pure, a place to forget all one's own insecurities at that age. And he had been like Sam, conscious of being a minority in strange situations because of his colour. He could understand that fully. 'We're airborne. Okay?' He looked at Van who was smiling at him to hide her relief. 'Do you think I help with Sam a bit?' he asked her.

'Oh, yes. That was another lack. He now has a daddy like other boys. I once heard Mrs Fairbairn say to him that his daddy would soon be home. I thought he'd say, "Do you mean Hal?" But he nodded smugly and said, "Yes, in three days." ' They laughed together.

'He still calls me Hal.'

'That will change.'

'You think so?'

'Yes, when he has a little brother or sister. He'll fall in love with it then. Wait and see.'

'Okay,' Hal said, 'I'll wait and see.' He leaned back, thinking, this must be one of the happiest moments of my life, linked in some way with that boy who had flown between school and home and kept his anxieties to himself, and this man sitting beside the woman he loved and discussing a possible child who would be the expression of their love. No longer Hal Purvis, the homeless one. He beckoned a hostess. 'Could we have a bottle of champagne opened, please? It's my wife's first transatlantic flight.'

Mish met them off the plane at Kennedy Airport, and it touched Hal to see the affectionate greeting between the brother and sister. Mish had always been there for

111

her, in theory if not in fact, never taking sides, never critical, his very detachment making him reliable.

Mish had told him how, when younger, Van's unconventional behaviour had been a thorn in Anna's flesh. He would have to remember if they had children of their own that tolerance was a virtue. And yet he had suffered in his early life from too much tolerance on the part of his parents, a tolerance which had been close to selfishness. Who ever got it right, he thought, shaking hands with Mish, slapping him on the back, saying, 'How's the doting father?'

They couldn't have seen Westchester County at a better time. The fall colours flamed on either side of them, the maples striking the high note, the laurels with their glossy leaves providing a rich, dark background, broken by the feathery fronds of the sumacs with their variegated colour.

Karin might not be in when they got home, Mish told them. Today was one of her busiest clinics, and in addition she'd had to see a long-term patient at the last moment.

'She never refuses?' Hal asked.

'Not Karin. She wouldn't risk that. Once she did and had a suicide on her hands, well, on her conscience.'

'It must be time-consuming. She never wanted to give it up when Benjamin arrived?'

'Karin? Not for a moment. Work comes first. I've learned that.'

'Her mind's too active,' Van said. 'I know. Most women, if they're honest, heave a sigh of relief when the early part's over.'

'Then there's her strong sense of debt,' Mish said.

'Debt?' Hal echoed.

'A debt to society, daftie,' Van explained from the back seat.

112

Mish laughed. 'Daftie! I haven't heard that word for years.'

'What would *you* say, then, Yankee?' she teased.

'I guess, "mutt". I don't know. Here's Ossining. This is where the old Croton aqueduct used to carry water to New York. And Sing Sing prison is here. We'll soon be home to our ain wee hoosie.'

'There's hope for you yet, Hamish Laidlaw,' Van said.

'Yeah, plaid's in this year. If you both look you'll get a great view of the Hudson.' They both did.

'Marvellous!' Hal exclaimed.

'Like the Firth of Clyde,' Van said.

'Snap.' Mish grinned. 'It's even more majestic after Peekskill. We're into painting territory, *your* painters, Hal, after Bear Mountain Bridge. Frederick Church, one of them, built his mansion there, called Olana. I expect you've already seen it.'

'Yes, but I'll take Van. I've still some stuff to do on him.'

'Let me know if there's any way I can help. I might be able to locate some of the paintings for you. But now that Benjy's here, I want to be more around the place in case Karin is held up at her clinics. There's got to be one of us.' And is that just a tiny bit resentful, Hal thought. Some men were like that.

'But you wouldn't want her to give it up?' he asked lightly.

'Good God, no! Not when she's happy and fulfilled. How do you feel about *your* work, Van?'

'Happy and fulfilled.' She laughed.

'And I don't go through any angst about that,' Hal said. 'Must move with the times.'

'Yeah ... once when Benjy ran a temperature and kept wanting his mummy I could have killed Karin for

113

not being there.' Hal felt Van's hand on his shoulder. 'Not rational, I know, but you get so damned protective. Complete surprise to me. It must be the old caveman syndrome.'

Van said, 'In the Glasgow slums some of the couples I had to deal with went out and left a mere child to take care of three or four younger ones. How does that compare?'

Mish didn't reply. He had left the freeway and begun to climb a hill. He slowed the car and pointed. 'That's a bird sanctuary there. I'll have to read up about birds for Benjy.' Hal felt Van's hand again.

'Good idea,' Hal said. 'It's a nice piece of country, this Mish.'

'Quite rural.' And a minute or two later, 'Our road.' It was quiet and tree-lined. 'We're further on. Fall's the best time to see this part. It gets a bit too bosky, too humid, in the height of summer, and the river looks dead, lumpen, the colour of wet clay. I think I'll have to give in sometime and have a pool made, but I'll wait till Benjy's older, more responsible.'

'Wait a few more years and you'll be buying them *all* waterwings,' Van said, laughing.

'Hey, don't rush me!' Mish laughed with her.

The house stood on a plateau, sturdy and uncompromising, not beautiful, but functional, Mish said, leading them into a large hall. A pleasant-faced woman came through the door at the end to greet them.

'Mrs Strickner comes in each day to look after our creature comforts,' Mish explained introducing her. 'She'll show you to your room.'

'Could I see Benjamin first?' Van said.

'Sure. Where is he, Mrs Strickner?'

'In the nursery.' She smiled. 'Ruth is getting him ready for bed.'

114

They all trooped upstairs, but when Van took the baby in her arms, Mish's pride was obvious.

'He's lovely, Mish,' she said, 'just like you except he's dark-haired.'

'It's his mother's hair.' The dark-skinned Ruth was just as proud as Mish. 'And he sure has a headful! Sometimes they can be nearly bald at this age.'

'What do you think of him, Hal?' Van asked. 'Isn't he lovely?'

He tried to match her enthusiasm. 'As babies go he seems fine. But, of course, Mish, any child of yours . . . need I say more?'

'No aspersions, if you don't mind. Just wait. You'll find yourself drooling one day, just like me. Give him back to Ruth, Van, and come and have a drink on the terrace.' The baby whimpered in the exchange.

'See, he knows his Aunty Van already.' Hal thought her look at him was faintly questioning.

They had dinner on the terrace later when Karin came home.

'Well, I take it you've seen the son and heir and been duly impressed. And Mish has bored you to death telling you how perfect he is.' She had joined them again after going upstairs.

Mish smirked. 'We all saw you streaking off to the nursery like a bat out of hell.'

'I don't deny it. Yes, he's lovely, adorable, I could die for him. That's the end of the baby talk. Tell us about your trip, Van, and then all the Glasgow news. Then Kirkcudbright . . . have I pronounced it properly?'

'We've all evening,' Mish said. 'Were you held up?'

'Yeah, I'm sorry. This patient, he's being difficult. But aren't they all? You know something of this, Van?'

'Oh, yes. Some you just don't warm to. It's no good pretending they're all angelic.'

'That's it. And yet the ones you don't warm to won't get out of your hair – as is evident.' She laughed at herself. 'But you know who I'm talking about, Hal. I can say this between our four walls. He lives where you have an apartment.'

'Do I? What was he called?'

'Paul Laskins. There I go. Blame this good wine you brought us.' She held up her glass.

'Ah, yes. Paul Laskins.' Hal nodded. 'I can't remember meeting him. But I dropped a clanger with one of the tenants, Ellie Kaplan – I think I told you about her, Karin – she was entertaining him one evening and she'd asked me to look in but I forgot. That landed me in a spot of trouble.' He laughed.

'What happened?'

'The said Ellie came down to my apartment to tick me off, the worse for wear, I'm sorry to say. I had a hell of a time getting rid of her.'

'See the shady life he's been leading, Van?' Karin smiled at her. 'Are you calling in to see her when you're in town?'

'Not on your life. And don't give Van funny ideas.'

'I told you before she was lonely,' Karin said. 'It's the New York disease. Almost worse than drugs and that's bad enough.'

'Did I ever tell you what Ellie told me about this Laskins chap?' Hal asked her. 'And his girl?'

'No, you didn't.' Her eyes were eager. 'I know it's unprofessional, but shoot.'

'The girlfriend's name was Bobbie.'

'Yes, I know that.'

'Ellie said she was quiet, didn't talk much, didn't socialize except to baby-sit for another occupant. Is that any help?'

'Everything helps. Anything else?'

'She lived with Laskins for two or three years and then left suddenly. Ellie said she sometimes looked as if she had been crying, that there were rows – of course Ellie could dramatize any situation.'

'Did she make any comments about Paul?'

'She referred to him as a weirdo, that he didn't work ... oh, yes, after his girl went away she asked him to her apartment to cheer him up – and possibly to satisfy her own curiosity – but he went into a kind of fugue in the middle of what she was saying and it was a waste of time being kind to him.'

'You never actually saw him?'

Hal shook his head. 'But you could live there and never meet other residents for ages. Funnily enough, I was always running into Ellie Kaplan, but I don't think that was entirely a coincidence.'

'Maybe she passed her time going up and down in the elevator,' Mish said.

'You could be right.'

'Ah, well. New York, New York ... have another drink and tell us about your plans. What do you want to do, Van?'

'All the touristy things, go up the Empire State Building, sail round Manhattan, play with Benjamin, and explore this area,' she took a breath, 'lie in the garden and sunbathe and play with Benjamin ...'

'It's our proper honeymoon,' Hal said. 'We only had a weekend in Paris. And don't forget, we were parted for six months.'

'But you had Ellie Kaplan.' Van smiled at him.

They sat talking on the terrace. Across the Hudson they thought they could see the lights of moving cars. It was a warm, still night and the sky was navy blue, an American sky, Van said.

'Why American?' Mish asked her.

117

'It's bigger than ours back home.'

'Serves me right for asking.'

'Everything's bigger here, including the mosquitoes. We've all had a long day. Shall we go in?'

They tiptoed upstairs and tiptoed in to see Benjamin asleep because Van wanted to.

'You couldn't be getting broody by any chance?' Hal asked her when they were in bed.

'Not yet.' She said, turning to him, 'This is good enough.'

During the day it was not too warm to do all the things they wanted to do, Van's touristic leanings were fully satisfied, and Hal trailed along blissfully. He agreed with her that the ferry which sailed round Manhattan was incredible, and that the Staten Island one was equally colourful and exciting. And he marvelled at this other girlish side of her, so different from the conscientious mother of Sam, the competent social worker, the loving wife. She'll never grow really old, he thought, congratulating himself on his good luck.

As always in New York it was the people more than the sights which impressed him with their liveliness and vitality, their *newness*, as if they'd received some kind of electrical charge simply by living and working here. 'You could see the triumph in their faces,' he said to Van.

'You'd be triumphant too,' she pointed out, 'if you'd come from poverty to a place like this with all its opportunities. It's the American Dream, although they don't all succeed.'

They took a boat trip from West Point to the Upper Hudson and saw a microcosm of the people, mostly young, of all races, and felt the infection of their gaiety. 'They're quite something,' Hal said, leaning on the rail under a striped awning, 'with their capacity for enjoyment.'

She laughed at him. 'You're the unfortunate product of a public school education. You've never been on a Clyde steamer at the Fair Holidays. You've never danced to the band, worn a cap with "Kiss me" on it. You haven't lived. My father would be completely at home here.'

'Okay, okay.'

He told her of his researches, how the Hudson Valley painters had impressed him with their reverence for nature, what an education it had been for him. They were explorers as well as painters, he explained to Van.

They roamed further, to the little towns, went beyond Albany to Lake George which lay pale blue and placid outside the chalet they hired for the night so that they could row on the lake most of the day.

And in between they took days off and spent them in the garden with Benjamin, leaving Ruth to loll contentedly in a garden chair, her fat thighs exposed in her minuscule, too-tight skirt. Hal said the Malaysian servants in his parents' house would never have dared to relax like that. His mother and father insisted on correct behaviour.

'The English took their class system with them wherever they went,' Van said.

They got to know each other, never, it seemed, having had the time. Hal told Van about his childhood, and how he had come to recognize it as a deprived one although there had been no shortage of material comforts. 'I think that's what attracted me to you to begin with,' he said, 'your capacity for love. I was starved of it.'

'We were poor judges of each other,' she said. 'I thought you were sophisticated, utterly sure of yourself,

119

a real man-about-town,' she laughed, 'a bobby-dazzler. And my self-esteem was so low because of living in the midst of a talented family that I thought someone like you would never look at me in a thousand years.'

'How long did it take you to discover the lonely little boy behind the façade?'

'Not long. When we made love that night in the Barcelona hotel. There's no better way.'

They got to know Karin, admiring her for her honesty and forthrightness. They teased Mish about his new role of doting father until he took the wind out of their sails by freely admitting it.

Van noticed, because she was closer to her brother, his occasional resentment when Karin was late. Once, when they were sitting waiting for her they heard Benjy crying upstairs while Ruth was getting him ready for bed. 'I want Mummy!' he was wailing. Van saw Mish's lips tightening. He got up and went into the house and they could hear him running upstairs.

'In theory it's good,' Hal said.

'What?'

'Women having careers. Sometimes men's belief in it is only skin deep.'

She put her finger to her lips.

When Mish came back again and Karin had arrived, he was falsely hearty, but there was the barb. 'Benjy nearly brought the house down tonight,' he said, 'crying for you.'

Karin's eyes were shrewd. 'Yeah?' There was to be no letting down hair in public.

It was obvious to Van and Hal that Karin's work was her passion. 'Each patient is a challenge,' she told them, 'like a crossword puzzle. You have to find the key. With some it takes longer than others.'

And another time: 'Take Paul Laskins, for instance.'

120

They both noticed that this man seemed to be at the forefront of her mind. 'Now that I've established that he's a pathological liar I have to go on from there, I have to make him come clean, not force him, or rather, not let him see that he's being forced. Sometimes when we're both in the room at the same time there's a strange kind of bond. He's intensely interested in me. He knows I'm intensely interested in him. It's a relationship of a kind.' Van saw her brother look away. Did he feel uncomfortable at Karin airing her professional problems? Would he have preferred a more domestic conversation?

'Do you feel that with other patients?' Hal asked.

'No, strangely enough I don't, but then most of them are more malleable than Paul. There's a hard shell there, but in the core of him he's as soft as butter. It's a question of peeling off the layers.'

Van looked at her, the bright, intelligent, brown eyes, the firm mouth, the determination even in her hairstyle, its neat, strong shape which rarely varied as if she put on a wig each morning. No, she thought, she's definitely not an earth mother.

'He says life holds nothing for him,' Karin continued, 'that he's a nihilist. I have yet to meet one. You just have to find the soft part, like a crustacean.'

'Couldn't that be it, simply?' Hal said, 'that he has no zest for life? We had a boy like that at my prep school. He couldn't be bothered with games, was effortlessly clever, so didn't have to study, lived life in a low key, then one day this terrible thing happened. He got into the janitor's room late one night when he'd gone home and hung himself from a rafter.

'The headmaster gathered us together the next day to tell us about it. He said that Raymond – I remember his name now – had left a note which said, "Life is not

121

worth living". Looking back, that man took quite a risk telling young boys about that note. He had advanced views. We had to think of this terrible admission, he said, and take an interest in everything because there were so many wonderful things in the world. And when we were in chapel we had to pray for his soul.

'I remember thinking, well, it was true about Raymond. Nothing interested him. I once showed him my stamp collection, which was pretty good, and he said, "So what?" I wondered if he was so clever that he didn't have to discover anything or aim for anything. But I was pretty young.' He laughed at himself. 'I mean, I used to lie awake at nights practising in my mind how to hit a six at cricket! It's about having a goal. Isn't that right, Karin?'

'To a point, but I think Raymond was clinically depressed. It's a crying shame it wasn't spotted. Perhaps there had been a trauma in his life.'

'His mother died suddenly and his father remarried.'

'There you are. That was the carpet taken from under his feet.'

'Could we make that enough of psychiatry?' Mish said, getting up. 'Have you forgotten we're going out tonight, courtesy of Hal?'

'I'm sorry.' Karin got up too.

'Fascinating stuff all the same,' Hal said.

'We'll be ready in ten minutes,' Van smiled to ignore the tension. 'That just gives us time to peep in at Benjy.'

The two women went out together. Hal noticed Karin's arm round Van's shoulders.

'Good that they get on together,' he said to Mish.

'Yes, we're lucky.' He nodded. 'They're both unique.'

Thirteen

Hal and Van flew into Renfrew airport in order to pick up Sam and take him back home. They had spoken to Ritchie on the telephone and said not to meet them as it would be past Sam's bed time.

Glasgow lit up was a wonderful sight, Hal said, the slums blotted out by the darkness, the streets delineated in a neon pattern of light. The most humdrum of places gained a magical quality, and Glasgow was far from humdrum with its hills and valleys, its many church spires reminding you of its Calvinistic background. The gridlike streets crossing and recrossing were like those of New York. They spotted the University on its hill. 'There's something to be said for old Gilbert floodlit,' Hal remarked.

'Maybe one day Sam will be a student there,' Van said. 'That would please Anna and Ritchie.'

'Unless he follows in their footsteps and goes to the Art School?'

'He shows no aptitude so far. Just like me. He says he would like to be a doctor. He hears me talking about them.'

Anna and Ritchie welcomed them enthusiastically when they arrived at Clevedon Crescent after ten o'clock.

'Sam did his best to stay up,' Anna said, 'but he went

to sleep on the rug so Ritchie carried him off to bed. Come and sit down and have a drink. And there are sandwiches.' And when they were settled comfortably, 'Now, tell me how Mish is, and Karin, and Benjamin. It's a big name for a wee lad.'

'I can see it being shortened to Benjy. He's an angelic baby. Lively. He lies and crows and they love him to death.'

'Oh, he'll be spoiled!' Anna cried, with satisfaction.

'Not by Karin,' Van said.

'Any spoiling will be done by your son,' Hal added. 'He needs someone like Karin to keep him from going over the top.'

Anna raised her eyebrows. 'Mish? I wonder if I neglected him when he was small. Did I, Van?'

'Terribly. Both of us.' She smiled at her mother.

'Do you hear that, Ritchie?'

'She's pulling your leg.'

'No, you were great, Mother, but maybe now I can say it. There was always the feeling that your work was . . . sacrosanct. We didn't come first. "Mummy's working," I remember Mish saying to me. "Don't disturb her."'

'Poor wee things.' Anna bit her lip, laughed.

'Don't feel sorry for them,' Ritchie said. 'They were as snug as bugs in a rug. We worked our fingers to the bone for them, slaved away . . .'

'Now you're making *me* feel sorry.' Van looked at Hal, laughing. 'And Hal's got tears in his eyes. Anyhow we're all good friends which is better than anything. I've no complaints.'

'Anyhow you had a grand time in America?' Anna asked.

'Yes, we did everything we meant to do, didn't we, Hal, and had lovely evenings together, the four of us.

Karin was often later than Mish getting home. I think he left his gallery early to be with us.'

'He could do that, being the boss.' Ritchie nodded with satisfaction.

'You two really ought to go,' Hal said. 'You'd see some wonderful art. The museums are fantastic.'

'We've done enough gallivanting for the time being, but we're planning for next spring. We've a lot of work on the stocks, requests, functions, but after Christmas we'll make a space. Did you find out any more about your Hudson Valley lot, Hal?'

'Oh, yes, I saw one or two people, and Van and I went to museums where we knew their work was, the Met, and Poughkeepsie, of all places, that's where Vassar is, and there's a lot in Washington. We didn't get there.'

'Wasn't there a Rocky Mountain School? I read about that.'

'Yes, they went West as well. The call of the wild. I suppose the Hudson began to get too domesticated for them as it got built up. They lost favour after the Civil War, maybe because of the popularity of the French stuff, then about nineteen-hundred and forty they bounced back and their stock's steadily rising.'

'I bet Mish is in there.'

'Oh, yes, your son is shrewd. Figurative stuff's coming back.'

'Painters like me are going to be on the scrapheap in a few years.' Ritchie looked doleful.

'Poor wee laddie,' Anna teased.

'Oh, I'm no' worried.' He blew her a kiss. 'I'll just live off you.'

'I'd like to know what's been going on here,' Van said. 'You're an avid reader of the *Glasgow Herald*, Mum.'

'Well,' Anna considered, 'Not much. Between them Mr Heath and Enoch Powell are doing precious little to solve the Irish question. Here, as you know, there's a lot of sympathy for the IRA. What else? Hugh Fraser goes from strength to strength, but then, everybody knows Glasgow has the best shops and the kindest shop assistants in the country! We're glad we came back, aren't we, Ritchie?'

'Aye, we have the best water.'

'Well, there's precious little in this,' Hal said, taking a sip of his whisky. 'But maybe I can't express any opinions around here being a Sassenach.'

'I like Richmond,' Van said. 'It's gentle. It's selfish but I'm glad to be in a gentle place after working in drab ones. All the same, since Sam was born here, this must be my first love . . .' She turned at the sound of the door opening. Sam stood there, his pyjama trousers untied, showing a fair amount of his private parts. He was rubbing his eyes. She was out of her chair in a second and had swung him into her arms, 'Well, look who's here!'

'I got up to have a wee,' he said. 'You were making an awful row.'

'Were we? Come and sit down and Grandma might give you a sandwich.' She tied his pyjama cord. 'You didn't have to tell us where *you*'d been.' He looked sheepish.

Hal was beside them, bending down to give Sam a hug. 'It's great to see you again.'

'You were away an awful long time.' He was cross with sleep.

'But I bet you were spoiled rotten while we were away. Come on, admit it.'

He looked at Anna and Ritchie, his mouth turned down, smugly.

'Well, tell them all we did,' Anna said, giving him a sandwich. 'That's your favourite, salmon.'

'But don't spill all the beans,' Ritchie said.

'We had dinner in the Mal ... Mal ... in the big hotel at the station.' Sam spoke proudly through his sandwich.

'Hey,' Van protested, 'that isn't fair! I was more than twice your age before they took me. Remember that, Dad? Mish and me?'

'I remember you weren't impressed. Worried about the poor with only crusts.'

'*I* was impressed,' Sam said, fully awake. 'What is it anyhow?'

Van laughed and hugged him. 'Get on with your sandwich then we're all going to bed.'

That night in the bedroom with the balcony above the door, she and Hal lay close in each other's arms. 'I'm happy,' she said, 'and I'm not going to feel guilty about it.'

'You mean, guilty about this "my cup's-full-and-running-over" kind of happiness? Thank God I'm English. I've never suffered from religious guilt.' He rolled over on top of her, whispered in her ear, 'Unless you're too tired?'

'Not when you tug my ear like that with your teeth.' Her arms went round his neck.

Gordon, Wendy and their children, also Nancy and James, came to see Hal and Van on Sunday morning before they left for gentle Richmond. Nancy and James were just back from a cruise in the Philippines, and they were both tanned, James tanned and thin, Nancy tanned and plump. It could not be denied, Van thought, that her aunt was becoming a clone of Queen Victoria, except that she wouldn't have been seen dead in black with jet trimmings. Rather the reverse. She had 'gone for pink a lot recently', she told Van, because it 'did something' for her complexion at her age.

'And your hair?' Van suggested, admiring the bright gold shining cap which was so well permed and set that it had lost all connection with the real thing.

Wendy was the surprise. She had lost weight and her demeanour was brisk tending to authoritarian: 'No, Gordon, that's not how it happened,' or, 'Gordon always gets the story the wrong way round.'

'Have you noticed?' she said, pleased with Van's admiration of her svelte figure, 'I'm going to Keep Fit classes, and I've taken up swimming. I must say it's done wonders for me.'

'You certainly look wonderful,' Van said, looking at her glowing skin, but it was the general air of purposefulness which most surprised her.

'Yes, I think I've improved. You may not realize this, Van, but I've always admired *you*.'

'Admired *me*! Oh, come off it, Wendy. You swept Gordon off his feet. I can remember you at the tennis club, now I can tell you – it's been one of my shameful secrets – how I envied you and hated you for being so blonde and beautiful and daring to wear red instead of baby blue . . .' She laughed. 'And admit my gawkiness in comparison, and falling full length when I tore after the ball. Oh, I suffered the tortures of the damned!'

'Maybe you did, but you were only fourteen at the time and young for your age. Look at you now, holding down a responsible job in London, driving all over the place to different hospitals – Aunt Anna brags about you like mad. And look at the man you're married to. What a dish!'

'Well, I'll give you that.' And being polite, 'But so is yours.'

Wendy looked disparagingly across the room at Gordon, who had metaphorically buttonholed Hal and appeared to be laying down the law about something. 'He bores the pants off me. He's so pompous.'

Van giggled. 'Oh, Wendy!'

'Well, he's all right, really, pays the rent, but at times . . . well,' she turned a bright, determined face to Van, 'I've worked it out. I have to bring up the kids and I have to be a good wife to him, but I'm going away on my own next year. I've told him and he's furious and said everybody would laugh at him, but when I said I might write a book about my travels I could see his eyes lighting up – something else to boast about. ''Guess what the wife's getting up to now, lads?'' '

Van's eyes were round. 'Years ago you told me that you had got yourself pregnant before you were married just for a bit of excitement. At the time I didn't believe you. Now I do. Where are you going?'

'Middle East, Greece, Turkey. I'm busy planning routes. I have proper help in the house and he can take the girl with him to look after the kids if he goes to Arran. It's a *fait accompli*. He can't do a thing about it.' She called out loudly, 'Gordon! Van and Hal have got to get started. Where's wee Gordon?'

'He's romping about downstairs with Sam. I was just having an interesting conversation with Hal.'

'I hope *he* thinks so. Aunt Anna warned us Van and Hal had only an hour before they left.' She got to her feet, a leaner, fitter Wendy, head high, her eyes roaming round the room as if searching for the nearest mountain to scale. Once Van had thought of her as an Amazon. Now Diana, the Huntress, might be nearer the mark.

'Wendy's right, Hal,' she said, getting up too. 'We've a long way to go.'

She admired Hal afresh when they were on their way.

129

His profile was towards her as they bowled along the A74. She remembered Wendy's remark about him although she had no intention of telling him. Men loved praise. 'When you were living in New York,' she said, 'I bet you had dozens of girls falling for you.'

'Dozens,' he agreed. 'Especially one with dyed red hair who spent her time trying to seduce me.'

'Oh!' she said, 'we didn't go to see her after all. That woman who lived in the same apartments.'

'Ellie Kaplan. Yes, we might have got some more information for Karin about her patient. Do you think Mish was a tiny bit impatient when she was talking about him?'

'Maybe. But it's difficult to know what Mish thinks.'

'Except when it comes to Benjy.' He drove on in silence for a time.

BOOK 3

1972

Fourteen

Towards the end of March the following year Anna decided she would drive to Kirkcudbright and see Jean. They hadn't come to the annual Christmas party at Clevedon Crescent and Nancy had commented on it. She was plaintive.

'We three sisters have stuck close to each other. You even moved up here to be nearer us.' This was not strictly true as Rose, their mother, had left the house to Anna, but she let it pass. 'But Jean's drifting away these days. I suggested James and I paid them a visit and she didn't take me up on it, said to leave it as she was very busy. Well, it's only painting, and I'm her sister after all.'

'She's a successful painter, Nancy, but yes, we don't hear much from her. I'll take a run up before we go off to America.'

'To see your grandson?' Nancy was dewy-eyed, 'your first . . .'

'There's Sam.'

'Well, Sam . . .' She looked into the distance, as if searching in remotest Africa for Sam's birthplace.

Now, driving through Galloway on a bright, sunny but cold day and seeing the familiar landmarks and towns, Newton Stewart, Gatehouse of Fleet, she asked herself why they went abroad at all when they had beauty like this so near. And it was only a taste of the Highlands and their grandeur.

What was it that tempted people to leave the familiar for the unfamiliar? Weather, certainly; sunshine was a scarce commodity in Scotland, but that very scarcity gave it, if anything, more charm. Its sudden brilliant flashes were lighting up the coastline like a searchlight, the whiteness of the cottages newly painted for the summer visitors hurt her eyes, the green of some of the trees was at its most tender and fresh.

But there was the appeal of a different culture. Ritchie had a strong link with and a love for Spain ever since he had fought in the International Brigade, and he was as well-known in Barcelona as he was in Glasgow. In her case was it the chance to get out of one's skin, to live an exterior life instead of an interior one? Which brought you back to the weather.

But she too had grown to love the Spanish way of life, the difference in temperament of the people, the vibrancy, the colour, and, you always came back to it, the penetrating warmth of the sun to her chilled northern bones.

Those lovely lazy afternoons with Ritchie at their pool, the wicked delight she still took in swimming under his admiring gaze – he was a dry-land swimmer he always said ... her dreaming was interrupted by finding herself in the broad High Street of Kirkcudbright, and she drove circumspectly but more purposefully at the thought of seeing Jean, who next to Ritchie was closest to her heart.

Jean's welcome was as warm as ever. There was no doubt about that.

'You didn't come at Christmas so I've had to come to see you,' Anna said. 'Ritchie was too busy but I wanted to have a look at you before we go off to America.'

'Come in, come in!' Her eyes were moist. 'We'll have time for tea and a chinwag before John gets home.'

'How is he?'

They were in the cosy sitting-room, one of the few places where Anna always felt at home.

'He's not a hundred per cent. Sit there and toast your toes. Never mind your chilblains. What a suit! Trust you, Anna, to have the best. Put your feet up. Do you drive with shoes like that? Yes, on the footstool. Every time I trip over one it reminds me of Aunt Jessie. I couldn't part with them for the world.'

'Happy memories. What's wrong with John?'

'It's his heart, but he won't admit it. Or maybe he's growing old like the rest of us. Getting on for sixty now, and he's worked hard all his life.'

'You can't persuade him to give it up?'

'I've tried. I'm painting most of the day and he'd be at a loose end.' The selfishness of artists, Anna thought, but she was in no position to criticize when she and Ritchie happily ignored each other all day. But, then, they were both doing the same thing.

'I can see that. Great cup of tea, Jean. Well, you could try and persuade him to take longer holidays. You could copy Nancy and go on a cruise.'

'God forbid! It would kill me.'

'What about John?'

'Well, he likes people, of course. In no time they'd be coming to him with their aches and pains. And he could play bridge, I suppose. He occasionally plays here. Alan McAlpine tells me he's good.' She changed the subject. 'How are Van and Hal and Sam?'

'That's like the best romantic novel, a happy ending. They're blissfully happy, it shows in their faces, and

135

she's chosen a man who has taken Sam to his heart. They like Richmond. Van's working in hospitals not too far away, Sam's happy at school . . .'

'Maybe she's going to be like you. Everything running smoothly for ever and ever . . .' Jean's voice was bitter.

'There have been a few bumps for her on the way, Jean, don't forget. There was Sam's father . . .'

'But at least Sam is alive, unlike Roderick.'

'But you have three grandchildren to take his place.' Here we go, Anna thought, the old story.

'Ach, yes, I know. I'm having a grouse because you're the only one who'll tell me off if you get fed up with it. John is so long-suffering.'

'Why, then,' Anna looked at her sister, making her eyes clear, 'are you making him suffer?'

'Yes, that's me. A thorn in the flesh. You're the one that's all sweetness and light.'

'Hey!' She made herself laugh. 'I haven't driven a hundred miles to quarrel with you.' She looked at her. 'Is there anything you want to tell me, Jean? If there is, now's your chance.'

'Why should there be?' She stared her out. How well I know that look, Anna thought, Jean against the world. 'Come into the kitchen. I'll have to get the supper ready. You can help me and we'll have a swig of the cooking sherry.'

Anna watched them later at the dinner table. John was certainly thinner, but he was cheerful enough and dismissed any enquiries about his health. 'I had a touch of 'flu around Christmas, that's why we didn't come to your party, Anna, but I'm fine now.'

'Aren't you thinking of retiring soon? You have a fine assistant in Alastair.'

'Partner now. And there's a young lad in the town,

136

in his last year of medicine at St Andrews. His father has already approached me.'

'Well, what's stopping you? Look at Ritchie and me. We're off to Spain any time we get the chance.'

'But you have work there too. Jean needs her studio.'

She shut up. She saw the signs of strain in their eyes, how Jean banged dishes, smoked between courses, replenished her glass without asking anyone else. Oh, she's a wild thing, she thought, always will be. You'd have thought by this time she would have calmed down. She went to bed feeling uneasy.

The following day Jean said to her, 'A friend will be dropping in about teatime. Actually he's a client of Alan McAlpine's – funny how that man gets into your hair.'

'Thank goodness he isn't in Van's.'

'Yes, that was a near thing. Denis Carter.' She wasn't bothered about Van. 'He's divorced. He's an estate agent. Has a house up here although they lived mostly in London. Doing well with the landed gentry since he established a branch in Kirkcudbright.' It seemed to Anna too much of a preamble.

'So?'

Jean looked at her. 'He's taken up painting. Gets my advice from time to time when he's here. He's turning out some quite decent stuff.'

'Good for him. Has he become a regular visitor?' Still clear-eyed.

'More or less.'

'What does John think of that?'

'He knows him. You don't think he'd mind me having a pupil, for God's sake?'

'You who used to say that you hated the idea of teaching, that it was a waste of good painting time?'

The blue of Jean's eyes deepened. It was always a sign of anger. 'Have you come all the way here to criticize me? I thought it was a genuine desire to pay us a friendly visit?' There was a nerve at the side of her mouth.

'I'm sorry, Jean.' Anna retracted. 'I'm nit-picking.'

'Well, cut it out.' Jean got up and went out of the back door. She would be off to her solace, Anna thought.

Denis Carter came for tea, and there was no doubt he was charming, amusing, smiled a lot, but not with his eyes, Anna noticed, after the first few minutes. And she noticed those eyes followed Jean as she spoke, as she moved, and that they softened, and that he was younger than her. And she noticed Jean's elaborate casualness and knew it was overdone. The air between them was humming, as if there was some kind of conductor there. She felt that if she stood in its direct path she might be electrocuted.

'I hear you're taking lessons from Jean,' she said.

'Yes.' He smiled at Jean, his chin down, his eyes glancing upwards. 'Six lessons from Madame Majonga, or something. What was that song?' None of them could remember. I bet it's been more than six, Anna thought.

'He's not bad,' Jean said, 'in spite of the tuition.' The light in her face was exclusively for Denis Carter.

'I'm a metal worker,' Anna said. 'Not in the rarefied heights of high art, but Ritchie says I'm a good critic. Has Jean any of yours?'

He looked at Jean, eyebrows raised.

'There might be some in the studio. Would you really like to have a look, Anna?'

'I really would.' More and more she felt as if she had got mixed up with a play in which there was no part for her.

'She'll tear you in shreds,' Jean said to Carter. Later, Anna knew she would say to Ritchie, 'Have you ever felt completely unnecessary?' She hoped she *could* tear him in shreds.

But his paintings weren't nearly as bad as that, in fact they were good for an amateur, uninhibited. Ritchie would like them. They were mostly abstract, he had a poor sense of colour but a better than usual sense of form.

'Six out of ten,' she pronounced. 'No wonder Jean's prepared to give you lessons. She wouldn't waste her time on rubbish.'

'Oh, he's good,' Jean said. Her face had an innocence, a familiar look, puzzling Anna. She pondered over it, holding it in her mind until she was in bed. That incandescence, a highlighting of her features as if her face was held up to a source of light somewhere, an intensity in the blueness of her eyes.

It came to her as she was tossing and turning around three in the morning. Her twin had the same look long ago when she came in from those secret meetings with Frederick Kleiber. He too had been dark, with that charm which had been more than mere handsomeness. Jean had been obsessed by him. She realized she had been watching history repeating itself.

Anna said she had enjoyed meeting Denis Carter, but thought he shouldn't give up being a house agent yet. Some people painted by a lucky fluke which didn't last.

'This is a new one on me,' Jean said, calm now.

'They have little knowledge or understanding of why they paint, what they're trying to find out. They think it's just a case of hand-eye co-ordination, like in games at school, that it's a matter of confidence, maybe over-confidence, in some cases.' In Denis Carter's case, she thought.

'As a form of therapy it doesn't count? He had a

messy divorce, there's a little girl, Katie, whom he misses badly.'

'He's the wrong type to resort to art therapy. Why,' she said, eyes clear, 'are we always discussing this Denis Carter?'

'You brought it up.'

She went to see Sarah while Jean was busy in her studio – even Anna's presence didn't stop that – and she was greeted warmly. Safe dependable Sarah, she thought. What's the point of spoiling her contentment? But it was Sarah who spoiled hers.

She sent the children out with the girl and shut the door of the kitchen. She was eternally busy in the kitchen, Anna thought. You would have thought she was catering for the entire British Army.

'I'm glad you came, Aunt Anna. I'm worried about Mum,' she began. 'I thought of writing to you.'

'Isn't she well? I thought it was your father?' She wanted to dismiss any appearance of suspicion.

'Alastair's keeping an eye on him. He has a dicky heart. No, it's Mum. She's having an affair.'

Anna dropped the pretence. 'Denis Carter?'

'Yes. It's been going on for ages.'

'How did you know?'

'It was awful.' The girl's face was white behind the brown splash of freckles. 'Sandy and I went to see her one evening over a year ago. It was a special treat for him being allowed up past his bed time, also I wanted to borrow a jelly pan. She wasn't in the house, so we walked down the garden path to the studio, on tiptoe, to surprise her – that was Sandy's idea – well, we *did*. They were both there, lying on the sofa. It was obvious . . .'

'Oh, heavens! What happened?'

'Everybody was covered with confusion. It was terrible. I told Sandy they were playing games . . .' Her

140

face went red. 'I didn't want to tell him not to say anything because that would have made him guilty. I played it down.'

'Oh, Sarah!' Anna bit her lip. She couldn't laugh with Sarah about it. She hadn't a great sense of humour. 'He came to the house last night. Do you think anyone else knows?'

'I haven't discussed it, naturally. She phoned me the next morning and came here. She apologized. It was terribly awkward. I don't know if she meant it wouldn't happen again, or she was sorry we barged in.' The latter, Anna thought.

'There's nothing we can do,' she said. 'She's an adult. But even when she was young she never took my advice.'

'I keep hoping he'll stop coming, lose interest or something. He only comes to Kirkcudbright once a fortnight, or thereabouts. Maybe that's what keeps it going, with Mum, the excitement, I mean.'

'What does Alastair think?'

'He thinks she "forgot herself", just once. He's charitable about her fall from grace, but you know what the Wee Frees think of women caught in adultery. He's like Sandy, thinks it was just a game, a kind of gambol!' She smiled faintly.

Anna looked at her. 'I didn't think you'd be so broadminded, Sarah.'

'Well, I know Mum. Life has to be dangerous for her. I've always accepted that, and how she likes the grand drama. If she hadn't been a painter she would have been an actress.' Her face sobered. 'But you haven't heard the worst of it.'

'Gosh, can it get worse?'

'Yes. Sandy. Not long after the . . . occurrence, Dad had called to see Alastair – it was a Sunday – and Sandy

141

was in the room with them. He was bounding up and down on the sofa and Alastair told him to stop it. He wouldn't, and then he said he was just playing games like Grandma and the man . . . I was in the kitchen. Alastair came in and told me afterwards. Dad hadn't said anything, had pretended not to hear.'

'Your father isn't stupid. Oh!' Anna groaned. 'Oh, dear, oh, dear! But why on earth hasn't he told Carter not to come back?'

'Can't you see it? I know Dad, how his mind works. He knows if he did, she might walk out of the house and go to him.' Sarah's voice was low. 'He couldn't bear to lose her.'

'But that's . . . sick.'

'That's love.' The tears were streaking her face. 'Do you know what I think? I think he knows his heart's bad, and he'd rather have Mum beside him on any terms. After all, it's the second time for him. He was her doctor when the baby . . . Oh, Aunty!'

Anna put her arms round her. 'Maybe I should talk to her, try and get her . . .'

'No. You two argue a lot although you're close. Alastair thought of speaking to her, but I know he would give her a sermon and that would be worse.'

'And we both know your mother. She's as thrawn as the very devil.' Anna found herself speaking with Bessie Tait's voice.

'She's so beautiful.'

'Yes. So beautiful. I'm going home tomorrow. Ritchie's the one. He's not a member of the family. And he's very level-headed.' If level-headed meant keeping out of things which didn't concern him, that adjective certainly applied.

She thought Jean clung to her longer than usual when she was saying good-bye. She gave Anna an extra hug before she released her. 'That's for coming. You're the only one I can bear to have in the house these days.' And when Anna was at the wheel of her car, 'Love to everybody,' she said, 'especially to Van.'

Anna telephoned Van before she and Ritchie left for New York. 'We're off now to see that new grandson. I'll give you all the news when I get back.'

'And give them all our love. Wish I were coming with you. How did you get on at Kirkcudbright? Was Jean in good form?'

'You could say that. She's having an affair with a man younger than herself. Divorced.'

'No!' She could hear Van's surprise. 'Did she tell you?'

'No, Sarah did. She caught them at it. Sandy was with her.'

'Oh, God. Poor Sarah!'

'Sandy had been allowed up late and he wanted to surprise Grandma.' She badly wanted to laugh. 'And then he told John.'

'Oh, no!'

'You know children. He told him that Grandma had been playing games on the sofa with a man. Sarah hadn't wanted him to be burdened with a guilty secret and so had made light of it. This liberal upbringing they go in for nowadays! I'd have said to him that if he mentioned it he'd get a good skelpin'.'

'You would not. You prided yourself on being liberal when you were all at the Art School, throwing convention to the winds.'

'The extent of my liberal leanings in those days would have been to have a coffee on my own in the Regal Café!'

'So what's the position now?'

143

'John hasn't said anything to Jean, so Sarah thinks. Her theory is that he depends on Jean too much, and if he challenged her he's afraid she might walk out. He's not well, Van. His heart's bad.'

'So Jean goes on with the affair?'

'She's not heartless. Sarah hasn't told her about Sandy spilling the beans. Jean loves John, you know, but it's a different kind of love. I know her. She still hankers after passion. This is a last fling. And I'm sure she's made up her mind half-a-dozen times to finish with Denis Carter, that's his name, and then when she sees him . . . what would you do if you were in my place?'

She heard Van pause, then, 'Nothing. They're all suffering. It'll solve itself in one way or the other. A situation like that is self-terminating.'

'What big words!'

'I learn them from my work, and talking to Karin. She says people sometimes come to her because they're unhappy in their marriage. Well, some marriages *are* unhappy, she says. You either thole them or give them up.'

'The thing was, Jean wasn't unhappy with John.'

'But there was something missing for her. It'll work itself out.'

'Why are you so sure?'

'Because Jean isn't heartless. That's her trouble. She's got too much heart.'

'Yes . . . have a talk with Hal anyhow.'

'He'll feel the same. What did Dad say?'

'The same as you. "Leave it," he says, "it's not our business." I'm the only one who thinks I can manipulate fate, or whatever. Oh, dear! Well, can I speak to Sam for a minute? That'll cheer me up.'

'He's here, waiting. Don't worry too much, Mum. Enjoy yourself. Love to you and Dad. I'll keep in touch.'

Fifteen

'What's your impression?' Anna asked Ritchie. He was driving fairly cautiously even though they were now out of the city and heading for Westchester.

'The wideness of the streets in those small towns. When you think of villages outside Glasgow, Carmunnock, Strathaven, any in the Trossachs further afield – they're like twisting lanes in comparison. *They* haven't been altered for hundreds of years because the hamlets were there first. Here they've started from scratch, and it's a big country with plenty of space.'

'Not cosy, though.'

'No, you couldn't shout across the street to a neighbour coming out of a pub.'

'And you only know there are houses tucked away because of those postboxes at the end of a drive.'

'It's space again. A vast country, a new world. The breadth appeals to me. The thing is my murals might get even bigger here.'

'They're big enough. Look, we turn off here. Indian names. Have you noticed? Oscawana. We drive along for a few miles. Are you excited?'

'Aye, fairly excited. I used to think Mish was our success story. Now I'm changing my tune. Van's a grand lass. She'll go ahead now.'

'Especially with a husband like Hal. He won my heart when he took to Sam right away.'

'We're blessed. And Karin's a wee smasher. We'd better stop counting our chickens. It's dangerous. But we've been lucky all the way through.'

'Lucky.' She slipped a hand through his arm. 'And here we are, spreading our wings, going to visit our son in America. Look at that high sky. No drizzly damp here.'

'But tough winters. God, I'm happy, Anna! I don't deserve it.'

'Nobody does, but it's a bonus when you get it. We've done two miles along this road now. Keep a lookout. Karin says you'll see the house easily, that it's on a hill. They can see the Hudson. Slow down, Ritchie. Turn here. That's it. My, it's rough, and a climb. It wouldn't do for our retirement, eh?' She smiled at him.

'We're no landin' oorselves on oor bairns. That's what ma Ma used to say. And they never did.' He always lapsed into the vernacular when he spoke about Lizzie and Walter, Anna thought. Maybe it brought them closer, now that they were both gone. The salt of the earth.

They followed the drive and stopped in front of a wide terrace perched up on a vast rocky shrubbery. 'What a position!' Anna said. 'And not too far from New York. Trust Mish to get it right.' They climbed the steps and rang the bell. A small dark woman answered it, neat in a cotton dress, her hair pulled back in a bun. Mish had said there were a lot of Italians in the area. She greeted them pleasantly.

'You're Mr Laidlaw's folks.' She held out her hand. 'I can see the likeness. I'm Mrs Strickner, their help. Come in.' The hall was wide and light with rugs on the polished pale gold wood floor. Mish, Anna thought,

146

modernism. No clutter. 'They won't be in for an hour or so,' the woman was saying, 'they catch the home traffic, but I've strict instructions to make you a cup of tea. I'll show you to your room first. Leave the big cases, Mr Laidlaw, Ruth and me can handle them.'

Their bedroom was as wide and spacious as the hall with an even better view than from the terrace. 'Lovely, isn't it?' Anna said to Ritchie, 'It's a grand river that, like the sea. Different from Clevedon Crescent. There we're carpeted up to the walls.'

'It's the only way to keep cosy in Glasgow. Look at that.' He pointed to a small Cocteau etching on the wall. 'It was one of Mish's first purchases. Did you see that abstract above the staircase?'

'An American painter. I didn't recognize him.'

'Hopperesque anyhow. Even Mish couldn't afford a Hopper.'

'Come and look at the *en suite*,' she called to him. 'I'm freshening up, as the housekeeper said.'

'You look fresh enough to me.' He came into the small room and took her in his arms, then waltzed her out again.

'Be your age!' She was laughing. 'I feel I'm acting a part. "Ceremonial visit of grandparents." I don't feel old enough for that. Do you?'

'No.' He shook his head, smiling at her, and she thought, I'll never get enough of his handsomeness, his curly hair, his eyes, his loving, painter's eyes. 'We're impostors. We're really that young couple who went to Art School and had coffee in the Regal Café and went to the University Union hops on Saturday nights.'

'And spent more time in the sitooterie than on the dance floor.'

'My God, even yet I can get a vicarious thrill from that memory. The mystery. Maybe there's something to

147

be said for chastity before marriage.' He kissed her. 'You're still that girl to me, Anna.'

'Minus the mystery. And you're still that cheeky lad from Glasgow Road. Isn't it sad how time passes?'

'We've a lot ahead of us yet.'

'But that young ardour . . .'

'It's still there for me.'

'I'm not so jealous now. That's a sign of growing older. You need intensity for jealousy.'

He said, looking into her eyes, 'I don't know how I could live without you. It's time I told you how much you mean to me.'

'It's too painful to think along these lines. Don't. Remember the agony of Jean when Frederick Kleiber was drowned? I wouldn't like to see the like of that again.'

'And now she's risking her marriage with John.'

'I know her. There's a hunger in her that's never satisfied. Oh, I hope she doesn't regret it too much!' She pulled away from his arms. 'Do you think that wee soul will have finished his nap by this time? I'm going to go downstairs and ask. And there's that cup of tea we were promised.'

'"Ae fond kiss afore we sever . . ."' His hands wandered as his mouth held hers.

'You're another Rabbie Burns,' she said.

'Aye, he was a devil wi' the wummen tae. We'll awa' doon noo.'

'What's got into you?' She giggled like a girl.

'I'm fighting off the American influence. Let's mosey on down.'

Benjamin was brought in to see them in the care of his nursemaid. She seemed good-natured, Anna thought, the main prerequisite when it came to looking after children.

148

'Can I hold him, Ruth?' she asked the girl.

'You sure can, Ma'am.' Her broad black face was lit by a wide smile. 'He's some weight, I'm warnin' you.'

He was. Anna sat down with him and smiled with delight at the baby's face raised to hers.

'I'm not the crowing type,' she said to Ritchie, 'but he's beautiful, isn't he? Like Mish.'

'But with Karin's brown eyes. He's squirming like an eel. For God's sake, don't drop him! Give him to me.' She raised her eyebrows but handed the baby over. To her surprise he lay contentedly in Ritchie's arms, gazing up at him with obvious adoration. He looked over at Anna with a smug smile, rocking Benjamin gently.

'Yes, I see,' she said. 'You're won over right away. It's going to be "my grandson" from now on. He's lovely.' She turned to the girl who was watching them with amusement. 'Is he a good baby?'

'Good and bad, Ma'am. I don't like them when they're too good. He has a will of his own. Like his mother. Young Mrs Laidlaw knows what she's about, she sure does. And she don't spoil him. But your son!' She shook her head delightedly. 'He's just crazy about him, baby talk and everything, and him such a city gentleman. Well, you see all kinds in my job. Better that than a neglected child, a loveless couple. I've worked for some who hardly know they've *got* a child. Out all the time.'

Karin and Mish arrived together half an hour later. They greeted Anna and Ritchie enthusiastically.

'I see you're getting your hand in, Dad,' Mish said.

'He's chuffed because Benjamin has taken to him.' Anna smiled at this smart-suited sleek young man who was her son.

'That will be two doting men on the premises,' Karin

said. 'Shall I take him now, Ritchie?' She had always used their first names, Anna remembered with pleasure, admiring also the practised, loving way she lifted the baby, how she spoke to him. She wondered how it felt to go out each day and leave a child you loved, to be far away if anything should happen. A hard decision. She had been lucky that she worked at home.

Mish's contribution, leaning over Karin's shoulder and talking rubbish, made her want to laugh, but brought sentimental tears to her eyes. Fatherhood, she supposed, took men in different ways. Ritchie had not been a baby's man. His work always came first. Now, she thought, remembering his smug face, he was making up for lost time.

She and Karin went upstairs for Benjamin's bath-time, and again she admired Karin's loving but practical way of handling her son.

'This is my time,' she said, smiling up at Anna. 'It's important to me. If you're bored, go down and join the men.'

'Bored? No fear! It takes me back. Now I've all the fun with none of the hard work. We love him already, Karin. He's had a lucky start to be brought up in a place like this.'

'Yes, we want him to feel secure. But it doesn't do to be too possessive, or obsessive. That's why I don't think it's a bad thing to have Ruth and Mrs Strickner around while we're away. If Mish had his way he would have me hovering over this little guy all day in a white pinny.' She lifted the child out of the bath and enveloped him in a voluminous white towel. 'Although I must admit when you see them like this, all pink and shiny and cuddly, it's quite tempting.'

Later, over dinner, Anna told them about Jean.

'In a way I'm not surprised,' Mish said, surprising

150

Anna. 'She has a strange appeal, it's more than beauty, it's a promise of . . . secret delights. I had quite carnal leanings towards her myself.'

'Well, well!' Anna said.

'Sorry, Mother, but she's a seductress, your twin, a Circe, or maybe Deirdre of the Sorrows is nearer to it. Don't you agree, Father?'

'I can never see past your mother,' Ritchie replied, with innocent eyes.

'Liar,' Anna said. 'But leaving that aside, I never worried about Jean ousting me. I know her through and through, there's a hidden bond. There was utter loyalty between us. She would never have done any harm to me just as I would never have done any harm to her. If she's a seductress, it's an inbuilt thing, there's nothing premeditated about it. But I wouldn't know about her effect on the opposite sex.'

'She's a classic figure,' Karin said. 'Built for tragedy. Drawn by it. What's that Wagnerian tale about the lady on the rocks who drew the sailors to their death – Lorelei, wasn't it?'

'Poor Jean.' Anna looked sad. 'All those names she's being called. She's her own worst enemy, that's all. She can't resist this man, in fact, she probably wanted it to happen. She loves John in an entirely different way. He was her saviour at one time.'

'But her loyalty doesn't extend to her husband?' Mish asked.

'Well, husbands aren't blood relations,' Karin put in. 'Sisters are, especially twins.'

'Is that an excuse?'

'No, but it's an explanation of Jean's behaviour.'

She's sharp, Anna thought, needle sharp. 'Van thinks we shouldn't interfere,' she said.

'She's right.' Karin turned to her. 'Besides, it wouldn't

151

do any good. The sexual urge is much stronger than loyalty. Didn't she have a tragic love affair when she was young?' Anna nodded. 'She's reliving that.' You don't have to be a psychologist to know that, Anna thought, and changed the subject.

'Let's hear about your gallery, Mish. Ritchie and I are dying to come in with you some morning and see around it.'

'And I'm dying to show you.' He smiled at them.

'But he won't tell you how well-known he's become,' Karin said. 'I've got cuttings from the *New York Times* to show you. "Young Englishman has the smartest gallery in town."'

Sixteen

Karin went on with her work as usual, even though Anna and Ritchie were there. They understood, being workers themselves. They liked exploring the long narrow stretch of the Hudson Valley, the Catskills – pleasant enough but not to be compared with the grander mountains of the Scottish Highlands.

They spent some time at the Storm King Art Center, and while Anna looked at the sculptures Ritchie sketched happily away. They crossed the river to stay a night in the Mohawk Mountain House where everything was too big and too grand, and they missed out the palatial homes.

They preferred New York and 'making nuisances of themselves' in Mish's gallery where they met an elegant young man whose American accent had deepened since breakfast that morning, and who presided over some of the best modern paintings to be had. Was that our son, they asked each other when they were back in busy Madison Avenue.

They found an unexpected interest in the remaining iron-front buildings in SoHo which reminded them, so they agreed, of Walter Macfarlane's showroom in the north of Glasgow with its wonderful displays of gates, railings, fountains, bandstands and the like.

In the Lower West Side they located the site where

the Hudson Valley painters had worked, and they had occasional rests in the Plaza Hotel to compare notes.

'I paint because of what's inside me,' Ritchie said. 'I don't give a damn which medium people use, or which approach they take. The subject decides it. I only *seem* more sophisticated because cameras have taken over. But, when I look at, say, Gifford's painting of Kauterskill Cave in the Catskills, it's the man I see, his kind of poetic illumination, whereas in my Spanish murals I'm seeking the essence of Spain, its glamour, its colour and its cruelty.'

Although Mish left his assistants in charge to accompany them on their expeditions, Karin adhered strictly to her schedule. 'I've got to be regimented,' she told Anna, 'otherwise I encroach on my time for Benjy.'

This morning she sat at her desk, looking across at Paul Laskins and wishing he was out of her life, and feeling that discomfort at the pit of her stomach, like a pre-menstrual nag. Their eyes met. There was a half-smile on his mouth.

'How is your baby getting on, Miss Gottleib?' he said.

'I don't discuss my personal life with my patients, Paul.' She knew her tone was sharp.

'I only asked how your baby was getting on.' He was truculent.

'I appreciate your interest.' She met his eyes. 'He's getting along fine.'

'A little boy?' His eyes were full of candour.

'Yes.'

'He's a lucky little boy with a mother like you.' She drew in her breath, tightening her lips. 'And living in Westchester, far away from the dirt and noise of the city. It's a great place to bring up kids. I've never been there, often thought of it, I like the country . . .' She let him talk while she puzzled over who the hell his informant was. There was that sullen-looking cleaner who never responded to her greeting. Could she by any chance work at Paul Laskins's apartments as well? 'I thought of taking a boat up the Hudson from the Battery, just to see. You're on a hill, aren't you?' The nag had intensified, right down in the core of her. She interrupted him.

'I've been looking at your notes, Paul. I see you said to me . . .' She lifted her head to look at him, 'this was regarding your girlfriend – "It's over, the whole thing's over. She got tired waiting." What was she tired waiting *for*?'

'Did I say that?' He was playful. 'I can't remember.'

'Yes, you did. Was it that she was tired waiting for you to get a job?'

'Yes, that was it.' He looked away.

'You see, I didn't see how it *could* be because you said on that same date that she thought you *were* working. That you told her you got in before her in the evenings.'

'Okay, okay!' He was impatient. 'Does it matter?'

'Truth bears all investigation. That's an old saying. I want the truth. Did she want you to marry her? Was that it? Was that why she walked out on you?'

'Why? God knows. Women are funny.'

'And that worried you?'

'Of course it worried me. I told you I begged and begged . . .'

'And that got on your mind?'

'Sure it did.'

'Kept you from sleeping?'

'Why should it?'

'Because you worried about her refusing to marry you, because you wondered . . .'

'I worried period. Who can understand the contortions of the feminine mind?' From truculence he became playful again, the little rosebud mouth pursed, the eyes twinkled. 'You should ask your husband.' Karin concealed her annoyance. 'I bet sometimes when you go up that steep drive to your terrace he's wondering what sort of mood will she be in tonight.'

She said calmly, 'You were close to your girlfriend. You've told me she was a quiet home-loving girl. She didn't want to go out on the town. You stayed in most evenings quite happily . . .'

'Making whoopee,' he sang.

She met his eyes, staring him out until his fell. 'Isn't that so?'

'Yes, yes, that's what we did. There we were,' he had sobered, 'like two married people, like two peas in a pod, happy together . . .'

'Playing mummies and daddies . . .' the phrase came into Karin's mind. Everything in place except for the baby . . .

'I believe she sometime baby-sat for a lady in the same apartments?'

He sat up on the couch, turning his head to her. 'Who told you that? You've been spying on me!'

'That sounds like the pot calling the kettle black. Calm down. I gave you a warning before.'

'If people looked after their own affairs,' he was muttering to himself as he lay down again. 'Yes, she did sometimes. Once she brought it upstairs to show me, sat dandling it on her knee. She looked . . . right with it.' His voice rose. 'But I know why she did it!' He was suddenly weeping, hoarse, guttural sobs. 'She did it to taunt me. There she sat, holding it in her arms, tucking the shawl under its chin and she looked at me with those eyes of hers and I told her to get it back downstairs pretty damn quick . . .'

Karin sat, seeing the bald crown above the cushion

moving from side to side as he sobbed. She said after a time, 'There's a box of tissues on the table. Go over and sit on the armchair beside it. It's comfortable. Would you like some coffee?'

He got up and walked to the armchair with his gangling gait, collapsed into it, helped himself to a wad of tissues. He looked pathetic. His nose was red. His little mouth was trembling, the lower lip jutting out like a child's. 'No, thanks,' he said. 'It's a drink I'd like.'

'You'll have to wait for that, I'm afraid. Are you gay, Paul?'

He laughed, rubbing at his nose with the tissues, then rolled them up into a ball and tossed them towards the wastebasket. They fell short. 'I thought you'd say that. The usual conclusion. I am not gay.' He enunciated each word, slowly. 'Don't you think it's a ridiculous question to ask me when you know I slept with Bobbie for the best part of three years?'

'And you were having normal sexual intercourse with her during that time?'

'Often. Sometimes twice a night. Does that satisfy you?'

'Did you use normal means of contraception?'

'All the time, yeah, all the time.' He raised his head, swaggering.

'You're telling me the truth?'

'Why shouldn't I, for God's sake?' He looked out of the window, his mouth pursed, his chin lifted.

'Paul,' she said, 'even if you deny it I know you were adopted at the age of three by Mr and Mrs Laskins. Your real parents were in a car crash. I'm sorry. You were old enough to miss them, and it must have been traumatic for you. You're intelligent. A tragedy like that, losing them, going to live somewhere else, takes away one's awareness of one's own identity, lowers one's self-esteem.'

'Not so as you would notice.' He was still looking across at the window as if following the movements of a fly crawling there.

'Your adoptive parents were kind to you from what you told me but you accepted all they did with little sense of gratitude. You were thinking all the time how badly you'd been treated by fate. Isn't that so?'

'They took me in to make them feel good, is all. They liked Kathleen better. All I ever wanted was to get away.'

'Well, you did. They sent you to College, didn't they?'

'Yes.'

'And they're still paying out?'

'Yeah, yeah. I don't know why you harp on about this.'

'All right. All you ever wanted when you grew up was to make your *own* home with your *own* wife and your *own* family, the thing you felt you'd always been deprived of. But there was a snag, wasn't there?'

He had turned from the window as if wearied. 'I don't know what you mean.' His eyes didn't meet hers.

'You found a girl who wanted a home too, who wanted babies, but you couldn't give them to her. She found that out. Isn't that right?' He was looking at his hands. 'You shouldn't be seeing me,' Karin said. 'You're wasting my time and yours.' He muttered something she couldn't hear. 'I'll give you the address of a clinic. It's for men's problems. They'll sort you out. It may be something very simple. Will you promise to go there?'

'It could be Bobbie! I told her that time and time again. We had rows about it.'

'Well, make a start with yourself.'

'They'll laugh at me.'

'Why should they? That's their job. I'll write to your doctor. Let me know how you get on. We shan't make another appointment for the time being.'

He got up. He stood, his eyes unfocused, as if he had forgotten where he was.

'Oh, on you go, Paul.' She smiled at him, finding it difficult. 'You're behaving like a child.'

He put his hand on the back of his neck, swivelled it round as if to ease it. 'Some child! You're throwing me out, then?'

'I'm not throwing you out. I simply feel we should clear up things by you going to the clinic instead of wasting my time.'

He didn't move. 'You think that?' He was smiling, or at least the small mouth was turned up at one side.

'I think that.' The unease was back, an ache.

'This is how it goes. Always the same.' He nodded his head. 'Either they throw me out or they walk out on me. Everybody. You with your lovely house in Westchester and your husband and your baby don't begin to *know* how I feel, the loneliness, the misery . . .'

'Believe me, I do.' Karin met his look squarely. 'My life is spent feeling sympathy for people like you but knowing that that isn't enough, that I have to try and help. This is my way of helping, giving you some good advice.'

Her receptionist knocked and put her head round the door. 'The next patient's here, Miss Gottleib.'

'Send her in, please. Let me know Paul,' she said, dismissing him.

He was suddenly thirty-three years old with thirty-three-old eyes, mature. He shrugged, his mouth lifted at one side. 'You win,' he said. 'Have a good day.' He walked out with a swagger, shutting the door behind him.

159

She wrote on his card, 'sterile' and put it away as the next patient came into the room. She was a schizophrenic, steady under treatment now, Karin hoped. Anything would be easy after Paul.

Seventeen

'These are halcyon days,' Van said.

It was Sunday, and they were strolling in Kew Gardens after watching cricket. She had enjoyed that with what she called her 'English' eyes, but Sam had become restless, and they were now at the lake where he was dashing about watching the ducks.

The gardens had become a favourite haunt of theirs. Sam needed lots of scope, and the grassy areas on either side of the Broad Walk gave him plenty of room. He enjoyed identifying the trees, but beyond that wasn't interested in any of the formal gardens. He had liked the spring flowers, particularly the bluebell wood, and the rhododendron dell was a good place for hide-and-seek. He was a free spirit. The only glasshouse he could be persuaded to enter was the Temperate House because of its spiral staircase.

His colour seemed to meld with the background in summer, Van thought, watching him. People were tanned by the summer sun, and in any case in London and its environs there was a greater mixture of races. He seemed to have got over any worries about being different.

With her eyes on him she said to Hal, 'Mum and Dad seemed to have a fantastic time with Karin and Mish.' Hal said, spotting a vacant bench, 'I bags this!', like a schoolboy, she thought. They sat down. 'Dad's home with great ideas for a new painting. I still feel I'm lacking in one dimension with my family, their capacity to *use* what they see.'

'You do it in other ways. It's called experience. The patients you see get the benefit. That's your *métier*.'

'I suppose so. Anyhow, it's absorbing. Sometimes I actually forget you for hours on end.' She teased him.

'You're shallow-hearted.'

'Oh, no,' she said, looking at him, her eyes becoming luminous. She swallowed, 'This love . . . I feel like saying . . . Excuse me.' She went on, 'It's Sam's school holidays next week. What should we do? Can you get off too? You were going to find out.'

'What would you like to do?'

'Glasgow,' she said. 'I'm dying to go home, to hear of all their exploits.'

'Faithless wench. This is your home, with me.'

'My second home. I'd love to take Sam on a Clyde steamer. Mum and Dad would go with us. They're sentimental about "doon the watter". Would that be too much for a Sassenach?'

'Anywhere with you is right for me.' He paused, then asked casually, 'How would you feel if I popped over to the States instead?'

She looked at him, saw the endearing smile, the inherent charm, the insouciance which had first captured her, and thought, I've married my father. Both of them needed boltholes. With her father it was Spain, with Hal it was America. He would go with her to Scotland, willingly, if she wanted it, but he would never feel as much at home as she did.

He was a product of a different culture, the son of expatriates, early weaned from them, subjected to boarding school at a tender age. Any terrors he possessed had been smothered by the system, he was of a type known throughout the world, sometimes admired, sometimes envied, never fully understood.

But in the close darkness of the night and after love-making he had told her of his fears, of his loneliness, the long walks on his own round the school perimeters, of his sudden flares of temper which made him a valuable player on the rugby field because he could translate that temper into the game, an aggression which prevented him from being bullied. He had learned how to channel these outbursts, but his iconoclasm had shown itself in individual pursuits, pole-vaulting, cross-country running, where he had only himself to compete against, or the weather. The competition had always been against 'the system', his determination to vanquish it.

When he had gone home to Singapore for holidays, he said, he always realized school was not so bad, that he had friends there, that he had made some kind of mark. He disliked his parents' ritual showing-off of their son to their friends, the forcible teaming up with other children whom he had no time for because they didn't rebel against the colonial way of life.

School was better. He had learned to put games in their proper perspective once he had asserted himself, and had found, thanks to an understanding master, a love of literature.

He had lost all respect for his mother because he had seen her sometimes at cocktail parties (when he had been dragooned into passing round canapés and suchlike), so drunk that the drink lifted to her lips had trickled down the front of her dress. The remembrance of her face with the slack mouth and vacant eyes had stayed with him.

He went through a period of wishing for an 'ordinary'

163

mother, one like Wotherspoon's who arrived at school with her car full of children and dogs and whisked off his friend to a jolly household somewhere in Somerset. 'I've a soft centre,' he said to Van, 'bite me and see.' And when she obediently bit his ear he had made love again, fiercely. 'Was I too rough?' he had said afterwards, knowing he had used her.

They talked about having children, but she said she wasn't ready yet. Life was too good, Sam was happy at school, she was happy at her work, they were happy in their marriage. It would be time enough when they knew that a baby would add to their happiness. There was no hurry.

'You break up next week, Sam,' she began, going home in the car from Kew.

'You bet. Are we going to Glasgow?'

'Would you like that?'

'Yes, it's much better than Frinton. That's where most of the chaps go. One of them punched me when I said it was all candy floss and sand in between your toes.' They laughed.

'What is it you like about Glasgow?' Hal asked.

'It's exciting. I can do grown-up things with Grandpa. He even takes me into his coffee howff. His painter friends say, "Here's the wee lad from down there," and make a fuss of me. And so do the waitresses.'

'Your mother's thinking of taking you on a boat doon the watter.' Hal's accent was comical.

'Great! It's a noble river, the Clyde, Hal.'

'It is, it is.' Hal was straight-faced. 'Would it matter if I didn't come? I have to go to America.'

'To see the baby?' His tone was contemptuous.

'No, about the book I'm writing. I have to study painters for it. Did I tell you about them? The Hudson . . .'

164

'You told me. You're always telling me about them. I can tell you, I'm never going to be a painter.' He turned his mouth down in disgust.

'Really? I thought you might, since you hobnob with painters in Glasgow.'

'No, thanks, I'd much rather be in a hospital like Mummy.'

'I thought your experience when you were in a Glasgow one might have put you off,' Van said.

'No, it didn't.' Sam's brown eyes widened in recollection. 'When I began to get better I liked it. It was strange, but nice. I lay in bed and watched them, the nurses, the doctors in their white coats, all bustling about. It was like being at the pictures! And the doctors were pleased with themselves, always rushing about with those things hanging out of their pockets.'

'Stethoscopes.'

'One let me try it on. I could hear the sea. And the nurses and doctors were always laughing and talking with each other, and everybody's *important*. You're important because when they look at you, you know they're talking about you, and they're important because they know all the people in their beds make them *feel* important. And they look wise sometimes, then they have a wee joke with one another and a laugh with the nurses, and they dash away. Oh, I love it, but they don't know I'm lying there, watching!'

They both laughed, and Van said, 'Yes, I know just what you mean.'

Anna and Ritchie were delighted that Van and Sam were coming to stay, and sorry Hal couldn't come with them. 'Ritchie's smiling all over his face,' Anna said when Van telephoned her. 'He loves taking Sam around, showing him off.'

'He was telling us the other day that he wanted to be a doctor.'

'Was he?' She sounded pleased. 'That would be the second one in our family, Jean's John. Then he must go to Glasgow University and stay with us here! Mish did, with my mother. We'll make it a tradition. She and Bessie loved having a young man in the house. My, he got round Bessie! Offering to carry the tray for her, telling her he hoped he wouldn't be a bother. Mother said she was very impressed, and it took a lot to impress Bessie. Oh, he was a great success with those two ladies!'

Hal said good-bye to Van and Sam when she dropped him off at Heathrow. Sam was hopping about with excitement. He was a creature of change, Van thought, looking at him, never happier that when there was the prospect of a journey. 'Do you mean to say you'll be in New York before we're in Glasgow?' he said to Hal.

'Probably. It's a long way to drive. A plane's like a bird. It can take short cuts.'

'Well, anyhow, I like Glasgow better.'

'Just wait till you see New York. You'll be astounded.'

He looked at Hal doubtfully. 'Well, I might go with you when that baby grows up a bit.' Hal was tempted to ask what he would say to a baby brother of his own. Better not, he decided.

'Got to be off. Goodbye, darling.' They kissed, Sam dancing with impatience beside them.

'Come on, Mummy! He'll miss the plane.'

'Right,' Hal said, releasing Van reluctantly. He gave Sam a hug. 'Take care of your mother.'

'Have a good trip, Hal.' Van must have told him to say that.

'Sure, kid.' He wondered when he would call him 'Daddy'. He walked away from them, keeping Van's

166

smiling, loving eyes in his mind. She never made him feel guilty. But as he read the Information Board, made for the Departure Gate, his spirits rose with the familiar sense of adventure. 'New York, here I come!' he thought, going up the gangway into the plane, saying 'Hi!' to the smiling stewardesses. Years of being looked after by them when he was small made him think of them as surrogate mothers rather than creatures of desire. Besides, none of them was a patch on Van.

And Van, driving towards Glasgow that same evening, coming off the A74 and filtering into the traffic system fairly painlessly, saw the huge bulk of the city ahead, speared by church spires, broken by towering blocks of houses, factory chimneys, saw the pall, less dense every year as local government got its act together.

She had told Sam how she and Mish used to do the arm movements of the Highland Fling when they saw the 'Welcome to Scotland' sign. Now she felt her throat fill as she drove alongside the Clyde past St Enoch Square, past the new hotels, a changed Glasgow, but the Glasgow she still loved.

'Isn't it busy?' Sam said. 'You're clever to drive through it, Mummy. It won't be long before I can take the wheel.'

'My brother used to say the very same thing.'

'Uncle Mish?'

'Yes. He drove like an expert straightaway. I took longer. But I soon got used to traffic because Grandma let me use her car when we lived with them.'

'I like this better than Richmond. It's too quiet.'

'Everything's relative.'

'What does that mean?'

'Someone living on the Isle of Skye would find Richmond very busy. The commuters going into London every day probably think it's too busy. Comparisons.'

And, a little later, 'There's the Botanic Gardens!' Sam bounced about beside her. 'Is that relative to anything?'

'Well, it could hold its own with Kew Gardens any time.'

'I'm not missing Hal. Are you?' He was peering from side to side.

'Yes, I am, very much.'

'But you had me before you had him.'

'Yes, you're a good substitute. Look, Clevedon Drive. Remember we used to walk down here going to your school?'

'Oh, that baby school! I'm glad I'm rid of that.'

'She died, you know, Miss Clewes.'

'Tough luck. Here's your turning, Mummy. Great! Clevedon Crescent. We're there!'

Eighteen

This time, instead of staying in the city all the time, Hal moved about the Hudson Valley getting the feel of the river towns between Albany and Yonkers, and following the trail of the painters who had worked there. He'd had a lot of help from the museum at Yonkers, and he began to feel familiar with the landscape of the area and to like its forests, its green, rolling hills, but most of all the river itself, viewing it both from its banks and on it, driving to Kingston or West Point and taking one of the motor vessels which plied from there and wishing it was one of the old-fashioned Hudson River sloops, being a romantic at heart.

There were many stately homes to be seen built by the New York grandees of the nineteenth century, but he preferred the homelier attractions of Washington Irving's house which still had the imprint of its owner.

He drove happily up and down Route Nine from Yonkers as far as the Catskills, thinking that Karin and Mish had made a wise choice for their house, and looking forward to seeing them that evening, as they had invited him for dinner. He was staying in nearby Peekskill since it was a convenient starting point for the river cruises.

It was stickily hot. He could remember the same humidity in Singapore when he was a child, and how

169

he had been put to bed in the hot afternoons by his ayah. He remembered her brown arm drawing the curtains against the fierceness of the sun, and the welcome coolness of his room with the fan revolving above his head. He had learned early to like being alone. It was probably for him the beginning of a realization that the mind needed as much stimulation as the body, and that could be got from books.

What a pity the Laidlaws didn't have a pool to cool down in, he thought, as he drove up the steep driveway. He'd had a shower before he left his hotel, but the cooling effect had already worn off.

Neither Karin nor Mish were home yet, Ruth told him, when he walked on to the shady terrace. She was seated on a deck chair with the little boy playing in a sandpit nearby.

'You remember me, Ruth?' he asked, shaking hands.

'Yeah, I sure do, Mr Purvis. The folks will be in soon. Have a seat and cool down. That's what I'm doing while we wait for Benjy's mummy and daddy.'

Benjy showed little interest in his arrival. He was intent on one of the many seemingly pointless exercises indulged in by children of his age, filling a small bucket with sand and then immediately emptying it out again.

'My, he's grown!' Hal became a hearty and admiring uncle. 'What age is he now?'

'A month off his second birthday,' Ruth said proudly. 'Walks all over the place now. He was slow to start with, but he makes up for it with his chatter.' The child went on digging, filling his bucket, emptying it, as if he had been processed.

'Here's your uncle come to see you, Benjy,' Ruth said. 'Give him a nice big kiss.'

Hal, taking his cue, lifted the child into his arms, saying, 'Hi, there!' The result was a howl of anger, little

170

feet kicking against his stomach, and a scarlet face which had lost its attractiveness. Hal had the distinct impression that it was a smaller edition of Mish who was squirming in his arms, although he had never seen Mish lose his temper. 'Sorry, Benjy.' He looked at Ruth for aid.

'Maybe if you fill his bucket you'll win him over,' she suggested. 'Once he's on a project he doesn't like to be interrupted, just like his mummy.'

'Good idea.'

Half an hour later when Karin arrived, Hal was still filling buckets under the strict instructions of his small companion, who conveyed his wishes by pointing imperiously every time Hal emptied a bucket.

'Oh, Hal!' Karin came towards him, arms out-stretched. 'Great to see you! Is this son of ours making you work?' She smiled, shaking her head.

'What a task-master!' He hugged her. 'Great to see you! He certainly is. I've practically built a complete medieval castle with turrets, drawbridges and the rest. I'm putty in his hands.'

'Oh, Benjy!' She lifted the child and sank into a chair with him. He cuddled against her, seemingly forgetting his project because of her presence. 'Come and sit down, Hal,' she said. 'Do you see a difference in him, apart from his bossiness?'

'Indeed I do. He looks as if he'll be off to school before long.'

'Nursery school. Oh, he'll love it. It's rather lonely for him here. Has he been good, Ruth?'

'He's been Benjy, Ma'am, neither good nor bad. But ma feet are killin' me running after him all the time. Mr Purvis here has saved ma life.'

Hal laughed. 'I'm glad I was of some use.' And to Karin, 'Are you and Mish well?'

171

'Couldn't be better, except for the heat. The Hudson Valley is pretty humid in August as no doubt you've noticed. Next year we'll be able to go away at this time, I hope, and escape the worst of the heat. We've been too busy getting the house in order. I guess it's straight now. Is Mrs Strickner about, Ruth?' She turned to her, the little boy still in her arms.

'Yea, Ma'am. She'll be pushing ahead with dinner now.'

'Would you ask her if she would please set up some drinks for the terrace? Mr Laidlaw will be home soon.'

When she had gone, Karin got up with Benjy. 'Bath time,' she said, looking down lovingly on her son, now half-asleep. 'You sit there and wait for Mish, Hal. I'll join you when I've seen to this weary kid and had a shower myself. Unless you would like one?'

'À deux?'

'If you like.' She grinned.

'It's a tempting offer, but I have a jealous wife. No, I'm fine, Karin. I've not driven from New York, like you. I'm staying nearby.'

'But there's a bedroom for you here!'

'Thanks, but I'll be moving on. I've made several appointments, but I'll come again, if you could put up with me. Ritchie gave me a small painting for Mish and I've left it at my apartment in New York.'

Ruth came in with the drinks as he was speaking. 'Mrs Strickner is busy at the stove so I brought the drinks. Yeah, you come back, Mr Purvis.' She had evidently overheard him. 'You sure make some good sand pies!' She gave a high cackling laugh which was so infectious that Karin and Hal joined in.

They sat until the mist was rising over the river, almost obscuring the lights along its banks, talking, talking. Hal had a rare sense of belonging, of gratitude, that

172

through Van he had been accepted into a loving family with branches all over the place.

He gave them news of Anna and Ritchie. 'If our marriage is as successful as theirs, I'll be a happy man,' he said. 'Ritchie treats Sam like a buddy, taking him into all the holy of holies reserved for painters. Sam, of course, basks in the attention. Change is of the essence for him.'

'And how about Jean?' Karin asked. 'I've thought of her a lot. It seems obvious, in a way. John can't give her the kind of excitement tinged with danger that she craves. There must have always been in her a lingering regret that he wasn't like her old lover.'

'Yes, I think you're right. It's part of her nature.'

'You see it in her painting,' Mish said, 'a kind of abandon. Ritchie's is controlled, so he pulls it off every time.'

'A long way from the Hudson Valley School.' Hal smiled. 'You and I have to have some long talks about them, Mish. I've a few proposals to make to you.'

'Come into my gallery when you're in New York. We'll lunch together.' He looked at Karin. 'Going back to Jean, Van thinks that losing Frederick Kleiber's baby, coupled with Roderick, gave her a grudge against fate.'

'It's possible. Her resentment could make her determined that fate should cough up something in expiation, ie, this Denis Carter.'

'No one can help there?' Hal looked at Karin. 'She's an adult.'

'No, but *she* can. One day she'll realize that it's not worth it for the hurt she's inflicting on John. Hey, Hal, you must be starving! This is not Yankee hospitality keeping you sitting talking in the dark. I'm slipping up. And we didn't even have a Union Jack out on the terrace to greet you, another quaint old American custom. Come along.' She rose. 'You bring the wine, Mish.'

'I've got some special stuff from the Hudson Valley wineries for him. I'll want your opinion, Hal.' They went indoors.

Mrs Strickner had left a cold table, a tempting array of clams on the half-shell – some of the platters had to be explained to Hal by a rather smug Mish – broiled lobster tails, bluefish, barbecued chicken, salads and squashes and blackeyed peas, and honey ice-cream. The next time he came, Karin would do him some Cajun cooking, Mish assured him. 'She likes a little spice in her life!' He gave her a wicked look.

'You've chosen to live in paradise,' Hal said. 'What are the other inhabitants like?'

'Commuter Americans. We're keeping a fairly low profile. Karin doesn't want case histories from acquaintances – the perils of her job.'

'That reminds me, Karin,' Hal remarked. 'How about that man you were treating who lived in the same apartments as me?'

'Paul Laskins? I stopped seeing him until he followed my advice. I don't think he's taken it. That's gone off at half-cock, unfortunately.'

'If I see Ellie Kaplan would you like me to ask her if she ever runs into him?'

'Well, there's no harm in that, provided it's done real casual-like.' She laughed.

'Oh, I'm an adept at that!'

'I believe you. You British are so *smooth*,' and, looking at Mish, 'but I love it!'

A day or two later Hal was back in New York to consult with his publisher. He was full of information, ideas, suggestions. As always on a project, he felt elated.

174

Everything was going well, and he caught a cab after his interview to go to Forty-sixth Street.

New York suited him, raised his temperature, made him tingle to his finger-tips. If Van had been with him it would have been perfect. The first thing he would do when he got back to his apartment would be to telephone her, just to hear her voice. He sat in the cab visualizing her, those bluest of blue eyes lighting up the pale but glowing face, the air of sensibility she always carried with her, of trust. When he was passing through the foyer he was waylaid by Ellie Kaplan.

'Hi, Hal! I knew you were back. The mail man told me. How've you been? How's that lovely lady of yours who came to see me? My, she was a lady all right, through and through!'

'She's fine, thank you. I'm only here for a short visit. She couldn't come with me. Strictly business.'

'But you'll surely have time to come up and see Ellie? I could ask in a few folks. Maybe have a roof party – although the last one fell flat.' Her remark jogged his memory.

'Do you ever see Paul Laskins?'

'Oh, him!' She was dismissive. 'I'd like to tell you, Hal, there is no gratitude with some guys! I used to think he was a weirdo. Now I'm sure he is.'

'Why is that, Ellie?' He must listen, he told himself, remembering his promise to Karin.

'He won't open the door when I knock.' Not surprising, Hal thought. 'The mail man says the same. Tells him to leave whatever it is outside. I met him once face to face, just here, where we're standing, and I asked him straight out if he ever saw that nice girl, Bobbie, who used to live here.'

'And had he?'

'He said a strange thing, well, maybe it wasn't so

175

strange but it was the way he said it, looking way past me and with a sly smile round his mouth. "I'm working towards that, Ellie," he said. He looked as if he was trying to stop himself laughing, you know, as if it was bottled up inside, a private joke. "I think," he said, "I've got the right bait." "You going fishing, Paul?" I said. I was feeling a bit uneasy because of that bottled-up kind of *glee*. It was kind of spilling out of his eyes.'

Strangely, Hal felt uneasy too. 'What did he say to that?'

'Nothing. Not a thing. He just tapped the side of his nose, with that same sly smile, and then walked away. Never a goodbye. I tell you he's a weirdo. But don't let's bother about him. You and I must get together and you'll tell me all about England and that lovely lady of yours, Dan, wasn't it?'

'No, *Van*. Yes, we surely will. I'll call you, Ellie. Just give me a day or so.' Her rouged cheeks seemed to crumple, her full mouth turned down. He felt sorry for her. 'We'll have dinner again. That was fun. What's your best day?' Van would approve of that, he thought, heading for the elevator. And he'd try and find out more about Laskins so that he could pass it on to Karin. The uneasiness Ellie had talked about seemed to have been transferred to him.

Nineteen

This evening she would tell him. She would say, 'Although I love you, although from you I'm getting all I've been missing for so long, I've come to the conclusion it isn't worth the price ... how pathetic that sounds, like a heroine in a cheap romance, but it isn't, and I'm not. I have to balance the elation, the joy I feel with you, a thrumming joy running along every nerve in my body, against the happiness of my husband and my family. Daily I see him grow away from me, my daughter looks at me with hardly restrained disgust and so she should, I'm no long comfortable in my skin. Can you understand?'

'What are you working on tonight?' In spite of her hurting heart the painting was absorbing her, and she had not been aware that he had come into the studio until she looked up and saw him standing beside her.

She felt light-hearted for a second, still in that other world of colour and sensation. In any case, Denis's voice or touch always elicited physical responses in her, she would feel a softening, a melting in her bones, her skin would tingle, even her hair seemed to become more alive and springier. 'This cemetery where my son is buried. I go and look at it in all weathers, in all seasons. The stones speak to me, sometimes the turf seems to rise ...'

The broad brush she was using was loaded with black paint. She held it poised until her hand steadied.

'Jean,' he said, 'I have something to say to you.' Her heart sunk as she remembered.

'So have I, to you.'

'It's going to be difficult for me ...' Difficult, she thought. It was as if he was reading her mind. Had John spoken to him? Sarah?

'Go on.'

'I am going back to my wife.' Without her volition the brush plunged forward like a striking adder and scored the painting in a vicious zigzag of black paint.

'Look what I've done. My poor painting ...' She heard her voice, thin, Ophelia-like, a woman she had always disliked.

'Come and sit down.' He took the brush from her hand, put it into a pot of turpentine on the bench beside her and led her to the couch. She wanted to say, 'Not there, not there,' but she had become a mute. She sat, knees together, hands clasped, elbows pressing into her sides to hold herself together, like stays. He put an arm round her shoulders, a friendly arm.

'You see,' he said, 'it's Katie. Not you. She's getting into trouble at school and her headmistress says she is disturbed about her mother and me. I've met Blanche a few times, discussed it, and now that the heat, the acrimony, has died down, she has agreed to try again, for Katie's sake.'

'Quite,' Jean said.

'You can guess how sorry I am. I made a clean breast of our relationship to her and I've promised her to start with a clean slate.' Clean slate, and clean breast ... Would he tell Blanche, who sounded snow-white, in detail of their shameless behaviour, how once she had daubed him with paint, and *where*? 'She makes only one proviso. That we give up the Kirkcudbright house and pass the agency to someone else in the firm.'

'That you show a clean pair of heels, in fact?'

'Jean,' he said, looking reproachfully at her, 'you know I loved you . . .'

'Shamelessly.' Now he registered disdain, a slight curl of his lip.

'If you like.'

'Tell me one thing, did you love Blanche like that, or . . . ?'

'No.' He shut the door on that topic. 'But I should never have taken you away from John. That was understood.'

'It's strange,' she said, conversationally, 'that I had made up my mind to say much the same thing to you tonight, but, to use a cliché, you've taken the wind out of my sails. And in any case you'd never believe me now that you got in first.'

Jean had the strange sensation that her eyes were going to fall out of her head. She squeezed them shut as if to push them back into place. 'My noble gesture, in a manner of speaking, pipped at the post by yours.' He didn't believe her. She knew by the pretence in his eyes, the faint smile hovering round his mouth.

'It's breaking my heart to do this,' he said.

'Don't let's talk a lot of crap.' She kept her face averted. 'On you go. It was good while it lasted.'

'You were a wonderful lover.'

'I didn't have to prove it. Just go, Denis. It's over, let it go. Do you remember "That Was the Week That Was?" They don't come like that any more.' She got up. 'I have to get on with my painting.'

She crossed the room, stood with her back to him, took up a rag and dipped it in spirit. If she cleaned off the black zigzag she could see the damage. She heard the door close quietly.

She kept a make-up kit in the little cloakroom she had had installed off the studio. She first washed her face then meticulously applied foundation, powder, lipstick, eye shadow, rouge. She always slightly overdid it, she realized, looking at the result, Anna was the one for subdued perfection. The Painted Ladies: Nancy, Anna and herself, Rose before that who had set the example. It was a good cloak.

She would go into the house and say to John, 'I'm going to give up painting for a time. Let's go off on holiday somewhere. We'll get a locum. Alastair would love being in charge. Just up his street.'

It was a clear summer night, breathtaking, poignant, with a luminosity because the moon was lurking behind the trees. Perhaps she and John would take a little run out in the car to the sea, sit on the cliffs along the coast and hold hands. 'John Anderson my jo, John,' she said to herself, thinking of Rabbie Burns. A poem for every contingency known to man. She could see them, white-haired already, tottering about the house, Sandy now junior partner to his elderly father, Alastair. Oh, it was foreordained! Why could she never accept what was for her?

The house was quiet and at first she thought John wasn't in. But there was a light under his study door. She knocked and went in.

'I'm back, John,' she said, and though of adding, 'back for good.' But there was no point in being dafter than she had already been. He didn't move. She could see the top of his sandy pow, 'frosty pow' she thought, still with Rabbie Burns, 'But now your brow is beld, John, Your locks are like the snow . . .' Above the chair his head was not white but ginger in the light from the

180

lamp. Sarah was so like him, that thick white skin with its spattering of freckles. Romantic types like Frederick and Denis never had sandy hair, nor freckles. But then they had no staying power.

'John,' she said, 'are you having a nap?'

She went to the chair, went round to the front of it. His mouth was open unbecomingly, so were his eyes. He was a stranger for a minute, then she touched his hand. Those nearing sixty often slept with their mouths open. But not their eyes. She touched his hand. It was as cold as death. It was death she was touching.

She felt sick, very sick. She swayed on her feet. And she sat down. Even her bowels were reacting. She might have to go to the lavatory before ... before she dealt with this terrible situation, before she telephoned Alastair.

She put her head in her hands to try and combat the sickness and saw her daughter's accusing eyes. Anna was the only one who wouldn't judge, nor condemn. Maybe her twin would believe her now, that fate had it in for her. But suddenly, with the thought of Anna, the resentment went from her mind, her body quietened, and she felt only a deep and bitter remorse because she had thrown away the substance for the shadow.

181

Twenty

Van and Wendy had arranged to take Gordon and Sam on a Clyde steamer for the day. It was Van's suggestion. A bond was forming between the two young women, initially forged by, to Van, the astounding fact that Wendy admired her. It was mutual. Wendy's extreme practicality, bordering on self-absorption, interested her. How easy it would be, she thought, if one didn't concern oneself with what other people thought.

Wendy's attitude to her children exemplified this. The younger children had been left at home. She paid for good help, and there was no use in keeping a dog and barking oneself. As far as Gordon was concerned, she said, she saw that he got his meals on time, she accompanied him on any official functions he was required to attend, she entertained his friends and business acquaintances, but, as she said to Van, it was no longer the sum total of her existence.

As they sailed away from Ardrossan to head around Arran – even for Sam and Gordon's sake Wendy had decided not to board the steamer at Broomielaw because of the 'sheer tedium of it' – she outlined her new philosophy to Van.

'I wouldn't dream of leaving Gordon, unless I fell in love with another man. But the truth of it is, Van, sex is no longer all that important to me. I have bigger fish to fry.' Van looked at her, her Amazonian (or Dianesque) beauty, her rose-like dewy complexion, her round blue eyes, the astounding air of general but asexual comeliness. She was a tall girl, dwarfing Van. She would intimidate most men with her confident demeanour, her powerful physique, not sloppily fat but looking as if the muscle and flesh of her body had been packed into too small a skin, giving an air of compactness and strength. She would have been perfect for the prow of a ship, or even the bonnet of a car, Van thought, locks streaked back from her strong-featured, classically beautiful face.

'I had a wonderful time in Greece and Turkey,' she said. 'I didn't go with a group – all that sitting about in cafés and watching dancers from the Glasgow Empire transported along with their dance routines! I study maps, I read up on the literature. Sometimes when the going was too difficult, for instance in the mountains of Lycia, I hired a driver. Not that I don't trust myself at the wheel, but some of the roads weren't mapped, and I didn't want to find myself in a ravine with the carrion crows picking at my bones.'

'Right,' Van agreed, inadequately.

'There's this place, Letoon, the official sanctuary of the matriarchal society of Lycia – the goddess Leto, you know, was the mistress of Zeus. She was someone quite after my own heart. She was chased away by some angry shepherds when she was drinking at a fountain, and she came back later and turned them into frogs!' Her teeth were a perfect curve of white, bordered in pink gum, when she laughed. She's in such good *nick*, Van thought.

'I think the woman you worship most must be Freya Stark,' she said.

'Yes, she's okay, but give me Alexander the Great

any day. The Great Romantic. You must have a vision.'

'Did you ever feel afraid?' Van asked her.

'Sometimes. I began to think it would be better to be dressed as a man. Some of the women explorers in the nineteenth century discovered this. Once a driver tried to rape me.' She looked at Van, head on one side, smiling.

'What did you *do*?'

'Used my head. I pointed outside, implying that it would be more comfortable, and once we were in the wood I beetled back to the jeep and drove off, leaving him! More by luck than good judgement I found my way back to the house where I was staying. I cleared out of that village pretty damn quick in case they wreaked vengeance on me – you think like that in Turkey – but on the whole I find the Turks and Greeks wonderful. And the country! Well, it makes this,' she swept her hand over the broad reach of the Firth of Clyde, 'look tame.'

'Tame?' Van echoed the word, Van who, coming from the unexciting but pleasant blandness of Surrey, was bowled over by the beauty around her. 'Tame? Well, I suppose so.' She turned to look back, and saw beyond the ship's wake the low coast of the Gareloch. 'And over there's Kilcreggan, where Aunt Jean's boating tragedy occurred.'

Wendy nodded. 'Funny the commotion that caused at the time. I don't mean the drowning, but her being pregnant and not married. How long ago is it now?'

Van calculated. 'She's fifty-eight now, and I think she was twenty-three when it happened. Thirty-five years ago.'

'Ages. Your grandmother was horrified, I remember hearing. In my case they got me married in double-quick time. I thought of digging my heels in and

refusing to get married, but Gordon nearly had a fit!'
She laughed. 'Ah, well, I didn't know my mind either.'
She looked around. 'Where are those two devils?'

'They asked me if they could go below deck. It was
really exciting with the old paddle steamers, my father
told me. "Going to see the engines." Mum and Dad's
happiest memory was of meeting on the *King Edward*.
Bessie had made her a packet of sandwiches, but *his*
mother had given him half-a-crown, and he treated her
to haddock and chips! She chucked the sandwiches to
the gulls when he wasn't looking!'

'If I'd married someone like your father, I don't think
I would be doing what I'm doing now, getting away
from Gordon.'

'Oh, Gordon's all right.' Van remembered how she
had longed for him, dreamt about him, her beautiful
gilt-haired cousin.

'A damning indictment. If he were an out-and-out
scoundrel it would be easier. But he's never looked at
another woman. Atonement, probably. And he thinks
too much of his reputation.'

'You're hard on poor Gordon.'

'No, just realistic.' Wendy turned to Van where they
stood at the railings, looking towards the blue coast of
Arran. The water danced and sparkled, a gull flew
ahead of them like a courier, the pure Scottish air was
soft to Van, different from the south, it seemed to stroke
her face with caressing fingers, and she thought, it's the
conquest Wendy wants, like her hero, Alexander, far
places rather than men (well, perhaps not so like Alexander), she doesn't give a doo's dab (since they were
on Scottish waters) for a man now. 'I've found what I
want to do.' Her crisp voice claimed Van's attention.
'Travel. Explore. It's the most important thing in my
life, nearly as important as the kids, more important

185

than Gordon. Honestly!' She lifted her chin. 'I have to quarter the globe – don't smile – find the place that speaks to me.'

'So it has to be unfamiliar?'

'Oh, God, yes. It has to be mountainous for a start.'

'What's wrong with Skye?'

'I speak the language there. It has to be strange, and untouched by tourism. The interior of Spain, perhaps. For the moment I'm not interested in the East but that might come later. And my travel books have got to be hard-edged, full of information for the people who travel off the beaten track.'

'That would be a good title for the series, "Off the Beaten Track."'

Wendy looked at Van. 'Quite good. I'm not intending to write wishy-washy soul-searching stuff – who wants second-hand musings – they'll be for real explorers, people who think like me, who want to find their own Shangri-La.'

'You'll have to know languages.'

'Oh, I thought of that. I was always good at them at school, and I'm going to classes at Berlitz every morning, and going to a gym, and photography classes. I've discovered I've a good eye as well as a good ear.'

'Well, you've certainly laid your plans.'

'I've thought long and hard about it. You know, Van, it's absolutely marvellous to have found a purpose in life.' She leant on the railings, looking beyond the nearing bulk of Arran which was far too 'tame' for her. Perhaps it was those summer holidays with the 'right people' in which her family must have indulged which had turned her against the sequestered Glasgow life of the middle classes.

Van looked at her, the shining skin, the bright eyes fixed on some far horizon, certainly not Arran, the

186

strong arms in the short-sleeved blouse. She felt puny in comparison, slack-muscled, drab. But only for a second, because there was Hal. With Hal and Sam and her work she was fulfilled. At this moment, she thought, I'm the happiest of people, a happy marriage, my mother and father on their own smooth, successful path, Mish happy in America with Karin and his son. Everything in the garden was lovely.

But, being Van, she immediately thought of the tragedy and sorrow in the world around her. Did Wendy never think of that? Van remembered the desolation in the shipyards, the rusting hulks and unused gantries along the banks of the Clyde, and how so many lives were hanging in the balance because of lack of employment.

Wendy is a romantic, she thought. Her dreams are centred on far-away places. What if she asked Wendy what she thought of that terrible picture of the fleeing children in Vietnam with their clothes burned off their bodies by napalm dropped by the American planes? But sounding smug was worse than sounding selfish.

'You make my life seem very dull compared with yours,' she said, smiling, but not really thinking that.

'Oh, no!' Wendy was vehement. 'I told you I envied you. Always envied you. You had the courage to sow your wild oats before you were married. It's now full with your work and that dishy man of yours. It's because my life is so pointless that I decided I had to do something about it before I was too old. The scales dropped from my eyes before I married Gordon! Look, Van, most of the girls like me growing up in the Sixties in Glasgow knew there were changes coming. They could feel it in their bones. The Beatles sang to them of it. I couldn't run wild because I was locked up in a boarding school I hated, and then I had this pash on

Gordon because I thought he looked like a Greek god, can you beat it, and then I let myself get pregnant because I liked this totally new sensation I had with him in the backs of cars, and then I let myself get pushed into a marriage because my mother is a pretty strong personality. Believe me, she couldn't have done it now.'

'You're very much alike,' Van smiled, remembering the way Mrs Armour had sailed into a room like a Cunard liner.

'But I keep telling you, you're lucky! And, I don't know how to describe it, but there's something about you, something different, a depth – I've thought about it and I think, well, your parents are different from the run-of-the-mill parents, they're so talented, your father's famous, they live exciting lives, they've broken barriers ... look at your mother marrying a man so much beneath her but she recognized his worth, and then Hamish is so *different*! He makes Gordon look like a country bumpkin, and ...'

'Oh, Wendy! Gordon's a smart man-about-town!'

'Man-about-Glasgow! He'd be like a fish out of water in New York because he needs his own background. But Hamish has no qualms, and he's successful, and he's married this fantastic American girl. No, *you* lot couldn't be ordinary if you tried. Let me tell you, you'll make your mark!'

Van was bemused. 'I never thought of us that way ...'

'And then you've got this husband who'll probably take you about the world because Glasgow or London are certainly not going to be the be-all and end-all of *his* existence, like Gordon, and you'll see strange things and meet people miles away from the smug lot I know with their ideas that McDonald's in Buchanan Street is the only place to go for clothes and the Grosvenor in Gordon Street for dinner, and the Perth Hydro for a family weekend . . . oh, those family weekends with the children herded together like prize heifers and bulls, and St Andrews for golf, and the Clyde coast for sailing, and the coming back and exchanging news over lunch at the Automobile Club! For God's sake, the men still wear bowler hats in their coffee howffs!'

'You certainly have got it in for poor old Glasgow. I love it.'

'That's because you're one of the ones who got away. Look, we're coming near Lamlash. We'd better get those boys. You know what it will be like. "Where can we go for something to eat, Mummy? I'm starving!" Did you ever feel like a bloody canteen?'

'You're great, Wendy,' Van laughed. 'You do me good.'

They parted at Central Station after a 'fabulous day doon the watter'. Perhaps Wendy didn't scorn it as much as she pretended, Van thought, as she and Sam sat in the taxi taking them to Clevedon Crescent. Sam was tired and over-excited, full of the exploits he and young Gordon had got up to. Gordon had been best at 'skiffing' stones along the water, six was his record where Sam had only managed four, but *he* had been better at climbing rocks and in that race they'd had on the sands, with their rolled-up jackets as markers. Next time they would probably climb Goat Fell.

'When can we go doon the watter again, Mum?' he asked, his accent comical. 'Gordon says that's what the Glasgow keelies call it.'

'We'll try and fix up another day before Hal comes home. Do you like your Aunt Wendy?'

'She's all right. Gordon says she's a bit bossy, but he can always get round his father. What's that, "get round"?'

189

'Wheedle. There's doesn't seem much point in it. Best to ask straight out. We'd always tell you straight out too, Hal and me.'

'Okay. Wait till I show Grandpa my collection of pebbles! I think a few might be semi-precious.' He produced a knotted, dirty handkerchief, untied it, and gloated over its contents. 'That speckled one. Gordon says it might be an agate. He goes to Arran every year. He knows. Do you think we could go there next year for our holidays?'

'Would you prefer it to Spain?'

Sam thought. 'No.' He shook his head regretfully. 'I like the sun.' His dark skin seemed to glow in the dim light inside the taxi.

Mrs Fairbairn met them in the hall with a set face when Van let themselves in. 'You come into the kitchen with me, Sam,' she said. Her eyes signalled to Van over his head.

The boy drew back. 'No, I've got something to show Grandpa.' Van held him.

'Is there something wrong?' She was trying to be calm.

'*They*'re all right.' The woman nodded upwards.

'Sam,' Van said, 'go into the kitchen with Mrs Fairbairn. There's something Grandpa and Grandma want to tell me.'

'I want . . .'

'Later. Do what I ask.'

'I've a cream pastry horn and a glass of ginger in the kitchen.' Mrs Fairbairn held out her hand, and Sam took it reluctantly. Van took the stairs two at a time.

She met Anna coming to the door of the drawing-room. She must have heard their voices. 'Is there bad news, Mother?' Van asked. She saw Ritchie getting up quickly from his seat at the fireplace.

'Yes, it's bad, Van.' He came to the door behind Anna, put his arm round her shoulders. 'Your Uncle John has died suddenly. Sarah phoned half an hour ago.'

'Oh, no! What . . . ?'

'Jean found him sitting in his chair, dead.'

'Oh, poor Jean!' She looked at Anna's white face. 'Come and sit down, Mother. You're shaking.'

'Am I?' She smiled faintly. 'It was a shock, Van.' They sat down, Anna still talking. 'It's terrible for Jean. Sarah says she's stunned. She's with her now. She wanted her to go back with her to their house but she wouldn't. She had to be taken away from John. Alastair couldn't get her to leave him.'

'Was it a heart attack?'

'Yes. Not entirely unexpected, but still terrible to happen so suddenly. It's the effect it will have on Jean. Sarah says she keeps on saying it was her fault.'

'Had she been out when it happened or something?' A dreadful suspicion was raising itself in Van's mind, images which might be in Jean's, guilty images.

'Not out. She had been in the studio until quite late and come into the room where he was sitting as usual in his chair, spoke to him, and . . .'

Anna looked at Van. 'I see your mind is working along the same lines as mine.'

Van returned the look, not answering. 'Was it you who answered the phone, Dad?' She turned to Ritchie.

'Yes. Alastair was with Jean, making the necessary arrangements . . . he was having a difficult time, apparently.'

'How did Sarah sound?'

'Too tight-lipped even for grief. That will hit her later. She was devoted to John. She said she knew this was going to happen. "I could have told her," she said.'

'Jean must be in agony,' Anna said. She wasn't crying.

191

'We know John was a fine man, no one appreciated that more than she did.' She looked at Van. 'I'm going to drive up there right away.'

'It's late, Mum.' Van went and sat beside her on the sofa, put an arm round her. 'Supposing you and I start off early tomorrow morning? That will give you time to let the family know. And we should phone to America, tell Mish and Hal.' She looked at her father. 'You could take care of Sam if I went with Mum?'

'Sam will take care of me. Anna, my love, be persuaded by Van. We'll have an early night after we let people know and you can get off as soon as you like tomorrow morning.'

Anna's eyes were still wide with shock. 'That girl, that poor girl, she always says fate has it in for her. She needs me, needs me . . .'

'Alastair will have sedated her.' Van took charge. 'Have either of you eaten?'

Anna shook her head impatiently. Her voice was dull. 'Where's that wee lad? Champing at the bit with Mrs Fairbairn? My, we miss Bessie at times like this.'

'I'll go down and get sandwiches and coffee and send him up to you. Tell him about John. He hates being kept in the dark.'

'Do you think he'll stay with me?' Ritchie asked.

Van smiled at him. 'He'll be as pleased as punch. He likes being spoiled. You phone Nancy, Mother, and Wendy – we had a great day, she's some girl – and I'll get the sandwiches. When I come up we'll phone Mish and Hal. Keep yourself busy, Mother. It's not like you to be . . . defeated.'

'It's not John. He hadn't been well for a long time. It was bound to come, sooner or later. It's Jean. My heart bleeds for her. I feel her agony *here*.' She put her hand on her breast, her voice rising in a wail.

Ritchie got up and motioned Van to give him her place. She got up and went out. He came first with Anna, always had and always would.

Twenty-one

They found Jean sitting in the studio in front of her easel. She was staring at the painting on it, at a large jagged score through it, a broad zigzag of black paint. Anna, standing behind Jean, her hand on her shoulder, even at such a time regarded it critically.

'The score could be intentional, significant. It's cold in here, Jean,' she said. 'Come into the house.' Jean didn't turn.

'I thought you would come. Anna rides to the rescue once more.'

'Stop that.' Anna's voice was calm. 'I've brought Van with me as well.'

Jean got up shakily, turning towards them. 'Excuse me. I'm being rude.' She hugged them both briefly, almost perfunctorily. She spoke to Van. 'It was good of you to come.'

Van said, 'I'm so sorry about Uncle John. What a terrible blow for you.'

'A terrible blow.' Her face was white, her hair black, both matt, without any vitality. She had bothered to put on lipstick as if she had felt her face should still make some sort of statement.

Anna, looking at her, saw through it, saw to the heart of this stricken sister of hers. The situation was in a way some kind of repetition of the one long ago when

Kleiber had died. Jean, she thought, looked like someone at home with grief, who inhabited a familiar
country.

'Come on back to the house,' she said again, 'and
we'll have a cup of tea. It will be more comfortable for
you, Jean. It's cold here.'

'All right.' Jean glanced at the painting. 'That black
score . . . I was given bad news, and the brush slipped
away from me.'

'About John?'

'No. That was later. Denis.' Her face twisted. 'You'd
laugh if I told you.'

'I doubt if I would. You know me. I never laugh at
anything obvious.'

'You mean you cry at weddings and laugh at
funerals?'

'Maybe. Come on back to the house,' and as Jean
lingered, she said, 'I think you could make that black
stroke meaningful. It could work for you.'

'It was meaningful all right. My God, it was meaningful to me.'

'Well, if you could make it meaningful to others, I'd
keep it in. Randomness is never really random.'

'Don't give me the old Jackson Pollock bit.' She
looked at Van. 'I bet you're saying to yourself, this is a
funny set-up. Your mother and I discussing painting
and my husband lying dead.'

'No,' Van shook her head, 'it's just what I would
expect of you two.'

The three of them walked up the garden path, one
after the other like Indian coolies. Anna noticed how
the chrysanthemums were tossing in the wind, how the
foliage had lost its vitality, its greenness, as if waiting
for the signal to take on its autumn colours or pack it
in for the winter. But the muted ochres, browns and

greys, she thought, were in sympathy with the occasion.

'Do you remember how you and Aunt Jessie all those years ago used to exchange plants and cuttings with the painters in Green Gate Close?' she asked.

'The Glasgow Girls?' Jean looked round, 'Or what remained of them. Yes, it was good therapy for me at the time. Now that it's John I could take it up again instead of painting.'

But when they were going in Anna and Van could see that the tears were running down her cheeks. She made no weeping noises, no groaning noises, nor snuffles nor sniffs, it was like a steadily running stream over smooth stones, over the contours of her face. Occasionally she raised her hand and wiped at the tears or deflected them as a small boulder might. Once Van saw her take a strand of hair and mop the tears with it.

When they were having tea in front of a bright fire Anna asked her, 'When is the funeral?'

'Tuesday.' The tears were gone now. She had absented herself when they had gone into the house and had come back with a hard, tight, white complexion and a new red mouth. 'Sarah and Alastair are making all the arrangements. Sarah says it's her father so she wants to do it. Sarah,' she said, looking over her cup, 'can hardly bear me at the moment.'

'Why?' Van asked, and regretted her question immediately.

'Because she thinks I'm responsible for John's death. I know your mother must have told you of Denis Carter, Van. There's no need to be coy.'

'I don't know how to be coy. Yes, I knew.'

'She thinks his discovery of that hastened his death. But *I* think Sarah, my own daughter, played a dirty trick on me. She told him about Denis.'

'You're talking rubbish as usual,' Anna said, 'down-right rubbish. Sarah, your own daughter, is incapable of playing dirty tricks on anyone, least of all you.'

'I thought so too, but nevertheless she cliped. I know, deep down I know.'

Anna put her cup noisily back in its saucer. 'What are you saying now? Honestly, Jean, at times I wonder at your mentality!'

'Oh, I'm sure you do. I'm sure you often wonder at my mentality. But do you know, I often wonder at your capacity to be always there at the right moment, chief mourner. That's you.'

Anna looked at Van, her eyebrows raised, as if to say, 'Now you see what I have to contend with.'

'Would you like me to clear out, Jean?' Van said. 'I can go and see Sarah, maybe help her with the children if she's busy . . .'

'Clear out to the enemy camp? Why not? I'm sure this must be distressing for you. John not yet buried and your mother and me going on at each other like a pair of fish-wives. But that's us. Anna knows what I'm like inside, she feels it too. She knows I have to circle round and round this hole in my heart left by John's death, castigate myself, castigate her, because, believe me, I have ample need to castigate myself before I let the flood-gates open.'

Van got up and kissed her cheek. 'Do you remember Uncle John used to say, "You two have a good chin-wag?" Well, I'm going to take a walk over to see Sarah and Alastair. I'll be the go-between. Can you put us both up until the funeral or would you like me to stay with Sarah?'

'There's plenty of room here, but you please yourself.'

When Van had gone Anna poured them both another cup of tea. 'Kirkcudbright tea always tastes better,' she said, 'than anywhere else's. It's this room, and the coal fire. We've done away with them, as they say, in Clevedon Crescent. I was filled with shame when I remembered the years Bessie carried up sticks and coals to the drawing-room one, carried down the ashes every day. Mrs Fairbairn would leave at the bare idea. They don't come like Bessie now . . .'

'What are you leading up to?' Jean asked, drinking thirstily from the hot tea.

'Have you convinced yourself that Sarah told John about Denis Carter?'

'I know she did. I could see the knowledge on his poor face. Day after day I saw it, the sadness, the defeat, and I had decided, on the night he died, to give Denis up . . .'

Anna interrupted her. 'You're barking up the wrong tree. It was Sandy who blurted it out to John. You know the way children do. Sarah told me. He was playing on the sofa when Alastair and John were talking together, and out it came. Think of a child's mind. He comes into the studio and sees you on the sofa with a strange man. Then when he's bouncing on the sofa . . .' she regretted that word but it was said now, 'he remembers. Sarah told me that if she didn't make a fuss about them finding you with Denis Carter he'd probably forget.' She watched Jean. Her eyes had closed, now they were wide open, distraught. Her voice was a whisper.

'You're telling me it wasn't Sarah?' She spread her hands. 'You see, that's what makes life so difficult for me. I never learn!' Her voice was a shout. 'Never bloody learn!'

'That's not you. That's life. Who does? Well, do you feel better now, or is there something else before you can make a proper job of grieving for a dearly loved husband?'

'Yes. This is where you laugh. Oh, you're going to like this! Denis forestalled me. He got in *first*. Told me he was going to try again with his wife because of their daughter. Pipped at the post, eh?'

'I'm not laughing. It's sad. It's even sadder when you think that you yourself are the only person who really *knows* that was your intention. Other people might just think you were ditched, and that you were making it up. But I believe you. Though thousands wouldn't.'

'You go right to the nub. Now you're going to tell me it's my problem, that I have to live with it.'

'Yes, I am, and yes, you have. But you have your family, your grandchildren. And you know you have always got me. You know I'm always there for you.'

Jean looked at her. She sighed. Anna could have wept for her, could have taken her in her arms, but this wasn't the time. Jean spoke slowly. 'You're a beauty, Anna. I look at you just now, dealing with my tragedy – what, another one? – in your own inimitable way, and I think what I've always thought about you, that you're beautiful. I've loved having you for a twin.' Her eyes were so bright that Anna felt like turning away from their glittering brightness.

'Okay, okay. And you've got your painting.'

'Oh, God, yes, there's my painting. But there's the problem now of how to get rid of the black zigzag?'

'You can work on that.' Anna looked at her watch. 'It's six o'clock. What do you say if I drive you over to Sarah's and you can make your peace with her. She'll be a good friend to you. I've discovered that with Van, a good friend. She'll be able to take the place of John.'

'Yes, and conveniently, they're alike as two peas.' Jean's smile was one to remember, rich, enveloping, strange and seductive, even when there was no need

199

to be seductive. 'You think of everything, Anna. The great solver.' She got up. 'I'll go as I am. ''Just as I am, without a stain.'' Do you remember going to Sunday School, dressed alike by Mother, with our straw Sunday hats and barred patent leather shoes. You rubbed Vaseline into yours to prevent them cracking.'

' ''Without *one* stain.'' '

'How right you are. What a comfort it must be to be always right.'

Anna couldn't sleep that night for her heart hurting. It was so sore, she thought, putting her hand over her left breast to soothe it. It had been all right at Sarah's when Jean had apologized for misjudging her. Sarah was generous, warm-hearted. She put her arms round Jean and wept, and said she would never have done that in a hundred years, but it was behind them now and she would care for Jean as a devoted daughter should and she was welcome to stay with them any time she felt like being cheered up. The children would do that for her.

Anna had met Van's eyes over the embracing couple and saw there the same doubt as she felt, not that Sarah hadn't forgiven her mother for imagining that she would 'clipe', but that Jean would never forgive herself. And Van had still to hear how Jean had been thrown over by Carter.

If my heart's hurting as badly as this, Anna thought, what can hers be like? At three o'clock in the morning, still sleepless, she got up and went along the landing to Jean's room and got into bed beside her. 'Are you sleeping?' she asked.

'Would I answer if I were?'

'Lift your head.' She put her arm under Jean's shoulders, felt the mop of hair brushing its bareness – wire-black hair – and held her in her arms until daylight.

But nobody can heal Jean's heart for her, she thought, not even me.

Hal flew home a few days earlier than he had intended to attend the funeral. He hired a car at the airport and was in Kirkcudbright on Monday evening, only stopping to pick up Ritchie and Sam, who, with his high spirits, was treating the journey more as a jaunt than anything else. Ritchie was quite at ease with the idea of taking Sam along rather than leaving him with Mrs Fairbairn. In his own boyhood there had never been any segregation of children either at weddings or funerals since there was no staff in the background with whom they could be left.

Van was as excited as Sam at seeing Hal but tried to hide it. When they were alone she said to him, 'It's awful to be so full of joy at a time like this, but to have you here with me now is as important as being with me on happy occasions.'

'Happiness has many sources. Who said that? I believe I've just made it up! It's almost worth being away from you to feel like this.' They were lying on her single bed, close-locked. 'I'm standing in for Mish and Karin. I offered. I think they were glad not to leave Benjy yet. His nurse, Ruth, is all right, Karin says, but her kindness outweighs her intelligence. In another year he'll be at nursery school and it will be easier.'

'They're very punctilious. Did you see them before you left?'

'Unfortunately, no. I had so much to clear up in New York, and see about the apartment – and try to avoid Ellie Kaplan ... remember her?' He smiled. 'I hadn't time to drive out to their house. I still had Ritchie's picture to give them. I had to apologize to Ritchie about that when I got back, *mea culpa*. But I left it in the safe in the New York office, and called Mish to tell him to pick it up from there.'

'You'd forget your head!' Already she was discovering that Hal was a 'putter-offer'. Anna's word. 'Have they made friends with any neighbours yet?'

'Acquaintances, rather. There are a lot of artistic people around them, but you know Mish, he's not rushing into any commitments. When winter comes I expect he'll be badgered to speak at all their literary and art societies and so on. Most of his friends are New Yorkers who've moved out there.'

They couldn't sleep together. Van was in the box room with a narrow bunk, and Hal and Sam were given a double bedroom in Sarah and Alastair's house. Ritchie moved in with Anna, to their mutual satisfaction.

The day of the funeral dawned bright with a whippy wind which made the fishing boats dance in the harbour. Hal, calling for them before the service – Jean was being taken by Sarah and Alastair – said that the streets seemed unusually empty. It was explained when they got to the church which was packed to the doors and beyond. There were small knots of people standing in the street, possibly in the hope of seeing the cortege arrive.

The address by the minister was moving. 'A well-beloved figure,' he said of John, 'following in the tradition of his father, except that old Dr Whitbread lived to the ripe old age of seventy-eight.

'By his devotion to duty, his care for the sick over and above the call of duty, he had won the hearts of the people of Kirkcudbright. His place can never be filled, but we have in Dr Alastair Campbell a worthy successor who has already made his mark in the community.

'We extend our heartfelt condolences to his family.

When Mrs Whitbread came amongst us from Glasgow, we recognized that in her we had someone who was unique. She has had her own sorrows, but all along she supported her husband in his daily tending of the sick, while at the same time fulfilling herself in her own calling. Here in Kirkcudbright we have a long tradition of appreciation of the arts, and this was evident when those famous women, the Glasgow Girls, chose to make a little coterie of their own at Green Gate Close. Mrs Whitbread added lustre to our artistic tradition with her paintings, which were sold as far away as London.'

Van remembered that Jean had once commented to her that there were precious few of her paintings hanging on Kirkcudbright walls.

'She will have her daughter and son-in-law to support her in her sad loss, and I know you will join me in saying that all the love which Dr John Whitbread inspired in our hearts is now freely given to her.'

Van watched Jean, her pale profile visible from where she sat through this lengthy eulogy. No widow's veil for Jean, you might have known, not even the regulation black toque favoured by most of the ladies with the exception of Anna in her dashing black sombrero. Jean's coat was black, buttoned to the chin, but she had tucked in at her neck a multicoloured silk scarf, as if, when surveying herself in the mirror, the sombre outfit had demanded it.

Her demeanour was faultless outside the church and afterwards at the cemetery and afterwards at the old doctor's house which Sarah and Alastair made open to anyone who wished. Jean spoke, it seemed, to all the mourners. Van, who was at times beside her, was surprised at her knowledge of their background and ailments. She seemed to deflect sympathy from herself by showing it to them. How many evenings she must have sat listening to John telling her of his day's work, until she began to spend them with Denis Carter. This was a different Jean from the one who had bickered with her sister, who flew into rages. Van wondered if she had seen the bouquet of pink roses with a card which read, 'All our sympathy in your sad loss. Denis and Blanche.'

They were exhausted at the end of the day and went soon to bed. Hal went off to his bedroom at Sarah's – Alastair had to be up early as he was single-handed now – and Hal didn't want to disturb him. He, Van and Sam had arranged to travel back to London the following morning. Anna and Ritchie were staying on with Jean.

They were sitting over a late breakfast when Hal and Sam arrived at Jean's house the following morning. Jean, Anna said, was in her studio. 'You have to leave her to do it her own way. I know her.'

'Will it be all right if we interrupt her?' Hal asked.

'It would be worse if you didn't.' Sam was induced to sit down with them and have a piece of toast, buttered thickly by Ritchie.

Jean was sitting in front of the painting again. This time there was no brush in her hand. The room was cold, the white light streaming in added to the chill.

'We're going now, Jean,' Van said quietly.

She got up immediately and came towards them, her face serene although her eyes were black with fatigue. 'I'm sorry we didn't spend more time together, Hal,' she said. 'I should have liked to hear about the Hudson Valley School.'

'That's easily remedied,' he said. 'Come and stay with us in Richmond and we'll chat about them. We'd love to have you for as long as you care to stay. Will you promise to come?'

'My, he could charm the breeks off a Heilanman, that one,' she said, smiling her slow, beautiful smile. She was unnaturally calm. It was more than serenity.

'Aye,' Van agreed, recalling some of the vernacular she had learned in Glasgow, 'he's a dab hand at it. But he means it, Jean, and so do I. You'd like the river, it's symbolic, for me at any rate, of England, a pleasant thoroughfare winding its way through London. In summer we can sit at its banks and have a drink. You'd like that.'

'It sounds like a fair-weather river. Nothing against the old Thames, but I like a bit of roughness with my water, a bit of swirling and gulls flying. I get it here.'

'She's calm, and so beautiful,' Hal said when they were driving through Galloway.

'Did you think too calm?' Van asked.

'A strange calm?'

'Yes.' She paused, seeing again the indestructible quality of her aunt in her mind's eye. 'Still, she's got Anna.' She left off worrying then and concentrated on Hal, when Sam would let her.

Twenty-two

There had to be, Hal said, several nights of unalloyed passion before they settled down to their busy life in Richmond.

This day, a week after their homecoming, had been busy for her. She had driven to three different hospitals in her area, and in each had to deal with cases which required a lot of time and thought, and the filling in of unending forms.

She had unfailing patience. In her happiness with Hal there was a tinge of guilt that she should be so fortunate while others were often bereaved or bereft of support, as well as being ill. It required a staunch spirit to withstand the vagaries of fate, or bloody bad luck as one old man had said to her. Wife dead, son too busy to bother about him, only his meagre pension to live on, and now with cancer of the prostate.

She would think of Jean alone in the cottage at Kirkcudbright, secure, certainly, financially, and blessed with a great talent. But she had always been a loner, and Sarah had told her on the telephone that her efforts to interest her mother in the activities of the town had failed.

'But that's all right, Sarah,' Van had said, 'if she's happy with what she's doing. Can you see your mother organizing jumble sales or raffles or charity teas?'

'Oh, I know,' Sarah had agreed. 'But she's so quiet. She's not like herself. Smiling, composed, but with a ravaged face. Alastair says that it is grief, that it will pass . . .'

Anna, when telephoned, accepted the situation more easily. 'We stayed on until she seemed to be on an even keel. I must admit some of the old fire had gone, but what do you expect, losing two men from your life at one go. But, remember, Jean is an artist through and through. Ritchie feels the same as I do. She'll find her salvation in her work, he says – when I see him at all! He's absorbed in his Medley Americana morning, noon and night. The Barcelona Museum are waiting for it. Manuel was in London recently and flew up to see it. We'll be going there after Christmas to have further talks.'

'Why don't you take Jean with you, Mum?'

'I've already asked her. She says she'll see.'

'And she's said she'll visit us.' She had to be content with that.

Hal was another person who was absorbed in his work. At night when Sam was in bed they talked about the places where the Hudson Valley School had painted, Storm King Mountain, the Catskills, Frances Silva's luminous painting on the Tappan Zee, and how that to stand in these places was to see them through their eyes.

'I remember reading that the Victorians used a viewing glass,' Van said, 'rather like my father who holds up his hands to make a square.'

'He thinks he's miles away from their work, you know, but he's an old romantic at heart.'

She told him of her problems and anxieties with some of her patients, but eventually their talk always came round to Jean and how she was faring in her cottage alone in Kirkcudbright. And when they felt sad about her they would cheer themselves up by laughing at Wendy and her metamorphosis. 'She asked me how the fellow-author was getting on,' she told Hal, after one of Wendy's calls. 'Meaning you. I like her. It's a long time since I had a girl friend.'

It was a pleasant time in their life; there was the thrill of being house owners, of congenial work, of seeing Sam happy, of being in love. Sometimes they went downstairs to see how Mr Elder was getting on and take him some books and food. His grumpy thanks was enough. Hal said it made him realize how lucky he was now, being part of a family. And yet there was Jean, surrounded by a family and a sister who cared deeply for her but still felt alone. He imagined he empathized with Jean more than the others because of his own lonely childhood.

'I remember reading somewhere that lepers used to wear a bell round their necks which rang as they walked,' he said. 'Perhaps *she* feels like a leper, that she might taint others.' Van smiled at him.

'You're developing a romantic imagination like your Hudson Valley painters. She's got Mother, don't forget. They're so close. They confide in each other all the time. It's a very symbiotic relationship. They know what the other is thinking. They're very close.'

'Yes, but Ritchie has always been a contender for your mother's affections. Who do you think she would choose, if she had to, between Jean and your father?'

'I don't know ... You're making me uneasy, Hal.'

'Sorry, I'm being introspective.'

But there was one evening when they decided to clear up after supper and go to bed early.

Sam had said, 'You know my chum I was telling you about?'

208

'The new one, James?' Van asked.

'Well, he was my best, but I've got others as well. The thing is, James is bringing his little brother to school with him, and instead of playing football at play-time, he goes off to the Infant School to see how the little thing is getting on!' He looked at them both with amazed disgust. 'And he *waits* at the Infants' gate to take him home. We used to have fun!'

'Are you jealous of this little brother?' Hal suggested.

'Me? Jealous! Some hope!' He sighed and blew out his breath. 'He's got a sister as well. She's older. Pamela. She's quite nice, actually. Yellow hair and a cage on her teeth. You have to laugh.'

'She sounds lovely,' Van said, subduing a smile.

'You don't have to laugh, Mummy!' Now he was indignant.

'I wasn't. I like yellow hair because mine is black, and she'll have a lovely smile when the wires come off. One of the most beautiful girls at my school had braces, that's what they're called, on her teeth, and I met her in London not so long ago. She was gorgeous!'

'How many are there in James's family, as a matter of interest?' Hal asked.

'Four. His mother drives them in a brake to school with a special place for two dogs at the back. She says, "Isn't this a madhouse?" when she gives me a lift, and she wishes sometimes she had only one like us, so quiet, she says, with only me and you two.' Van and Hal exchanged looks as if accused.

'Would you like there to be more?' Hal asked. Oh, cunning man, Van thought.

'Well,' Sam looked doubtful, 'I know there's the business of them being babies, but James says they grow up like anything and then they say funny things and they waddle about the floor in their nappies and they're quite nice and cuddly when they don't smell . . . he said he would bash me if I told anybody that . . . and you get to read them stories at night as the big brother, and his mother says, "Remember you are an example to Neville." What a name!' He looked down at his hands, blew out his breath, looked up at Van. 'Could I get down now?'

'With my body I thee worship,' Hal said, leaning on his elbows above her in bed, 'With my . . .' She snorted with laughter and drew him down on top of her.

'I told you. You make it too much fun and we're supposed to be engaged on a serious project here, pro-creation.'

'Is that what it's called?' He moved inside her, and she bit her lip.

'Don't do that . . .'

'Procreation is a very serious word. Spell it.'

'I,t. That's the original joke. Eve must have told it to Adam.'

'Ah, but do you know what it means? Have you looked it up in the dictionary?'

'I don't have to. I know.'

'It means, to beget, to generate. So?' He moved inside her again.

'Don't rush. We want everybody to savour and remember, including the begetee. We want a little . . . procrastination. Do you know what *that* means?'

'To put off, to defer action?'

'Mmmh . . .' She made that kind of sound, moving her head, afraid to speak.

'Not that procrastination is all that simple, given the way I feel, to defer action, to be dilatory, to wander down the paths of love, to linger, to pick a few nosegays on the way, to see ahead an even more wonderful

210

panorama of delight and sensation – see what the Hudson Valley Romantics have done to me – to, as you said, savour . . .'

'We aren't gobblers,' Van agreed.

'Only at the beginning. Do you remember that first time in the Barcelona hotel in that cool dark room near the Liceu theatre? My God, just thinking of that makes me want to hurry along a bit, reach that panorama of delight and sensation, just a little faster, and a little faster.' His breath quickened as did his movements . . .

'Don't,' she said, 'I'll die of delight, I mean it, I'll die . . . die . . .' There was no sense left in them now, no dallying, she dug her fingers into his back, bit her lip hard to prevent herself groaning, Sam was next door, she remembered, unaware of what they were doing for him, making a little sister, or a little brother, as the case might be . . .

'Well,' Hal said. His voice sounded a long way off although she knew he was lying beside her, limp, exhausted. 'Yes?'

'Yes.' Men's exhaustion was a physical manifestation, she thought, smiling, women's was inward, a sensation of having been inflated like a balloon which had drifted over some delectable, strange, far-off country of delight, and then someone pulled the cord and they found themselves lying flat on their backs. 'It's strange.' She, turned to him when she could speak. 'I feel pounds lighter somehow, as if I have to be tethered, in case I fly away.'

'Perhaps,' he said, kissing her with cool tired lips, 'we'll have to read a sex manual to have it all explained.'

'No,' she said, 'I like the mystery.' She took his face in her hands and found herself crying. 'Greetin',' she said, 'when I'm feelin' great.'

Twenty-three

Jean was in her studio. The weather outside made it a refuge. It was a blustering late October day. She could see leaves whirling about in an autumn kaleidoscope of colour, the trees tossing fretfully, as if protesting against the sadness of approaching winter. It was a day for the sea, she thought, not to sit in here staring at a painting which was so deeply scored in her mind and in her heart that even in bed she could shut her eyes and see it, etched on her retina. This, she thought, looking at it, although there was no need, is the picture of my life, a disaster area.

Alastair had come to see her the night before, slightly embarrassed, but with that stubborn look of determination, lowering through his thick sandy fringe like one of his Highland cattle, a 'this hurts me more than it hurts you' kind of look.

'It's Sarah. She's very worried about you, Jean. The baby's ill and she couldn't come to see you herself – it's whooping-cough – and she thinks you aren't eating.'

Jean was filled with guilt that she should give Sarah extra anxiety. 'I'm sorry about the baby. I can well understand Sarah's up to the eyes. But assure her I *am* eating. I buy lots of food. I'm really looking after myself.'

'It's Mrs Begg. I know she's a gossip, but she told

Sarah she was always throwing stuff away out of your fridge because it had gone bad, and she thought there was . . . something wrong with you,' he laughed apologetically, 'the common expression with them from a headache to having a wean. But you can see . . .'

'Mrs Begg shouldn't carry tales.'

'Well, you know her type. She only does the rough for us. But Sarah was in the surgery and she just happened to say . . .'

'Yes, I know.' She could just see the woman's red face raised as she scrubbed away, her eyes almost invisible behind the fat cheeks, (she was the antithesis of most fat women in that she was far from jolly), 'And she shouldn't ferret about in my fridge.'

'Sarah was saying . . .'

'Did Sarah send you here, Alastair, as a doctor or as a son-in-law?'

He looked sheepish, and then defensive. 'She's lost her father too, don't forget, and I a dear friend and colleague. She feels, we both feel, that you are our responsibility . . .'

Jean held up her hand. 'Alastair, I'm no one's responsibility, nor do I want to be a thorn in your flesh. I know how much Sarah has to do with the practice and the children. She's had it much harder than me because she's a better doctor's wife than I ever was.'

'In some ways, maybe.' He accepted that. 'But you have your other attributes.' His face softened. She looked at the long square chin, the deep-set blue eyes which always seemed narrowed as if perpetually viewing far horizons, a heather brae, maybe, the scattering of freckles over his long, narrow nose, the square hands.

'Do you ever wish you hadn't left the Highlands, Alastair?' she asked. He looked surprised at her question.

213

'And go back there? Goodness, no. I worked hard to get my degree at St Andrews. This was always my aim, general practice in a small friendly town, and I've got it, and the doctor's daughter as well!' He nodded, smiling, mouth closed.

'Are you telling me you planned that too?' She smiled back to take the sting out of her words.

'Well, it all fitted. I knew Sarah was the one for me as soon as I saw her,' he waved a square hand which would have looked well wielding a spade in a peat moss, 'but that's beside the point.' He looked at her with a doctor's steady gaze. 'Sarah says I have to ask you if you'll come and stay with us for a while. She'll feed you up. And maybe you could take on some of her duties while she's looking after the bairns. When one catches it they all do.'

'What kind of duties?' They had been over all this before.

'There are one or two old patients she calls in to see every week – they depend on her – and maybe it would take your mind off your own troubles. She's busy from morning to night, you know. People wonder how she does it all with a young family.'

Jean thought of their stirring household, the surgeries still held in a wing of the house, the children rushing about, the various helpers she had, the big table with Alastair pontificating at the head of it – she had never used that word to herself before – and how they kept open house to Tom, Dick and Harry, there was no doubt they were kind. Her heart shrivelled inside her like a prune (black-coated workers, John used to call them with his dry sweet smile). There was no room for her in that house, no room anywhere.

Ritchie and Anna were too happy and too busy to be disturbed by her presence, and were in any case due to go off to Spain any day, Van and Hal were too happy in their marriage to want her, Nancy was too set in her ways – she thought of Nancy's pattern of setting out most afternoons to have tea at Fullers and then a 'trail' through the Buchanan Street shops. No room there.

'Will you thank Sarah,' she said. 'I appreciate her kindness and yours too, Alastair, but it wouldn't suit me, and I wouldn't suit you, nor indeed the old ladies whom she would like me to visit. Here I can do what I like, potter around, and I have my studio.'

'But you're not painting!'

'How do you know that?

He looked shamefaced. 'Someone said . . .' It was that bitch, Mrs Begg again, sneaking in there to look around, to meddle. She had seen signs, paintings disturbed, a duster left by mistake.

'I understand how you must miss John,' he went on. 'We miss him too, don't forget that. I know you've had difficulties in your life, Roderick dying, but – and I hate to say this – it's selfish to go on as you're doing, making us feel . . . well, just a little . . . impatient. I've told you how Sarah worries. If you can't get to grips with being here on your own and don't want to come to us, go and visit your sister in Glasgow, even go and see Hamish and his wife in America. Sarah told me they had invited you. Then there's your other sister, Nancy. Look at the interesting life she leads, away into Glasgow every day, I'm told, if she isn't away on a cruise. There are many houses open to you in Glasgow. You could really enjoy yourself . . .'

She was suddenly tired of this man who was her son-in-law planning her life. He knew, of course, about Denis Carter from Sarah, but losing a lover didn't count in Alastair's philosophy. It had been sinful. It was a good thing he had gone back to his wife.

'I'll think about what you said.' She tried to think kindly of him, although his well-intentioned interest smacked of moral superiority. How could he know of her sleepless nights, the feeling of worthlessness, the disappearance of her creativity which in its own way was as great a loss as John's death? 'It was good of you to spare the time to come and see me,' and, waving aside herself as of no account, 'How is the new assistant doing?'

'So-so. It will be difficult to fill John's place.' He got up. 'So what have I to tell Sarah then?' His dogged persistence annoyed her.

'That I'm better off where I am. But thank her, and tell her I'm sorry about the children – that dreadful coughing and choking and getting up in the night, poor soul. I'll get some books and toys when I'm in the shops.'

'Well, if you reconsider, remember, we're just a phone call away.' It sounded like a television advert. He went off with a springing step, reminding her ridiculously of a dog which, having done its business, bounded away, relieved.

She spent the rest of the day putting things in order. In the studio she meticulously cleaned her brushes and left them in a dry pot, bristles up. That flat inch-and-a-half one, worn down on one side, had been her favourite. She took the ruined painting off the easel and stood it against the wall. She swept the floor, cleaned the little cloakroom with the materials Mrs Begg kept in a cupboard. She straightened the cover on the old sofa where she and Denis had made love, her face expressionless, although her hands lingered, smoothing the cushions.

Somehow she had missed lunch, and around four o'clock she made a cup of tea and ate some biscuits.

Perhaps Mrs bloody interfering Begg was right. They tasted musty, and she went out to the garden and emptied the remains from the tin on to the bird table. They weren't so greedy now because of the abundance of berries and fruit. Soon they would be circling around in the mornings, and sometimes a squirrel, lying in wait, would run down the roof of the garage and help itself to the crusts when they had gone.

She tidied the house and then sat down and wrote a letter to Anna. The words flowed from her, telling her what having a sister had meant, how she had loved her all her life.

There have been Frederick, John and Denis, two who have given me passion, one devotion, but there has been nothing like the love we share – how we have always avoided that word! Perhaps our silly bickering was a denial of it, but you knew and I knew that it had been there since birth.

My life is over. You have so much ahead of you, Ritchie's successes – this latest mural he's working on will be the summit, he'll take the art world by storm, just you wait and see.

And you have Mish and Karin, both with brilliant careers and a son who is the apple of their eye, and Van and Hal with Sam and more to come. Their love won't be barren, I could bet on that. You have your house in Spain and your family to visit and a husband who loves you. Well, haven't I always accused you of being the lucky one?

I'm no longer living in the present, Anna. Often I'm light-headed. Alastair thinks it's because I'm not eating, but then he was never perceptive.

Often I'm back in Clevedon Crescent with you in that big bedroom we shared – Mother thought since we were twins we should share a bedroom – and once again I'm half-running along the Crescent with you to catch a tram to the Art School – Nancy is there too but I don't see her so clearly.

And other times it's Kilcreggan where Frederick came that day and we made love in the woods and then went out in a boat. This is the awful part that rises in my mind, seeing his blue fingers clinging to its upturned side and then not seeing them, or him. I go down to the depths as I went down and down again in that dark loch searching for him. And I feel again that despair, that agony, when I was back in bed in that grey house and you were holding me. Every night now when I waken I seem to be struggling for breath and I dread falling sleep again.

I've killed three people, Anna. Frederick, because I didn't save him, Roderick, because I allowed him to be incarcerated in that Home and he escaped, only to his death, and John, who knew of Denis and suffered, and suffered, while I was in the studio in my lover's arms. Sarah too thinks I killed him. She'll never forgive me.

I feel it's written on my face. A woman who works in the house, Mrs Begg, is afraid of me, Sarah thinks I could work out my own salvation by serving the poor of Kirkcudbright. She wants me under her roof where she can show me the way, but it wouldn't work. I know the only place where I'll find peace. Anna, I love you.

Look over my paintings with Ritchie and take what you think is worth taking ... particularly the one of Wigtoun Bay. And think of me as you look at it because you and I were always ... kindred spirits.

Now it was time. Jean dressed warmly, as if she was going for a good walk, although the night was far from cold, moonless, which was better, a close dark night without shadows.

She knew this route, she thought, driving through the dark streets of Kirkcudbright, over the bridge with its arches making a dramatic pattern. When she had been planning her painting of Wigtoun Bay she had often admired them. She had never been a Sunday painter, setting up her easel, drawing from nature, her method had been numerous visits to absorb the atmosphere and make sketches.

She had always needed solitude for her painting, the idea of anyone standing watching at her shoulder was repugnant to her – she thought of the ruined canvas she had turned to the wall, and Denis, behind her: 'What are you working on tonight?' But, even out of doors she would have felt she was on show, some day she might do a painting of a painter painting. Some day, sometime never ...

She recognized the landmarks as she drove along, the twisting road, up hill and down dale, an ancient piece of Scotland this, the dark mass of trees which was Forest Park, now Gatehouse of Fleet and over the bridge there, past Cardoness Castle against the skyline. Once, long ago, she had taken Roderick to see the holy cairns up on the hill, and he had said, after their steep climb, unimpressed, 'More bloody ruins!' 'Roderick,' she had said, and then they were both laughing, gales of laughter, they had been close in their laughter, all barriers between mother and son, damaged son, removed. She had been weak with a laughter which was close to tears, close to the meaning of life as they stood on the hillside with Cairnbarrow Peak rearing behind them.

She opened the window to see if she could smell the sea. It was that which had first attracted her, the wide expanse of the bay looking south towards the Solway, different from landlocked Kirkcudbright Bay, she had wanted a place where she could stretch her eyes because it was to be a basic painting of sky, sea and the distant spit of land on the opposite Wigtoun shore, now pricked by lights. There had to be no distractions beyond the desire to convey nature in its essence.

She parked the car behind a clump of trees where it would be unseen from the road, taking care to choose a gravelly patch in case it might be difficult to drive away. The side of her mouth lifted and she smiled at herself as she got out of the car and locked it, smiled again at the unnecessary foresight.

On her left was the gate she had often gone through and crossed the field to the shore. It was very dark but there was the knobbly pewter line of the stone wall to guide her as she made her way downwards. How soft the air was, she held up her face, like Denis's soft fingers stroking it, caressing, following the outline like a pencil over her neck, her breasts, stopping there, cupping . . . Oh, he'd had it to a fine art, she thought, but wishing with a sudden surge of desire which shook her that she was lying underneath him, feeling him getting to the root of her desire for passion, for remembered passion, for the meaning of life.

'Right, Jean,' she thought, reaching the shore, 'now I've got you where you wanted to be. You've thought enough, your poor brain is tired with thinking, peace is what you want.' She thought of Yeats's kind of peace which came dropping slow. Maybe she should have read more poetry.

Of course she would cause sorrow, to Anna first of all, then Sarah, but she was young as were Van and Hal, Karin and Mish, full of their own lives, absorbed in living them, working them out. Inconsequentially she thought of Wendy Pettigrew who wouldn't care a hoot, that lively golden girl who was too good for her husband and was now going to find her own destiny in faraway places. Wendy, she thought, although beautiful was androgynous, you could imagine her with a sword and a shield, or beads for natives. She was an explorer.

That's all *she* was doing, come to think of it, except that she was going further than Wendy, and there would be no way back.

She sat down on the wet sand, took off her shoes and stockings and walked to where the water lipped and lapped like a cat. She could see the outline made by the spume. Between her toes the wet sand squelched, separating them, an evocative feeling of summer holidays with pail and spade and dress tucked into knickers. With Anna. Try not to think of Anna . . .

It was so dark as she stood in the shallows, so dark, but as she strained and stretched her eyes she could still see, beyond the sea's glimmer, the dark bulk of the opposite coastline. Was there a lighthouse there? You had to wait, count twenty . . . no, no pinprick of light, and too late for the sunset. She had a fleeting regret that she hadn't come in time for it. She collected sunsets although she never painted them. There were too many painters at it.

This was a gentle introduction, she thought, as she began to walk forwards. Why didn't she feel afraid? Or cold? It hadn't been so comfortable for Frederick,

221

engulfed in the clammy waters of that Scottish loch. And unable to swim. She thought of his blue fingers and the hair like seaweed across his face, that once rich, thick, brown hair which had hung over his face when she looked up at him in the dark wood. This was easy in comparison with how he must have felt, chosen, thought out, even soothing. The movement of her body as she went slowly forward reminded her of the same movement when she had looked up at him in the wood, or was it Denis? Or were they the same? But now there was Roderick in her thoughts, that lovable boy who'd had a bad deal from God right from the beginning, with his round Asiatic face and his quaint sayings, 'Did you come on the iron horse, Aunt Anna?' 'Wee Chinky', Sarah had called him. And Sarah had nursed him and cuddled him as a baby when she had been unable to bear the sight of him. Another failure. But how soon that had changed into a fierce protective love which had been the mainstay of her life until his death.

John had known the agony she felt when she had agreed that Roderick must go to the Castle Home. 'I'm the king of the Castle,' he had said jauntily when she was driving him there. With the support of Anna. Always Anna. And then his face had crumpled as they drove up the laurel-edged drive. But this was no place to think of Roderick, except to be glad that her guilt would be gone soon. Nor of Anna. She could hear her scolding voice in her ears. 'What's this rubbish, Jean? Paddling in the middle of the night? What in God's name are you up to now? Come out of that! You'll catch your death of cold.' Or catch your death . . .

There was a coldness round her waist and she realized it was seeping through her sensible clothes in spite of the theory that they would be a protection against it. A cold clamping indeed. Not a lover's. But then their

222

heaviness was a good thing. And with that thought her body adjusted and it was like a comforting arm round her, warm, a solace, a support. Water is your friend, she told herself, not your enemy.

One thing, this couldn't hurt John, safe in the arms of Jesus, or whatever. Why did those hymns pop into your mind on every appropriate situation? Was it because of that Sunday-school regime Rose had insisted on? Would she go to Roderick, or to John, or to Frederick, who must be somewhere around, possibly in a Viennese heaven with Mozart playing in the background.

Sarah would be hurt. Alastair would try to console her. 'You even sent me to her when you were worried sick with the children, remember? And implored her to come to us. You know Mrs Begg said she was acting strangely . . . The truth of it is your mother could never take advice. She always went her own way.'

It's a lonely way all the same, Jean thought, as the water lapped round her throat, lonely, lonely. Would it give her the answer? That's what her painting had been all about and it had ended with a crude zigzag of black paint. She took her feet away from the bottom and floated for a time, trying to see some light in the sky. A signal? But there was none. Her last conscious thought was of Anna.

Twenty-four

'It's nice here,' Ritchie said. They were sitting at the pool with drinks in their hand, waiting for Manuel Folguera, their old friend who had been instrumental in Ritchie obtaining his first assignment in Barcelona. He was Director of Art for Public Buildings.

'I love it,' Anna said. She was wearing a white, slim-skirted dress – she invariably wore white in Arenys de Mar because she knew it set off her bronzed skin and her black hair. 'I'm glad you didn't tell Vincente to empty the pool. It's like holding on to the hem of summer.'

'I dare you to swim in it!' How well she knew that teasing, loving look. 'Go on, give your old man a treat.'

'Nothing doing. I'm not spending an hour getting ready for Manuel coming and then ruining my make-up. He likes to see me looking smart, purely from an aesthetic point of view.'

'Oh, I know I'm quite safe with old Manuel, but have I told you recently that I think you're still the most beautiful woman I know? Age hasn't withered you, as the Bard has it.'

'Hi! Where do you get this age bit? I'm still on the right side of sixty. We were First World War babies.' Her face saddened. 'Poor Jean! I wish she'd come with us. I hate to think of her in that cottage without John. It's so lonely for her with no one near.'

'Yes, she'll be lonely, but she's got good neighbours, and there's Sarah and Alastair. She can go there whenever she wants.'

'I know. But she's lonely in her soul. I feel it. I should have insisted on her coming with us.'

'You know you've never been able to insist on Jean doing anything against her wishes. I tell you what. Wait till Manuel comes and we have dinner, then you can give her a ring to say goodnight. That'll cheer her up more than anything.'

'Well . . .' She looked towards the patio doors. 'Oh, here he is! Yes, I'll do that.' She rose to greet the familiar figure of their friend, tall, with one shoulder higher than the other she noticed afresh. She had never known whether it was a pose or a slight deformity. He was wearing a pale linen suit, as usual too tight in the jacket – he worried about his thickening waistline. His shirt and tie were of palest lilac, the tie spotted with white. Manuel spent time always choosing the correct colour scheme.

'*Bella* Anna!' He greeted her by bowing over her hand which he kissed. 'Immaculate as always. Gilding the lily. And such a dress! The cut, the sheer simplicity, the perfection! What is the material?'

'Slub silk. Manuel, you are the only man I talk clothes with. Ritchie couldn't care if I wore a sack over my head.'

'For the joy of taking it off, maybe,' Ritchie laughed, holding out his hand, which Manuel shook vigorously, at the same time whacking Ritchie on the shoulder. He was always excessively manly with manly men.

'Sit down and have a drink.' Ritchie indicated one of the cushioned wicker chairs bright with its abstract

225

print of lime green and white. Soon they would be packed away for the winter.

Manuel sat down and accepted the drink Ritchie held out to him. 'You know, my dear chap, I should be kneeling at your feet. The Committee is ecstatic about your mural! It will be shown to the public next week in the Museum of Modern Art. After that, who knows? A prestigious site you may be sure, or it might go on tour. With this latest painting, my friend, you have arrived! If you never did another thing, your fame is assured. It is sublime!'

'Trust you to lay it on thick, Manuel!' Ritchie laughed, but Anna, watching him, saw the flush of pleasure. 'Ma heid will be too big fur ma bunnet!' Manuel looked mystified.

'What gibberish is that you speak?'

'It's Glaswegian. Have you never heard of it?'

'No, nor do I wish to. What does it mean, Anna?' He turned to her.

'Pleased as punch. Swollen-headed. Tickled pink, oh, I'm stumped. What would you say in Spanish?'

He shrugged. 'You barbarians. *Magnifico*, perhaps?'

'That sounds about right. Only more so.'

'Has Maria seen it?' Ritchie asked, his eyes clear as he took a sip of his whisky. He had never taken to iced sherry, Manuel's tipple.

'She's on the Buying Committee. I thought you knew that? No?' Ritchie had half-shaken his head. 'She intends to write to you. She's leaving us, by the way.'

'Is she?' Look at him, Anna thought, pretending that it is of no account.

'Yes. She's going to live in Madrid. Her friend, Largo Bellido, you met him, remember, has at last persuaded her. And, of course, her daughter is at school there.'

'Is she marrying him?' Anna asked.

226

'They would hope to, if there is a dispensation.' Manuel shrugged. 'So what? She's happy. A rich man who adores her, with whom she can travel. This is the man for her, older, powerful, and well-known in Madrid society. Didn't you do some work for him, Anna?'

'Yes. He has outlets. He's taken quite a few pieces.'

'So, there you are,' Manuel said, 'everyone happy, Maria and Largo, you and Anna, Ritchie, everyone happy except me.' He spoke lightly.

'How is Juan?' Anna had seen his eyes change.

'He has left me.' He looked down at his glass. 'It is finished, like my sherry.' He laughed as Ritchie took his glass from him and went to the side-table to replenish it. 'So it goes. Thank you, Ritchie, drown the sorrows, eh? He's gone to a mere boy, twenty-two years of age. I should have been prepared.' He took a sip. 'Another drink and I shall start to tell you how much I miss him. It's not the sex, you know, it is the companionship. We laughed at the same things. He cooked so well, creatively. We enjoyed the theatre together. He didn't know a thing about painting, but then I didn't know a thing about his work.'

'What was that?' Anna asked.

'He was a civil engineer.'

'Oh!' She was silenced for a second. 'Yes, it's sad for you. Loneliness is the worst to bear. I've been so lucky with Ritchie and the children. We were just talking about my sister before you came in. Her husband died suddenly, and she's had a lot of sadness in her life . . .'

'Perhaps she'll find another lover?'

'I doubt it. She had one, and she's now suffering from guilt as well as loneliness. She thinks her husband knew.'

'And so she thinks she killed him?'

'Well,' she raised her shoulders, 'that perhaps the knowing hastened . . . why deny it? It's what she *thinks*.'

'I remember her. A beautiful woman. A different beauty from yours, Anna, more fitful, but with sudden glimpses of a startling beauty. And yet, there was always the underlying sadness, those tragic eyes. But I'm making myself more dismal than ever. Self-pity is demeaning.' He looked at Ritchie, a smile on his mouth only. 'Next week there is a grand unveiling, champagne, and every important person in Barcelona has been sent an invitation. It's in your honour. You'll both come and you'll be the happiest man in the world that the accolades came to you when you were still alive to receive them. You and Anna.' He raised his glass. 'Fate has been kind to you.'

'Yes, we're lucky,' she agreed. Hadn't Jean told her that often enough? 'Let's go in and eat. It's getting chilly.' A cold little wind played round the pool, round her heart.

They ate and drank and talked about mutual friends, about Anna's work, because Manuel always showed a strong interest in it, and when he was mellow with the rioja Ritchie talked about the Civil War and the International Brigade and the comradeship in the high sierras, the misery and the elation, the fierce cold and the burning sun. Manuel hadn't taken part in the war against Franco. They had never known if it was from choice or because of his health, but he loved to hear Ritchie speak of it.

'It was my love of the Spanish people that made me glad to come and work here,' he told Manuel. 'You have to suffer together to appreciate each other.'

'I suffer. I think this is the end for me.' He was supporting his head, his elbow on the table. 'Losing Juan. The despair is unbearable at times. The end . . .'

'What rubbish!' Anna interrupted, fierce because her tongue was loosened by the wine. 'That's what I say to Jean when she comes out with remarks like that, "What rubbish!" You'll find another friend, Manuel. It's a down phase for you – maybe it's the male menopause. Ritchie gives that as an excuse for all manner of things. But, remember, you still have your work. You once said to me that it was the most important thing in your life.'

'Did I?' He looked at her, his mouth going up at one corner. 'You only say that when you have your work and your lover. But you're right. I must be cheerful. Life is a series of losses until the last one, so let's drink to your mural, Ritchie, "Medley Americana".' The telephone rang.

'Who on earth is it at this time of night?' Anna said. Her heart began to beat painfully. Don't think, she said to herself, don't allow yourself even to think it might be bad news, Jean, always Jean ... Juanita, who was washing up in the kitchen appeared at the dining-room door.

'Señora, the telephone. You hear?'

'*Si, si.* I'm coming.' She got up and dashed past the woman to the hall where she lifted the receiver from its hook. It's Jean, she thought, she's decided to come here after all. Yes, that's who it is. It was a man's voice, strongly Scottish, it was Alastair. How clear he sounded, all that way. Wasn't science wonderful? She swayed and sat down suddenly on the chair beside her.

'Alastair? Are the children all right? They had whooping ...'

'Yes, they're fine. It's your sister.'

The cheerful voice she had adopted wouldn't go away. 'Is she all right?' There was a pause. Manuel's last words echoed in her head, 'Life is a series of losses until the final one ...'

229

'Is Ritchie there? Perhaps I should speak to him . . .'

'No, she's my sister. Go on.'

'I'm afraid, Anna . . . Her car has been found abandoned at Wigtoun Bay.'

'Oh, yes? She likes it there. Her painting, you know. She might have driven there to make some notes . . .' The ball of pain in her heart was swelling, threatening to rise to her throat and choke her.

'You'll have to face up to it, Anna. You see, everything is tidied in her house. There is a letter for you. It looks as if . . .'

'As if what, Alastair?' Now her voice was high and fretful. There was something irritating about Alastair Campbell, always had been, his solidity, nothing volatile in his character, a rock, certainly, but like all rocks . . .

'That she has . . . walked into the sea. Her shoes and stockings have been found.'

'Walked into . . . ?'

'The *sea*.' Pedantic to the end.

Anna stood looking at the white receiver clutched in her hand. White for coolness, she had decided, for the hall decor. She whispered into the blurred whiteness, 'I'll come right away.'

Ritchie, coming quickly into the hall, found her sitting there. He replaced the receiver and took her in his arms and held her, went down with her into the depths. Manuel passed them quietly. There was the soft shutting of the door.

Twenty-five

Karin and Mish were entertaining their next-door neighbours, Sally and George Hoefer, next door in this context being a quarter of a mile away. Sally was small, with a sharp face and a poodle cut, George was stolid, florid, with the faint purple tinge in his complexion of incipient blood pressure, Karin's medical mind registered.

They had been quietly helpful since Karin and Mish had moved in. Sally had called to welcome them, and had left a list of the services available in the village. They went up to the city every day, but anything they could do to help, would they please let them know.

George Hoefer had a small but evidently lucrative printing business in New York, which he ran with the assistance of Sally as 'front man'. They were city types, born and bred, they knew nothing about gardens, they didn't play golf, nor do their own carpentry and such like, but they just wanted the Laidlaws to know that they were there if anything went wrong.

The four of them were sitting over their coffee inside the patio window of the lounge where Karin had arranged chairs. It was too dark, now that they were into October, to be outside on the terrace, but she liked to see the view, the faint glimmer of the river, the pricking of lights, the dark bulk of the trees.

231

'Lovely meal, Karin,' Sally Hoefer said. 'I'm really glad to know you're liking it here. You and I are unlikely to meet in the village since we're both working wives.' She laughed. 'I must say I'm quite glad to escape all the activity that goes on here, car boot sales, charity drives, pool parties and the like. We stay up in town a fair amount. We have a pied-à-terre in our business premises for overnight stops.'

'We're music buffs,' George offered. 'We don't miss many concerts at the Lincoln Center if we can help it. We have a season ticket there.'

'Lucky you.' Karin glanced at Mish. His look said, 'It's going fine. Glad we did it.' She said to the Hoefers, 'We were rather worried in case you thought we were inhospitable, but so far we seem to have so little time for social activities. What time we've left we like to spend with Benjy, our son.'

'Yes,' Sally said. 'I've seen him in the garden with his nurse when I've been driving past. He looks a lovely little boy. Perhaps you'd bring him over some Sunday afternoon. We have a pool, but George is having it emptied this weekend. Too cold now.'

'We decided against one until he grows older,' Mish said. 'Karin thinks I have a bee in my bonnet.'

Sally looked entranced, not surely about Mish's fear of installing a pool, Karin thought. 'Oh, I love to hear your voice, Mr Laidlaw! You were a wow when you came to our party. Honestly, Karin, the ladies were swooning over him, I have to tell you.'

'I'll have to watch out.' Karin laughed.

'You surely will. Some of our friends were asking who the distinguished Englishman was. You'll probably get a deluge of invitations.'

'You're embarrassing the guy,' her husband said. 'Where's your gallery, Mish? I might look in . . .'

While the others talked about modern painting, Karin's mind veered to the tragedy of Jean's death. Perhaps it was the mention of the Hoefers' pool which had started it. She and Mish had talked a lot about Jean's suicide, and the inevitability of it. Mish had said that was what made it a tragedy.

He was worried about his mother. His father had called him the night before to say that Anna was still taking it very badly, and how worried he was. Mish had offered to come home and see her, even to bring Karin and Benjy, but Ritchie had advised against it. It was better if everyone went on with their normal lives.

'And your Aunt Nancy,' Ritchie had said. 'She's like someone who's had a stroke. It's the first time I haven't seen her hopping about like a little bird. But James will take her on another cruise. That wouldn't work with your mother. The only good thing is that Van is pregnant . . .'

'I fell in love with New York,' Mish was saying, 'and I've got what I wanted, my own gallery there. We chose to come and live here because we wanted to be out of the city for Benjy, and the Hudson Valley has always appealed to us. When we've more time we'll get around to exploring. My brother-in-law is writing a book about the painters who worked around here.'

'We're rather the same as you,' George said. 'I was brought up in Yonkers and I always wanted to live further up the river. Its history appealed to me.'

'George is by way of being a local historian in his spare time,' his wife explained. 'Nothing he likes better than research.'

'I don't think you can put down your roots in a place until you know what its roots are,' he announced. This was evidently his hobby-horse. 'I've ferreted out old records going back as far as the seventeenth century. I

233

bet that surprises you, Mish. New one on me, your name?'

'It's Hamish, actually.'

'Actually,' Sally repeated. 'I *love* it!'

'We do the same, hon,' her husband said, 'Linc, Newt, life's too short to have long names . . . Yeah,' he reverted to his subject, 'I've got maps. I've studied the lie of the land on this hill long before our houses went up. I know all the stops for the stagecoach to Albany. There's one a stone's throw from here. And I've read some of the legends that have grown up over the years. Did you know there was a mill race here once, feeding into the pond above us? Long ago there was a saw-mill there, and there's a story attached to that . . .'

'Oh, I know the pond!' Karin exclaimed. 'We went up there one Sunday afternoon to see if we could spot any birds. Remember, Mish? You had some Audubon prints.'

'Yes, I remember. Spooky, wasn't it? Dense undergrowth. We gave up after a while.'

'We had heard a bird call we couldn't identify, and we pushed in . . .'

'You said, "Let's clear out of here," ' Mish said, looking at his wife, and to Sally and George. 'Very unlike Karin. She's so practical, and unafraid.'

'What *is* the legend, George?' Karin asked him.

'Well, maybe you were right about the atmosphere. It was during the Revolution, and the miller's daughter fell in love with a British soldier. Her brothers weren't at all pleased, and so one dark night they hid behind a rock, and murdered him. Some people say the place is haunted.'

A slight shiver went through Karin and she laughed to hide it. 'Tell us something cheerful for a change!' She wasn't usually so sensitive, she thought.

'Well, of course,' George was in his element, 'it was the railway that made all the difference. It was a lovely piece of land and the realtors got busy. It became known as the place to live for the beautiful people – that's how I think of them – artists and such like. Just up your street, Mish. And then after that nature lovers like yourselves. Some went right back, built a small cabin in the woods. There was even a quasi-religious cult for a time. The white house at the corner of Furnace Road became their headquarters. It was a kind of artistic Eldorado, I think, yeah, that's it, an artistic Eldorado, dancers, musicians, painters, various types of intellectuals. It was the music bit that appealed to us. Thought there might be some good societies . . .'

'Were you disappointed?' Mish asked.

'Well, I have to say there aren't any Aaron Coplands around, though we've toyed with starting something up ourselves when we've more time, some kind of musical salon, perhaps, to give it a grand name. No, the folks who live here seem to be the usual well-heeled commuters, with their pool-side parties, tennis parties, country clubs. We haven't met with any authors, but we keep on hoping we'll make a sighting. We heard of a Self-help Group, but perhaps that isn't in your line, Karin?'

'I have time for anything that works. I have my failures.' She thought of Paul Laskins who had given up coming to see her, and hadn't taken her advice about attending a clinic. Unfinished business, she thought, and that feeling of unexplainable unease that she'd been feeling all evening came back to her. She was overtired.

'Our demands for somewhere to live were simple,' Mish said. 'Somewhere out of the city, a view of the Hudson, a place where we could bring up a family.' Karin saw a shadow pass over Sally Hoefer's face.

'We haven't any children, nor likely to,' she said, and then, brightening, and turning to her husband, 'Can you remember that old advertisement you copied out about Amberlands?' She looked at Karin and Mish. 'That's what they call this estate.'

'You mean that one, "A Community of Your Kind"? Yeah, that really tickled us. I believe I could just about recollect it, in spite of this tiptop wine you keep plying me with, Mish.' George raised his glass in salute. 'Here goes.' He intoned, face solemn, '"Haven't you always craved to live in a community where your neighbours were the kind of people you care to invite to your home – even if you never did invite them?"' They all laughed.

Mish said. 'That's what I call a let-out clause!'

'It sure is, and there was more which I can't remember, about the area attracting artists, writers, liberals and radicals, the very ones you would like for your neighbours! Card carriers!'

'It's rather like a book I read long ago,' Mish observed. 'It stayed in my memory. *Erewhon*. Any of you know Samuel Butler? It was about a magical mythical land.'

'You got me there, Mish.' George looked at Karin and Sally. 'Any of you ladies?' They shook their heads.

Mish laughed. 'It's my father I have to blame, or thank. He buys old books at Barrowlands, that's a market place in Glasgow where he lives, in Scotland. Barrowlands, I have to tell you, is an Aladdin's cave of treasures. It's in the East End, a gigantic fleamarket where the bargains which people find are amazing. Dad's always looking for first editions, but I sometimes think he gets more ideas for his paintings than first editions . . .' George Hoefer held up his hand.

'Hey, wait a minute! Your father can't be *the* Ritchie

Laidlaw?' Mish nodded. 'He's famous! Listen to this, Sally. Well, we're honoured to know you.'

'Yes, we surely are,' Sally agreed. '*Everybody*'s heard of Ritchie Laidlaw!'

'Aw shucks!' Mish said, pantomiming, and then his pride made him go on. 'Well, I might as well be honest. I'm a fan of my dad's. I think he paints better than most painters whose work I sell, but then I may be a little prejudiced.'

'I should think you're a good judge.' Sally nodded at him. 'And just right for this community. Hey, George, we're outstaying our welcome. We must be going.' She got up. 'Karin, do you think I might have a peep at your little boy if it wouldn't disturb him?'

'Of course it wouldn't. He sleeps like a log. Come along.'

Benjy was lying in what she called his hedgehog position when they went quietly into the nursery. She straightened him on the pillow and brought up the covers which he had kicked off. 'They're like little animals, aren't they?'

'Yes.' Sally bent forward. 'So small, though, and . . . vulnerable.' She stood looking at him.

Going downstairs Karin said, 'I'm glad we got to know each other, Sally. It's comforting to have neighbours like you,' she laughed, ' "the kind you care to invite to your home." I'm quoting, of course.'

'But you've forgotten the, last bit.' She turned to smile at Karin. ' "Even if you never did invite them"!'

'How pretentious can they get! Anyhow, you and I have taken the plunge. I hope we'll see more of each other.'

'I'm sure we will.'

Later, when they were getting ready for bed, Mish asked her, 'Well, did you enjoy the Hoefers?'

'Yes, I did. There was a bit in the middle when I wasn't so sure, I guess I was suddenly tired, but then I thought they're really nice, complete in themselves, happy.'

'I liked George. Like you there was a bit when I thought, he's a little pompous, and then I thought, the guy likes music. This is the best bit,' he laughed at her, 'post-mortems. I expect they're doing the same in their bedroom.'

'And voicing their reservations too. I expect they thought you were an arrogant British artistic type and I was a plain, fuddy-duddy New Yorker who had captured you.'

'Now you're fishing!' He grabbed her and forced her back in the bed. 'Aren't you?'

'Do I have to?' She put her arms round his neck, pulling him towards her. 'But aren't you glad we chose such a snobbish place to live? So suitable for you with all those liberals and radical thinkers around?'

'More likely to be wife swappers. Hey, would you quit talking? We've got more important things to do.'

'Okay.' Suddenly she wasn't tired.

But after they had made love and she was lying quietly, she thought of the story George Hoefer had told them about the murdered man. So near them in place, so far away in time. Where was the mill race now? Did it still run under the hill, under their house? Why had she felt that unease?

Some landscapes made one's heart rise. The river always did that to her, but in that clearing above them, when she had gone bird-watching with Mish, she had felt a kind of oppression, the dense undergrowth, the semi-darkness, had felt a weighing down of her spirits, she who was so practical a person who, although she empathized with her patients, had never felt the same despair of depression, that worst of all illnesses.

Did spirits linger in certain places for centuries? Now that she knew of the murder of the girl's lover, she could believe this was so. Or was it that she was tired? She'd had a busy day, she had rushed home, seen to Benjy, cooked, entertained, the usual pattern of a working wife which nevertheless took its toll.

What disturbs me in this story, she decided, is its ugliness, the ugliness of revenge. She had come across it in patients, those who had harboured a grudge which had eaten into their souls, who believed that vengeance had to be satisfied to give them peace. An eye-for-an-eye had never been attractive to her in spite of having been brought up in a household which had been influenced by the Old Testament. Mish had never known this in his upbringing.

Paul Laskins came into her mind. She saw the small mouth, the sliding eyes, and wondered why she thought of him at all. She turned to Mish for comfort, and in his sleep his arms closed round her, protecting her from all harm.

Twenty-six

Ruth had never really liked this place, the river and that. It was too far from a bit of life. You needed a car to get down to the village, and even that was pretty dull after the Bronx, all those classy women chattering in the Cozy Nook tea-room with their classy kids, expensive sneakers and loud 'Hey Mom!' voices.

But she had to admit, on a day like this, it was something else. The view was really good, all that water down below like a sea, like Coney Island, blue as if you could have a swim in it. If they'd even had a pool here she could have had a few good dips all summer and tried out that snazzy bikini she'd bought the last time she'd gone to visit her folks.

Maybe if she saved real hard she would be able to afford a vacation in some fun place like Miami Beach. The Long Island ones weren't bad, except for Fire Island, no thanks, but being here it wasn't that easy to reach them on her days off.

Still, Mr and Mrs Laidlaw were really nice, okay. He was a real gentleman like that film star, Leslie Howard, in looks, and Mrs Laidlaw, Jewish but a looker too, and both so considerate.

'Benjy comes first, Ruth. Get Mrs Strickner to help you with any washing or cleaning that might take you

240

away from him for too long. The main thing is to enjoy yourself with him, be happy.'

And so she did, truth to tell. He was the cutest little kid with his big brown eyes and dark hair. 'Tootie', he called her, on account he couldn't say 'Ruth'. It was such an old-fashioned name – she'd always fancied 'Dawn' or 'Marilyn', but when she'd said that to Mom she'd told her she was lucky to have a name at all with that bastard walking out on them. Mrs Laidlaw said it was a nice name, from the Bible, and she didn't tell her she had been named for Babe Ruth on account of them living near the Yankee Stadium.

But was Benjy stubborn! He sure knew what he wanted, but then so did his folks. They had wanted him all right – that was obvious. But they took their work seriously too, driving off every morning so composed about it, so well-dressed, so polite but kind of jokey, grateful, but with a smile, oh, you couldn't do better than those two, and they paid her well.

Maybe if they had another one she might stay on, because she would have an automobile by then, and she could buzz along Route Nine, through classy River-dale and into the Bronx with all its things going on in the street, not like here with the houses like miles between them and no running in and out. Mrs Strickner said that was common, they didn't do that here. And maybe when she drove into the Bronx she would run into Bud Shulman who seemed to be taking a shine to her, at least Mom had said he was coming round to the house and asking how Ruth was getting along up the Hudson. Up the creek, more likely. She laughed out loud at her own wit.

When he bought an automobile – he only had his old truck and he'd said he wouldn't come calling on any lady with any old truck – he would come and see her right here and take her out to one of those swinging nightclubs in the Bear Mountain Park. She doubted if there were any nightclubs there, but she sure would like to go. Once, as a Sunday School treat the teacher had taken the kids there, and they'd sailed right the way up from the Battery . . .

'Tootie!' Benjy was pulling at her skirt. He had his red pixie hat on. 'Tootie! Out!'

'Okay, Benjy,' she said, 'I just have to go to the bathroom, then we'll go out and you'll play in the sand-pit and I'll get one of them nice garden loungers from the shed and we'll be as happy as chipmunks. That's what your folks want, and that is sure what I'm aiming to do right now to rest them weary legs of mine.'

Oh, it was lovely for October, hot, you couldn't believe it. She had nothing to do but keep an eye on Benjy and laze in this lounger, nice to let your knees slide apart and feel the heat up there, nothing to do until she set the oven at five o'clock and put in the casseroles Mrs Strickner had left before she went for her day off, maybe do a bit of ironing. She'd see. Be happy, that's what the folks wanted. The air was as soft on her cheek as Bud Shulman's fingers could be – she shuddered and giggled – and the colours down there at the river . . . my, it was a picture with the reds and golds and silver-greys and that blue sky hanging over it all like in a Western movie. There was sure nothing like it in the Bronx.

Yeah Ruth, you've made it here, she thought, lying back in the lounger, knees wide apart now, just keep an eye on that little kid making his sand pies, whacking away at the stuff, shouting, 'See, Tootie! See that big one!' from time to time. You wouldn't believe kids could get any satisfaction out of filling sand into a bucket just to knock it all out again with their spades. But maybe

242

there was method in Benjy's madness because he was putting his pies in a circle round a flag his daddy had brought him, a tiny Stars and Stripes.

He was so like his daddy, that quietness, so different from the kids at home, always jumping about and fighting and chattering like monkeys in the Bronx Zoo.

Take that friend of his folks, his uncle, wasn't it, Mr Purvis. Now, he had what Mr Laidlaw didn't have, sex appeal. It was in his eyes. He noticed you. You knew if your lipstick was on straight, if you were smelling right, the way he looked at you. Not a come-on look like the guys on the street corners at home, but recognizing you as alive and a different sex. You read about it in them women's magazines, an 'I see you' look, 'You have a place in this world just as much as I have', It had nothing to do with being handsome because Mr Laidlaw scored there, it was something in the eyes.

Hal, he was called, and that wife of his, Van – no great shakes, these names. Now, she was pretty good-looking too, pity she had to wear specs, but you could see they were wrapped up in each other, and it made her as if she was lit inside all the time. The air hummed around them. They had eyes for nobody else. It gave you quite a shiver to see all that love spilling out of them.

That's what she'd like if Bud Shulman ever got serious, that kind of look in his eyes, no foolin', a look that was full of love and not ashamed to show it, an 'I love you' look. Now she was getting soppy.

'Hi, Benjy!' she called, coming down to earth. 'Want to come inside with Ruth for a drink of milk?' He looked up with wide eyes, pursed his mouth and shook his head vigorously.

'Pies!' he shouted, pointing, 'Making pies!' He gave one an almighty whack with his spade and it fell to pieces.

'Now, that was silly, chicken,' she said. 'After you'd made a really nice one.' He tossed his head, making the bobble on his pixie hat dance about, and laughed out loud, 'Benjy bashed it!', then bent his head and began filling up the pail again with its Disney dwarves painted round the outside.

That's what I mean about kids, Ruth thought. Could you see *me* putting on my knickers then taking them off again, then putting them on and taking them off again? Maybe you had to have your own kids to get to understand their funny ways.

Beyond Benjy in his sand-pit she saw a man coming up the steep path towards the terrace. He must have come in by the wicket gate on the lower road. Most people parked at the front of the house and walked round the terrace that way because the road there was wider and there was more room for parking.

She watched him, a tall, gangling figure, nearly bald but with a fringe of fair hair and young by the way he climbed easily, taking long steps. She saw that he was carrying a flat parcel under his arm. They didn't usually get callers at this time. Most people knew the Laidlaws were out every day. He was covering the distance easily with those long, striding steps, now he was quite close.

'Hi!' he called, and then he was beside her. He had passed Benjy in his sand-pit, not stopping, which was strange. Most people always spoke to a kid, just the way you would pat a dog. 'Is this the Laidlaw residence?' he asked.

'Yes,' she said, suddenly remembering she had her legs apart. She banged her knees together and got up hurriedly, seeing Benjy's wide eyes on the man. He had stopped playing. She crossed to the sand-pit, lifted him in her arms, and then turned to face the man. 'Can I help you?' she said. She felt more secure now.

'That's a cute kid you got there.' He held out his hand. Benjy pressed against Ruth.

'He's not sure about strangers,' she said.

'Better that way. Hi, I may have something for him. Always carry . . .' He put down his parcel on the stone flags, carefully, she noticed, felt in his pocket and produced a neon-pink flat case. 'Coloured pencils. Most kids like them, but maybe he isn't old enough to draw?' He smiled tentatively at Ruth and, reassured, she set Benjy down.

'Oh, he likes to *draw*. His daddy encourages him, being in that line himself.' Don't shoot off your mouth, Ruth, she reminded herself, but cooped up here all day on your own you got to wishing you could talk with a grown-up. He seemed quite nice, really, but you had to be careful. Benjy's eager fingers snatched at the pink case, were already opening it. 'Say thank you to the man, Benjy.'

'Oh, it's nothing.' The man wriggled his body. He was really quite shy.

'Who shall I say called?' she asked in a posh voice, copying Mrs Strickner.

'I'm . . . Carl Williams. I've been meaning to deliver this,' he pointed to the parcel lying on the stone flags, 'it's a picture, but we just happened to be passing by and it seemed like a good opportunity. They're expecting it.'

'I don't know nothing about that.' Ruth looked at the flat parcel, and suddenly remembered. Hadn't Mr Purvis said something about a picture? 'Did a Mr Purvis give it to you?' She met the man's eyes. They slid away from hers. He was sure shy as hell.

'Yeah, that's it.' He didn't hesitate. 'Mr Purvis. That's right! We were going to Poughkeepsie and we were asked to hand it in. No sweat. Wow!' He ran a finger round the inside of his collar, 'It's sure hot for October.

245

Sun having its last fling before winter sets in, eh? Here!'
He felt in the pocket of his light poplin jacket and produced a square notepad. 'Not much good having pencils if you've nothing to draw on, eh?' He bent down
beside Benjy, opened the pad, took one of the pencils
Benjy was holding and quickly drew quite a good cat,
complete with whiskers. Benjy stood beside him, wide-
eyed with admiration.

'Cat,' he said, 'that's a cat,' pointing.

'Great kid!' Mr Williams said, straightening. 'You a
neighbour?' Ruth was flattered.

'No, I look after Benjy while his parents are at work.'
That sounded better than saying she was just a
nursemaid.

'About two, is he?'

'Thereabouts.'

'Just the same age as ours would have been if . . .' a
shadow seemed to pass over his face and he looked
away from Ruth as if he was trying to control himself.
If what? she wondered. Had *his* little boy died or something? That was sad enough. 'I'm sure glad I found you
anyhow. Will you apologize to Mr and Mrs Laidlaw that
I've taken so long to come? I know they'll understand.'

She looked at the parcel where Mr Williams had laid
it so carefully on the flags. Well, he knew their names,
so he must be all right. A married man who'd had a
child who would have been the same age as Benjy if
. . . poor souls! Yes, he seemed genuine but she still
wasn't going to offer him a cup of tea or anything.

'Lovely district, this,' he said, as if determined to be
cheerful. 'I expect you know it well.'

'Not as yet, but my boyfriend and me, we intend to
go to West Point when he has time.'

'You'll enjoy that. Men always do anyhow. We're just
boys at heart.' He laughed jauntily.

246

'I don't know about Bud. He's dead against fighting. He works with the kids in the Bronx. There's a club there for the ones with broken homes.' At the same time, she was thinking, his wife's in the car, why doesn't he hurry on back to her, or will Mrs Laidlaw say I should have given their friends a cup of tea or something?

'The most important thing in the world,' Mr Williams was saying, 'the patter of tiny feet in a home.' Again that sadness came into his eyes, pale grey eyes, flat, and again they slid away from her. He certainly changed his moods quickly. She could hardly keep up with him.

He bent down and lifted the parcel. 'This picture,' he said, 'you'll take good care of it? Well, I know you will. But maybe you should take it inside right away?' And then, turning to Benjy, he called, 'Say, son, have you plenty of sand there?' The child looked up.

'Sand,' he repeated. 'Sand for Benjy.' Ruth saw he hadn't used the pencils but had stuck them on top of his sand pies.

'I know where there's a lot more, lots and lots.' Mr Williams turned to Ruth and whispered, 'In the Sahara.' He sure was a joker, she thought. Should she take the picture in as he had suggested, make a quick cup of tea, bring it out and tell him to fetch his wife? If only Mrs Strickner had been here.

'More sand?' Benjy asked. He was smiling at the man. He had taken to him. That was a good sign. Maybe she should go inside . . . the telephone bell rang, settling it. It sounded very loud, very insistent, in the afternoon quietness.

'Oh, Gawd!' she exclaimed, forgetting her hostess image, 'Mrs Strickner's off . . .'

'You dash right in and answer that,' Mr Williams said, 'I'll wait till you get back, then I'll get off.'

247

'Okay.' Ruth ran inside, thinking, should I have done that, should I have given them tea long ago, should I have taken in the picture at the same time? They didn't realize the responsibility they loaded on to you, leaving you alone without Mrs Strickner. There should be rules . . . oh, give it a rest, Ruth! Mr Purvis asked him to hand it in when he was passing. Maybe Mr Williams had one of them galleries like Mr Laidlaw's, pictures all over the place.

It was the firm who were coming to make a pergola over the drive. 'Pergolas and Patios' they called themselves, in Peekskill. They were sending a man to take measurements tomorrow and they would like explicit instructions as to how to find the Laidlaw residence. Mr Laidlaw had said they were to ring before they came.

It took a little time to explain exactly where the house was. She would have liked to have said, 'the back of beyond', and the man was thick. But he got it right at last. How could she know the numbers of the freeways and the turnoffs? She was only a nursemaid, she told them, not a car owner. Yet.

She hung up and thought of preparing a tray while she was here, along with a glass of milk for Benjy, and thought again, no, Mr Williams had said his wife was waiting. She should have handled this better and told him to go fetch her right away. She rather liked the idea of pretending to be a friend of the owner, sitting on the terrace behind the tray, 'Milk and sugar? Or lemon?' like in one of those English films.

When Ruth got to the terrace there was no sign of Mr Williams. Or Benjy. Her heart gave a terrible lurch inside her body, sweat broke out all over her. There was something wrong with her eyes, that's what it was. Coming from the cool, shaded kitchen to the sunlight.

She squeezed them shut, swallowed and opened them again. The terrace was deserted. Benjy's coloured pencils were still stuck in his sand pies, but there was no spade nor pail. And no Benjy.

Now her whole body was shaking, shivering, she was talking to herself, 'No, no, it's a bad dream. It's the dark, and then the bright terrace . . .' *Benjy wasn't there.* Even if something had happened to her eyes she couldn't make a mistake like that. The scarlet of the pixie hat would have caught her attention right away. He wouldn't take it off. It was one of his little quirks.

She let out a shriek, adrenalin seemed to pour into her body, and she ran blunderingly down the path, sobbing, mouthing, incoherent. Once she fell, scraping her knees on the rockery stones at the side, and the pain made the sobbing louder.

She reached the wicket gate, went through it, but there was no car parked, only the terrible quietness, the afternoon quietness, a stretch of wooded ground bound by a high wooden fence, broken by a drive with a mailbox beside it with the name 'Streiger' on it. They were in Europe, Mrs Strickner had told her.

No one about. There never was until between six and seven o'clock when the gentlemen came back from the city, and the ladies, for it took two to keep those rich houses going. What a damn stupid place to live with no life, no life . . . she felt sick. Nausea at the back of her throat.

She turned and stumbled back up the path again, felt her breasts swaying, slowed down, took a deep breath. There must be an explanation. Maybe he had said to Benjy, 'Would you like a little run in the car with Mrs Williams and me while Ruth is speaking on the phone? Come and get an ice-cream.' Holding out his hand. Benjy wouldn't understand the whole thing, but he sure as hell would pick up the word 'ice-cream'. He loved the stuff but Mrs Laidlaw only allowed it as a treat.

Or maybe that nice Mrs Hoefer had come over when she was inside and said, 'Fancy meeting you here, Mr Williams! How are you? Do come over and have a drink with us. Your wife? Yes, of course, she's welcome. Bring the little boy.' She was mad keen on Benjy, anyone could see that. 'Ruth won't mind,' she would say. They would call her any minute. Everything would be all right.

But that was nonsense. Mrs Hoefer worked in the city too. You'd think they'd want to enjoy their nice houses. But the lights – you could see them through the trees – were never on till late.

She was in the kitchen now. It was like a morgue, no Mrs Strickner, no Mrs Laidlaw, no Benjy. She felt terribly sick now, another lurch of fear swept through her, and she could smell herself, rank, horrible, like from some swamp. Her hand trembled so badly that she could hardly lift the receiver.

What was she going to say, and who was she going to ring? It had to be Mrs Laidlaw rather than Mr Laidlaw, she didn't know why she thought that. Her tears were choking her now because the picture of Benjy in his sand-pit with his red pixie hat came up before her eyes. If *she* loved him, what would his mother's feelings be? 'May I speak with Mrs Laidlaw?' she said to the efficient voice at Reception.

'Speak up!' it said, already judging her.

Twenty-seven

After the first terrible shock when she heard Ruth on the telephone mouthing incoherently, choking, weeping, saying over and over again, 'It's Benjy, Mrs Laidlaw, it's Benjy,' her professional training helped her. She heard her own voice, harsh and ugly in her ears. 'Compose yourself, Ruth, just tell me what's happened.'

After she had got into her car in a daze – having rung Mish, who had implored her to wait for him, 'Just wait, Karin,' and she had refused, saying she must get home – she remembered through her misery the unease she had felt the evening the Hoefers had visited them. Their story about the murdered man so near in the woods above their house had been like the snake in the garden of Eden, an augury, and that in itself was stupid, unlike her.

She wasn't usually imaginative, sensitive, but not imaginative. Had it been Sally Hoefer then who had disturbed her, that childless woman who had made her feel guilty about Benjy? Why hadn't she asked Ruth if she had called the Hoefers, ran to them for help?

But she had no grounds for suspecting Sally. She had been pleasant, neighbourly, a business woman who was fully occupied all day with her husband, hadn't she said so? Had her feeling of unease, then, been some kind of premonition? There are more things in heaven and earth than . . . can be logically explained. She should know that, dealing as she did each day with the darker side of human nature, its fears, its anxieties and its guilt.

She was two people. The calm psychologist, Miss Gottleib, 'Keep calm, there must be a logical explanation, don't allow your mind to disintegrate, to fly into fragments, you need every part of it to face this situation, Mish will depend on you, Ruth, poor Ruth, Benjy,' but at the mere mouthing of Benjy's name and the image of him behind her retina, she was no longer Miss Gottleib, the therapist, but a distraught mother, full of guilt and recrimination.

Her erstwhile beautiful career, so important to her that she had to leave her child in the care of a kind but not very intelligent black girl! Ruth had been their own little personal anti-racist gesture, anything they could do. There had been another young woman, nursery-trained, efficient, white, but with a hard mouth. 'I'm a disciplinarian, Mrs Laidlaw,' she had said, 'you can leave your son safely in my hands.' Karin had decided on Ruth, a loving kind of a girl from a poor home with brothers and sisters and a warm heart. No, she shouldn't feel guilt there.

'Whom the gods love they first destroy . . .' Had she been too happy, too engrossed in her own career, too uncaring about the outside world? But hadn't she paid her dues first in Biafra, and wasn't she dealing with broken people all day long? And Mish too in his own way was contributing to the sum of human happiness. There was a need in people's lives for more than food and shelter. Mish was a purveyor of beauty . . . specious, she thought, that's for rich people, and heard herself moaning like an animal, crouched over the wheel, moaning, her foot hard down on the floor, regardless of speed limits.

252

She was running now alongside the river, having cleared the city traffic, Tappanzee Bridge, generally the Hudson calmed her, not today, not today. She drove in a daze of misery, fast but safe through habit.

She drew up the car in front of the house and ran inside. In the kitchen Ruth was sitting in a chair in an obvious state of shock, with Mrs Strickner bending over her. She had evidently just come in. Her bag and gloves lay on the table. She raised her face to Karin, her pale face framed by her black hair. She was happily blameless.

'Oh, Mrs Laidlaw! Am I glad I came back early! My friend didn't turn up so I took the four o'clock train back. I don't know what to do with Ruth . . .'

'I'll deal with her.' Reserves of strength and her training helped her. 'Make some tea, Mrs Strickner, please.' She put her arm round Ruth's shoulders. 'Come into the lounge with me, Ruth. I want you to tell me exactly what happened.' The girl raised a face, swollen with tears, eyes red-rimmed.

'Are you going to kill me, Mrs Laidlaw?'

'Now, what good would that do?' Karin was almost hearty. 'Come on, Ruth! Get up. You're in Mrs Strickner's way. Come along.' She helped the girl through the hallway and into the lounge, feeling the soft fleshiness of her waist under her arm. Of course Ruth had always been indolent, she had known that, and an indolent body often went with an indolent mind. But she had decided rationally, hadn't she, that it was better than a trained nursemaid with a hard mouth. Love was all-important, a big heart.

Had Ruth gone to sleep and Benjy had wandered off? She had said something on the telephone about a man who had brought a parcel, but that could have been a lie to cover herself. Wasn't Benjy perhaps at this

253

moment with some neighbour who would soon bring him back? But she knew their only near neighbours were in Europe. And Sally Hoefer. Was he with her? Now she was in danger of thinking irrationally. Sally was in New York, she knew that, and Ruth, in any case, had never been a liar, she was honest, incapable of deception.

She had just got the girl settled in a chair when Mish came bursting in. His face was so white, his eyes so sunken, that he was like a stranger. He came towards her and took her in his arms, speechless. She could feel his body trembling against hers, but when he released her he was in control of himself.

'Oh, Mr Laidlaw!' Mrs Strickner had come in with the tea, like a priestess, ministering but uninvolved in the tragedy going on around her. 'I'm glad you're home for your wife's sake. You poor souls! If my friend had turned up I wouldn't be here either.'

'Pour out the tea, Mrs Strickner,' Karin said, 'we can all do with a cup. Sit down, Mish. You must have been just behind me. Drink your tea, Ruth. Is there plenty of sugar in it? Yes, another spoonful.' Where was she getting this schoolmarmy tone? 'Now, Ruth, that's better. Mr Laidlaw's here and we're going to listen to you while you tell us exactly what happened.' She looked at Mish but his eyes were fixed on Ruth.

'That's right,' he said, 'tell us everything.'

The girl took the Kleenex Karin offered her, then a sip of tea, drew in her breath. 'We were in the garden, both as happy as sand boys. You know what you told me, Mrs Laidlaw, about getting Benjy plenty of fresh air and the sun was shining . . .'

'Just a minute!' Karin turned to Mish. 'The police! I haven't called the police!' She spoke wildly.

'It's all right. I did.' He was tense. 'Go on, Ruth, go

on.' He was more composed than Karin, except for that tiny flicker on the side of his left eye. And that startling paleness, as if the shock he had received had turned inwards, making the blood on his cheeks recede.

'Well,' Ruth wiped at her eyes, drew the same quivering breath, 'this man came and he had a picture for you. He said he had been asked to hand it in . . .'

'You didn't say a picture!' Karin interrupted. 'Where is it?' The girl looked startled.

'Where is it?' She looked confused. 'It must still be in the garden, near the sand-pit. He put it down when he gave Benjy some coloured pencils.'

'I'll go and look.' Mish got up and went swiftly through the patio doors and into the garden. Karin sat very still, trying to empty her mind. One thing at a time. See the picture first. Mish was back again.

'There's no picture there. I presume it was wrapped up, Ruth?'

'Yes, in a parcel. I didn't actually see it. He *said* it was a picture. He put it down, like, careful, when he went over to the sand-pit. Oh, Mr Laidlaw!' She had begun to weep again. 'Did you see the pencils stuck in Benjy's pies?'

'Yes.' He closed his eyes for a second as if he'd been struck by a blow. Karin wanted to get up and weep with him, more than weep, moan, even shriek.

'What . . . What happened then, Ruth?' she said. She had to clear her throat twice.

'The telephone rang, and I went in to answer it because Mrs Strickner was off. He said he would keep an eye on Benjy. Benjy seemed to quite like him. He smiled up at him, you know the way he does with that smile of his and his red pixie hat . . . Oh, Oh!' it was a primeval cry, deep-throated. 'Oh, Jesus!' She put her hand to her mouth, rocking, and Karin waited, holding on, her nails digging into her palms, wanting to join the girl in her cries. 'He said he knew where there was sand, lots and lots of sand. I remember that because he joked with me about it, but you could see Benjy was really taken about that sand.' She hit the side of her head with her hand. 'It wasn't ice-cream that tempted Benjy, it was that sand! He's crazy about the stuff, don't know why . . . and then when I came out from the house he wasn't there, little Benjy. He'd taken his pail and spade – you see, sand! I remember the man's joke now. "In the Sahara," he whispered to me. That was him. He joked one minute then he was serious the next.'

'You noticed that,' Karin said, 'that his behaviour was . . . odd?' There was a greater fear inside her now, like the onset of a terrible truth.

'Yeah, that's the word, Mrs Laidlaw. Odd. Oh, I remember it all now. And the man had gone and taken Benjy with his pail and spade, and I guess the picture as well if it isn't there. Oh, Mrs Laidlaw, Mr Laidlaw,' the tears were streaming down her cheeks, 'I hope never to have a shock like that again, never in the whole wide world.'

Karin straightened her back. Relieve the tension. She hadn't wept yet. That was for later. 'This picture, Ruth. Can you remember anything about it, anything else?'

'No, I can't, Mrs Laidlaw. It was all the time wrapped up. But he said it was from Mr Purvis, that I do recall.'

'He knew his name?' Mish demanded. He looked at Karin, 'Hal . . .' His face was suddenly distraught. 'Why in God's name don't these policemen come?' She shook her head, unable to look at him again. 'You're sure he said it came from Mr Purvis?' he asked Ruth again.

'No, well, maybe he did. Yes, he did, because when I asked him he said it *was*. You see, Mr Purvis told me when he called here the last time he would be leaving it. I remember that distinctly.'

'I got it.' Mish half-muttered to Karin. 'I picked it up from Hal's office. Some time ago.'

Now the pain was in her heart as if a knife was being slowly turned in it, piercing deeper and deeper, bringing with it a terrible certainty. Her feeble conjectures about Sally Hoefer were less than nothing. It had been Paul Laskins. Sally was sane. She might long for a child but it had to be her own.

'Did he give his name, Ruth?'

'Yes. Carl Williams. That was it. He seemed to know you the way he spoke. He and his wife were just passing, he said, on their way to Poughkeepsie.'

'Did you see his wife?'

'No, Mrs Laidlaw. I was bothered that I hadn't asked him to fetch her for a cup of tea, but I can't be expected to think of everything, can I?'

'No, Ruth. Will you describe Mr Williams to me, please?'

'He was tall, bald, but it wasn't an old baldness, like those old men you see. He had a kind of fringe round the baldness.' She lifted her cup and drank thirstily from it. She was recovering now. She was being supported in this awful thing that had happened to her. The Laidlaws were clever folk. She had done nothing wrong. They would take over now. Money talks, that was what Mom always said, usually bitterly, money talks. 'He walked funny, like . . . like long strides, and kind of leaning on one side and then the other side . . .'

'Like loping?'

'Yeah, that kind of thing, yeah, like a wolf, loping.'

Karin got up from her chair. 'It was Paul Laskins.'

She had her hand to her mouth. 'He's unbalanced. He's been snooping around us for ages. I never did find out how he got our address . . .' she heard her voice rising, going out of control. Mish was on his feet, holding her. 'I'm going to die . . . die . . .' She couldn't bear the pain. 'He took a grudge against me. I said I wouldn't see him again. Hal told me he and his girl wanted a baby. Oh, my God!' Her voice shrieked, whirled round the room. She was still in Mish's arms when two policemen arrived. They looked around impassively.

'Excuse us,' one of them said. 'Door was open.' He looked at Karin and Mish. He had released her.

'I'm glad you've come,' she said shakily.

'Mr and Mrs Laidlaw, is it?' the policeman asked. 'Sit down, Mrs Laidlaw. Now, you want to take it easy. Your husband told us what had happened. Don't you worry. We'll have your boy back here in no time. Now, we'd like to make a few enquiries.'

Karin sat. Controlled agony was worse, a searing agony which was so intense that it prevented her from thinking straight. She remembered the murdered British soldier at the mill above them, and the reason for his death. Vengeance. Ugly, ugly. Ruthless. What had happened was a demonstration of its power, its force for evil. Visited on her.

The agony abated and she was sane again, listening. Those loud rasping breaths were surely not her own. She saw Mrs Strickner in the room again with a tray and fresh tea. She poured out two cups for the policemen, gave one to Mish and another to Karin.

'It's fresh. Drink it, Mrs Laidlaw. You'll feel better.' And, confidently, nodding in the direction of the policemen, 'They'll find Benjy for you. Just wait and see.'

'We sure hope to.' It was the second man speaking.

He had laid down his cup and taken a notebook from his breast pocket. She put out her hand to Mish but his eyes were fixed on the policeman.

Twenty-eight

'It's impossible to imagine such a thing happening!' Van and Hal were sitting over a late dinner. Sam had been allowed to stay up to say 'Hello!' to Hal – he had been later than Van in getting home – and now he had gone to bed willingly, his eyes closing with tiredness.

'When the new baby comes,' he had said, 'I'll be allowed to stay up late because I'll be the boss.'

'Not the boss,' Hal had corrected him, 'the older brother, or sister. He or she will look up to you to show them the ropes, but not to be bossed.'

He had nodded. 'I get it. Well, I don't mind showing it the ropes.'

Mish had telephoned Hal during dinner, and he had been away for a long time. He had waited to tell Van the appalling news until Sam had gone to bed.

'I can't believe it!' Van reiterated. 'Can we help in any way? If you went?' She was shaken. The long days at the various hospitals were leaving her more tired now.

'I offered, but obviously unless I can be of positive help there's no point. Mish says Karin is convinced that Paul Laskins, her patient, is responsible. She's told the detectives who're dealing with the case, and they're trying to trace him. She gave them his New York address, the same as mine, remember? But needless to say they didn't find him there. You can imagine the state they're both in.'

'Yes. And Mish is quite dippy about Benjy. Almost more than Karin.'

'You wouldn't have thought it, knowing him. As long as he doesn't blame her for not being at home to look after Benjy.' He looked at Van. 'But you never really *know* people, do you? That was an eye-opener for me. He's usually such an equable bloke.'

'People have more than one side. Even Mish. Has he rung Mother?'

'Yes. We'll ring them later. Anna and Ritchie will be devastated. This on top of Jean's death!'

'It's too much. Too much. Poor Mother.' She paused. 'I'm thinking of that woman who knew Laskins. Ellie Kaplan. You went to see her the last time you were in New York, didn't you?'

'Yes, I did. I brought up the subject of Paul Laskins but she was fed up with him. Said he was a weirdo, that he wouldn't open the door to her.'

Van shifted her position in her chair. The baby seemed to be pressing against her ribs, but in spite of the discomfort of pregnancy, it had given her a new beauty, not only in Hal's eyes. Her face had lost its aquilinity and her skin seemed to glow. Her beautiful eyes were luminous, bluer than ever, emphasized by the dark smudges under them. One of the hospital staff had said to her today, 'Pregnancy suits you.'

What she had noticed herself in her dealings with patients was an even greater sympathy, a deeper understanding of their problems, as if because of this gift within her – she thought of the coming baby that way – she had an added sensitivity. And Mr Elder had said she was not to tire herself when she had taken him a flask of soup. At the same time as asking her to tell

Sam to be a bit speedier on his errands to the Post Office.

'Hal,' she said, 'I've forgotten the background to Paul Laskins. Tell me again.'

'According to Ellie he had this girlfriend, Bobbie, who used to live with him. And she wasn't very sociable. The only person she fraternized with was a woman downstairs whom she baby-sat for sometimes . . .'

Van sat forward. 'She liked babies?'

'It seemed so.' He met her eyes and was alerted. 'Laskins stopped going to see Karin in the middle of his treatment. Mish said so.'

'Did he say why?'

'No, I didn't ask. He was too upset. Are you tired, darling? You look . . .'

'No.' She was irritable, unlike her. 'I've never felt better in my life. Don't cosset me. But you know how this baby is very important to us?'

'It sure is.'

'It's become, much as I'm engrossed in you, Sam and my work, the most important thing in my life. All the time I'm visiting hospitals I think of myself as a kind of shelter. I find myself being extra kind, extra sympathetic, but at the same time, careful, telling myself not to hurry in case I fall, everything is directed towards guarding it. It becomes pretty much like an obsession.'

'That's natural.'

'Of course it is. But we're lucky, we're together, you've made me pregnant, we have a baby in here,' she patted her stomach, 'you've felt it, Sam has felt it – it's a living breathing object to the three of us, just waiting to be born, and we have nothing to do but wait, all safe and sound. We're lucky.' She said it again.

'Damned lucky. Where's this getting?'

262

'What about that girl who wishes desperately for a baby and can't have one? Or rather, her boyfriend can't start one in her?'

'Laskins's girlfriend?'

Van nodded. 'Bobbie. I never thought we couldn't. I had proved I could with Sam, I was pretty sure we were all right – and here's the living proof.' She looked down at her swollen stomach. 'Maybe we're arrogant. We started it when we wanted, when it suited us. Confident.'

'And I was arrogant. Most men are. But supposing Paul Laskins couldn't perform. Is that what you're saying?'

'Not exactly. Deliver.' Her mouth quirked. 'I've seen so many embittered women with their lives ruined because of their obsession about having a child. Men can't feel that despair, but they can feel humiliated, inadequate.'

Hal nodded. 'Right. I never thought of a woman's side of it. But when you think of someone like Ellie Kaplan, unfulfilled . . .'

'Don't get carried away.' She smiled at him. 'Maybe Ellie hasn't got any further than wanting a man. Even Paul Laskins would have done.'

'She was fed up with him. And he seemed to have become peculiar recently, shutting himself up in his flat.'

'Anything else? Think?'

He tried to recollect that last meeting with Ellie Kaplan in the foyer of the apartments, the buzz of people, talking, passing, repassing each other, doormen answering telephones, calling to each other, to cab drivers, New Yorkers always seemed to create a buzz of their own as if they packed away more adrenalin than the more contained English. He thought of that

263

anxious, pathetic look in her eyes, belied by her jaunty manner. 'Let me see. Yes, she said that when she'd last met him he'd had a sly smile round his mouth, looking past her, as if he was hiding a secret, trying to keep himself from laughing.'

'As if he'd found out something to his advantage?'

'That could be it.'

'Anything else?' She was sitting at the bedside of a patient now. She had discovered that if you were patient, but relaxed, people remembered more than they had thought at first.

'Yes, there was.' Hal's face brightened. 'She asked him if he ever saw that nice girl, Bobbie, and he said,' he closed his eyes in an effort to remember, 'it was some kind of fishing analogy, yes, this is it, "I'm working towards it. I think I've got the right bait."'

'Bait! Benjy! What he had always wanted to give her, a baby.'

'Steal Benjy for her! God, if you're right, he must be mad!'

'Unbalanced anyhow, obsessed, unable to give her a child himself. I'm sure that's it. He was a patient of Karin's and she'd know why. You should go and phone her right away, tell her.'

'Do you think so? She's probably worked this out already, told the detectives who're in charge of the case. It's where he is with Benjy that's the terrible part of it, or what he *does* with him.' He met her eyes. 'I'll phone.' He got up. 'Yeah, I'll phone.'

Mish answered when he rang. Karin was upstairs but she'd be down shortly since they were waiting for the detectives to come. Hal said, 'I rang because I just remembered a conversation I had with Ellie Kaplan, that's the woman who lives in my apartments in Forty-sixth Street. It's apropos Paul Laskins.' He repeated what Ellie had told him. '*Bait*, Mish. It sounds significant.'

'Maybe.' Mish sounded weary. 'It only confirms Karin's belief that he's the man we're looking for. She did ask him to go to a fertility clinic, but he didn't keep the appointment.'

'It's terrible for you.'

'No sympathy, please. It's difficult enough. Sorry, I'm edgy. We haven't slept since it happened. But there's no doubt that Laskins is the culprit. I could murder him with my bare hands!' His voice was harsh.

'I wish we could do more.'

'I wish it had never happened, that we hadn't come here, that Karin . . .' He stopped. 'This doesn't get me anywhere. By the way, Hal,' his voice calmed, 'that painting of Dad's that I picked up at your publisher's office. Got it all right. It's a little beauty . . . what a bloody schemer Laskins is! Did you say to Ruth that you would be handing it in, by the way?'

Hal thought. 'Yes, I did, but then I got rushed and didn't.'

'It's okay. I was just checking.' His voice broke. 'This devil is crucifying us!'

'I'll get off the line. Ring if there's anything we can do, anything at all.' He hung up, miserable that he was so helpless. He hoped they could comfort each other.

Twenty-nine

They were in the lounge waiting for the new detective. He had rung Mish earlier, saying, cheerfully, 'Bob Bruccoli. I've been assigned to your case from the Met Division. I'll drop by in an hour if that's okay.' They had been forewarned by the two local men who had sung Bruccoli's praises. 'A whiz kid on abduction cases.'

The strain was beginning to tell on them. Karin, at her desk, was making a pretence of being busy with some files, Mish was rearranging books on the shelves in a haphazard fashion. They were past talking to each other, each tightly encased in their grief.

Karin, glancing up from Laskins's file which she was going through for the hundredth time, looked at the mess Mish was making, the random piles of books on the floor. She wanted to shout, 'Why the hell are you doing that now, for God's sake?'

Last night when she had been lying sleepless she had turned to Mish, moaned, 'What are we going to do if we don't find him?' It was a cry for comfort. 'We would never get over it.' He lay rigid beside her. She knew he was awake. 'Mish,' she moaned, 'you're not blaming me, are you? You've gone away . . . what is it?'

He got abruptly and began to pace about the room. She put on the bedside light and sat up. She saw his usually sleek hair was dishevelled, his fists were clenched at his sides, his eyes were wild. 'I'm going to kill Laskins!' he shouted. 'I'm going to find him somehow and kill him! Those people you deal with, they've no morals, they're murderous bastards!' Even in her despair her professionalism came to the fore.

'Those people you refer to are sick. They come to me for help.'

'And this is the way they pay you back?' He wheeled to face her. 'Steal our child? Who *knows* what he's doing to our Benjy! You're right. They're sick. There are no depths to . . .'

She got out of bed and went to him. 'Stop that!' she ordered. 'You're letting your imagination run away with you. Would you rather I didn't work at all?' He turned away but she put a hand on his arm. 'We're together in this. It's my job. I never question yours.'

'Yes, I know it's your job.' He flung away from her. 'If it hadn't been for your job you might have been with our son, keeping him safe!' He went out of the room and she could hear him running downstairs, then the patio doors being opened.

Karin sat down on the bed because her legs had given way. This wasn't Mish, her equable, urbane British gentleman who she was secretly proud of because of the covert admiration of other women. Even Ruth and Mrs Strickner were under his spell. Was it a veneer or had this tragedy uncovered a hidden grudge against her for having a career at all?

But his mother worked, always had, and his sister. Was it that within him there was a displaced feminine element, the need to protect, to watch over, to be there? And was the urbanity a cover for some kind of inadequacy, unexplainable as all inadequacies were, until a lot of digging took place?

Van had said she always felt inadequate because of

her brilliant parents. Had Mish felt the same and, lacking their talent, had made a niche for himself as a buyer and seller of pictures instead of an executor? And what if he were right in feeling that she should have been at home instead of following her own career? On his showing it had led to this awful thing which had happened to Benjy.

And what if his suppositions were right and something awful had happened to Benjy, that at this moment he was being tortured, or even worse? She knew far more about that than Mish, with all his urbanity, could ever guess at. Now she was tortured by images of Benjy, the anguished face, the terrified eyes, heard him calling for her. She saw the red pixie hat and thought of blood.

A long time later when she had crept into bed and covered herself because she was cold, she became aware that Mish was beside her. He didn't speak. She heard him weeping. But she was too full of hurt and the guilt which he had imposed on her, and she turned away, her hand covering her eyes.

In the morning he was calm, his face ashen. 'I'm sorry about my outburst last night, Karin. I was off my head. Please forgive me.' She dismissed his apology, saying they were both worn out. He must work it out for himself. She knew the foolishness of too many words.

'Mr Bruccoli's here, Mrs Laidlaw.' Mrs Strickner was at the door. A young man came from behind her, small, swarthy, with lively brown eyes. He came forward to them. 'Bob Bruccoli. Glad to meet you.' He went swiftly with hand outstretched from one to the other. 'We spoke on the telephone, Mr Laidlaw.'

'Yes. Have a seat.'

'Would you like some coffee?' Karin asked. Mrs Strickner was teetering at the door.

'Thanks. Thirsty work driving from the city.' He jumped up from his chair and went to the window. He scanned the garden carefully, nodded, then went back to his seat. He moved as if he were on springs. 'This business about your little boy,' he said. 'It's half-solved already. Just a matter of finding out where he's being hidden.' He took out a notebook. 'I have Paul Laskins's Manhattan address here.'

'And I gave the other detectives his sister's address in New Jersey,' Karin said.

'Yeah, they're working on that. Tell me, do you think this patient of yours is a psychopath?'

'I didn't. I do now. That should be obvious.' She turned away.

'How did he present when he first came to you?' She noticed the correct verb even in her misery.

'Unbalanced, secretive.'

'C'mon now, Mrs Laidlaw, there must be more. Rack your brains.' Was he deliberately irritating her?

'Don't you think I haven't? A thousand times?' She got up and walked about, hands clenched. 'One's imagination runs riot during the night. And my husband is threatening to kill Laskins.' She looked at Mish.

'Why don't you discuss it with your wife, Mr Laidlaw?' Bruccoli's eyes were smooth. 'She's an expert. Go on, Mrs Laidlaw. Tell him what you think.' He'd felt the tension between them. 'I'm only too well aware how sleepless nights can churn you up.' He looked as if he had never known a sleepless night in his life but you could never tell. Everyone had their own life.

'First of all he's not mad,' she said. 'Obsessed, certainly, devious, cunning, psychopathic, but not mad.'

'But you never know which way he'd jump?'

'That's true. It's true that if I'd been with Benjy this wouldn't have happened.'

269

'True.' Bruccoli was still smooth. 'My wife was work-ing when our little boy was killed crossing the street. She couldn't take it. We're divorced.'

'I'm sorry.' She didn't look at Mish. 'How long ago was it?'

'Three years. It was tough.' *He* was looking at Mish. 'Plenty tough, but you weather it. It's behind me now.' Mrs Strickner was pushing at the door with a tray. Mish jumped up and held it for her.

'I'll do it.' Karin had made to rise. When he handed her a cup his eyes were full of suffering, but the coldness had gone. He gave a cup to Bruccoli. She saw the detec-tive take two heaped teaspoonfuls of sugar from the bowl on the tray.

'I take plenty of sugar. Keeps my energy level up.' He smiled cheerfully at Karin. 'You been seeing this Laskins a long time, Mrs Laidlaw?'

'Yes, over two years. It's not unusual. Some patients are long-term if they don't co-operate.'

'He saw you then when you were pregnant?' She was surprised at his shrewdness, remembering how she had felt when she had caught Paul looking at her.

'He did. I . . . resented the way he looked at me.'

'And he wasn't living with his girlfriend at this time?' She nodded. He was well-briefed. 'Did you come to any conclusion about him, medically?' The hot strong coffee was restoring her. It had taken the place of drink as a stimulant. She didn't want to go down that road, knew the dangers.

'Yes, that's right. I thought his problem was that he was sterile. When I told him that and asked him to go to a clinic, he didn't come back. Couldn't face it, couldn't believe it. You can see how his mind worked.'

'Sure. Girlfriend broody. He can't deliver the goods. Envied you.' Bruccoli turned to Mish. 'And you. We

270

don't realize the envy that causes in some. He's lying low in a place that's familiar to him. His parents have been contacted – the daughter gave us their address. Trouble is they haven't seen him in ages.' He turned again to Karin. She saw the lively brown eyes, the clear whites, their shrewdness. He'd make a good psychiatrist. 'I've always been taken by the way you lot get stuff out of people. It's like my own job. Just a question of finding the key that unlocks the door. I expect you did the whole bit, him on the couch, that kind of thing?'

'Yes,' Karin said. People always said they were sure they could do your job. Like people who said they could write a book if only they had time.

'And I expect you harped back a bit to his childhood, the reminiscence bit . . .'

'It's necessary.' Her anger flared. 'He was clever, obsessionals are always clever. He found out where I lived and came here on a pretext and took away Benjy!'

'For his girlfriend. Bobbie, wasn't it? We've contacted her too. She's been interviewed. I think she's in the clear if she's telling the truth. She said she grew afraid of him, he started bashing her about because he blamed *her* for not being pregnant, said she was glad she hadn't, to him, in the end, and cleared out. He used to weep a lot as well. She'd said she was going back to her folks, not to follow her. Then she had a garbled call from him one day telling her he had a baby for her, a little boy. She was terrified. Said she would tell the police and he said if she did he would kill it.'

'Oh!' Karin put her hand to her mouth. She knew she was wailing. Bruccoli went on.

'When she asked him where he'd got this kid he said he'd stolen him from someone who deserved it because of their lies . . .'

271

'He means because I told him he was sterile. He's paying me back. It's vengeance!' She put her head in her hands and Mish came over and knelt beside her.

'We're nearly there, Karin.' Mish's voice was steady, he was in command of himself now. 'Mr Bruccoli's just needing one other thing, where Laskins was likely to go to hide, where he might be already. Isn't that right?' He appealed to him.

'Sure.'

'Don't you think I'd tell him if I could?' She spoke from behind her hands. 'It's worse than ever! If this girl, Bobbie, has said she doesn't want Benjy, and he knows she might tell the police, then he's no use to him, my Benjy, no use . . .' The tears fell through her fingers, stinging them in the crevices. She knew despair. Utter despair. And the images were back.

They said if you went down to the depths, so profound that it seemed to be the end of everything, you had only one way to go, upwards. Slowly she saw a glimmer of light, far away and wavering, then it grew stronger, as if it was clearing the darkness from her mind, from her memory. She heard Paul's voice: 'Hot, and New York was full of stink. I'd think how good it would be to see the bay again . . . go fishing in my little boat, lobster . . .' At the time she had been reminded of a book she had picked up once on holiday, *Beautiful Swimmers*, about lobster fishing in Chesapeake Bay, a lovely book, evocative.

'He talked about fishing in the bay,' she said.

Bob Bruccoli got up and went to the window. 'That your little boy's sand-pit down there?' It seemed an irrelevant question and she didn't answer.

'Yes, it is,' Mish said.

'Laskins brought you a painting?'

272

'That's what he said.' Karin took her hands away from her face.

'By way of being a painter, was he?'

'I suggested it as therapy.' She raised her head, feeling it dull and heavy.

'But he didn't leave it, as it happened?'

'No, if it was a painting he took it when he took Benjy.' She tried to control her mouth.

'There's one of his in the cloakroom,' Mish said. 'I was going to stash it away in my gallery. Karin didn't want it here.'

'May I see it?'

'Sure.' Mish got up and went out, half-running.

'It's straightening out, Mrs Laidlaw.' Bruccoli smiled at her. His teeth were good and very white. They lifted the darkness from his face.

'My husband has taken it very badly. He's threatening to murder Laskins. I'm afraid.'

He nodded. 'I'll deal with that.' He stopped. Mish was back.

'Found it,' he said. He propped up the picture he was carrying against a side table. 'I had scarcely looked at it myself.'

Bob Bruccoli was doing just that. None of Mish's clients ever examined a picture more closely. 'Abstraction,' he said. 'Those curves. Sky, sea and sand, wouldn't you say, Mr Laidlaw?'

'Could be a bay?'

'A bay within a bay. But that's too vague for us. Easy to find out where. And that square? That black square?' He looked at them. They shook their heads. He looked at Karin. 'Is the nursemaid here who was with your little boy?'

'Ruth? Yes. She'll be in the kitchen with Mrs Strickner. Would you like to see her?'

'Sure would.'

Mish was out of the room like a shot, returning with Ruth. She looked pale, Karin thought, and realized for the first time that black people could look pale. Her eyes were red-rimmed.

'Sit down, Ruth.' She tried to smile reassuringly, 'Mr Bruccoli would like to speak to you.'

'Nothing to be scared of.' Bruccoli sat down opposite her, leaning forward. 'I know you've been interviewed before. There's just one thing I'm looking for. Did Mr Williams get kind of friendly with Benjy?' He sat back. 'Take it easy.'

'Lemme see.' Ruth licked her lips. 'Yeah, when I lifted Benjy up. Walked past him at first, though. He gave him some coloured pencils in a box. And a notebook. And he drew him a cat in it, quite a good cat, considering. That pleased Benjy. You know that smile of his, Mrs Laidlaw?' Karin turned her head away.

'Was there anything else he did that made Benjy happy?'

'Well, Benjy was making his sand pies, to tell you the truth he liked that better than the pencils, and Mr Williams, who was standing beside me, called over to him, "I know where there's lots and lots of sand!" His little face lit up at that, one big smile, and he said, "More sand? More sand?"' She shook her head. 'He was sure crazy about sand.' She swivelled her head reminiscently. 'That Mr Williams was kind of jokey. Leant near my ear and whispered, "In the Sahara!" He was like that, hard to keep up with. Funny, then kind of solemn, then his eyes trailed away, like as if he wasn't there. I didn't like that, kind of spooky, but him knowing Mr Purvis . . .'

'And Benjy's pail and spade were missing?' Bruccoli was going over his notes.

'Yeah, that's right. It was the one with all the dwarves dancing round it with the pixie hats, Mrs . . .' The look on Karin's face stopped her.

'And the picture wasn't there either?'

'What he *said* was a picture. Yeah, he took the parcel.' Ruth pursed her lips, looking pleased with herself.

'Thanks,' Bruccoli said. 'You've been very helpful, Ruth. That's all just now.'

She got up, turning to Karin. 'I'm very sorry, Mrs Laidlaw. Real miserable. When I see you folks so white-faced and not blaming me ever . . .' she put her hand to her mouth and blundered rather than walked out of the room.

'We're looking for something that lives at the back of Laskins's mind all the time.' Bruccoli got to his feet. 'Just a matter of pin-pointing the location. I'll set off right away to his parents'. I've a hunch they'll give us the answer.' Mish got up too.

'I'll go with you! I can't take any more of this. It's the second day!'

'It's the second day for your wife, Mr Laidlaw. Now you have to stay with her and think positive. That's the way I work. No emotion. It interferes with my thinking. Goes for you too. This man won't do anything in a hurry, if ever. He has a soft centre.' He smiled at Karin. 'I'm by way of being a psychologist too.' He shook hands quickly with both of them, strode to the door and turned before he went out. 'You'll hear tonight. Maybe pretty late but you'll hear. Think positive.' The way he shut the door was positive.

'You can still go after him,' Karin said.

Mish shook his head, chastened, Benjy-like. 'That was a temporary breakdown. Too much emotion.'

She held out her arms to him and he went to her, again like Benjy. Anyway, she thought, holding him,

275

I'm glad I saw him like that. Underneath. It might become a good marriage if they got their son back, or even if they . . . No, she musn't think any further. Bruccoli had said they were to think positive.

Thirty

Bob Bruccoli, along with two local policemen, set off late that same evening after he had seen Paul Laskins's parents. He had spent quite a time talking to them, and his father had marked the place on the map for him.

'We call it Paul's Bay, don't we, Mother?' He found them a quiet, level-headed couple. 'He was always as happy as a sandboy there. He sometimes went off for days at a time. We didn't stop him. We could see that was where he was most at peace. And he always brought us back some soft-shells. He was a grand fisherman. Knew exactly where to go to find them, he studied waterways, a real waterman, but handless in a farm. We had to accept that. But he loved his bay, could tell you all the birds. Ospreys were his favourite. Once he said to me, "Pop, it's the only place I'm happy." That's right, isn't it, Ada?'

She had agreed, wiping her eyes. 'We chose him, so we weren't going to go against fate if he didn't know the back of a heifer from the front. If he had just stayed here instead of going to the city. He needed that bay.'

It was nearly midnight when they parked the car and began to make their way across the marshes. 'Chesapeake's special country,' one of the policemen said. 'It takes years to know your way about it, but it gets into your blood.'

277

A phrase Bruccoli had read somewhere swam into his consciousness: 'The Great River in which fish with hard shell coverings abound.' Wasn't it a translation from Indian folklore? And only an Indian, or nowadays a local fisherman, could find his way through a marshy swamp like this. The shapes of the loblolly pines were still visible because of the moon, but underfoot was tricky. He was glad he had been loaned a pair of waders.

'Paul's father pointed out the place on the map,' he said, 'but I couldn't have found my way myself. I'm city bred.'

The elder of the two men answered. 'You have to be born hereabouts. I was brought up on the Chester river. Paul's boathouse is on a creek off it. No distance, it just seems that way.'

'Did you know him well?' Bruccoli asked.

'As well as most, but he was a loner. Here we respect folks' inclinations. Mind this bit, Mr Bruccoli. It's real swampy.' His warning came too late. Bruccoli felt the mud slipping down his legs, oozing between his toes. You needed waders up to your armpits here.

'Could do with some Indian blood in me,' he joked.

Quite suddenly, it seemed, they were on a small cliff, overgrown with bushes, and nestling beneath them they could see the dim, square shape of a building. Bruccoli remembered the painting the missing child's father had shown him, with a similar square shape.

There was a path leading down the slope to it, and as they drew near, Bruccoli saw a light wavering inside, not very bright, possibly a candle. He realized now that the building was a boathouse, sitting on stilts above a small creek, a wooden shack with a slate roof. In front of it was a bay, Paul's Bay, the pale sand gleaming, the soft slap of the waves on the shore in their ears.

Bruccoli held up his hand to halt the two policemen.

278

He looked at them and they nodded. He put his hand under his jacket and his fingers closed on his revolver. He hoped he wouldn't have to use it. They stood silently, listening, but the only noise was the same soft slap of waves. Nothing came from the house. He took a few steps forward, put his hand on the latch and the door gave way as he pushed it open. He walked in, followed by the two policemen. A man sat on a chair with a child in his arms. He heard the elder policeman say, 'It's Paul okay.'

After Laskins's first startled glance, a small movement in the chair, he didn't seem afraid, indeed to Bruccoli he seemed relieved. 'Hi, Brisby!' he said, 'You the guide? Didn't think you'd track me down so soon.' The man didn't reply, looked at Bruccoli.

'Is the kid all right?' Bruccoli kept his voice level. He saw Laskins had wrapped Benjy in a man's jacket, probably his own. The red bobbled cap on the child's head had been pulled down over his ears. It was cold in the shed, a dank, clammy coldness. He could hear the water lapping under his feet.

'Sure thing.' Laskins was cocky. 'Got him to sleep at last. He kept on whimpering and I had to wrap him in my jacket. Wouldn't shut up.'

Maybe we've just got here in time, Bruccoli thought. He remembered a man who'd killed the kid he had abducted because he said he'd cried too much. He went forward and squatted down beside Laskins and the boy. He would play this one carefully. He didn't trust the look in Laskins's eyes, his sly half-smile.

'This is some hideaway,' he said. 'We'd never have found it if your father hadn't given us directions.'

'You didn't go bothering Dad, did you?' Laskins tilted his head up at Bruccoli. 'Frighten the life out of Mom, that would.'

279

'Your mother had seen your photograph on television.'

'Smart work, eh?' He looked pleased, momentarily, then, 'Was that the cops or that bitch, Bobbie?'

'It upset your parents. You didn't think of that, did you, when you took away that kid. Not to mention what it's done to his.' He watched Laskins carefully, although he knew he couldn't make a move since he was holding the child.

'Well, they shouldn't have adopted me, Mom and Dad, should they? And that Miss Gottleib. She needed bringing down a peg or two. Smart ass!' His appearance belied his jaunty air, white-faced, sunken eyed, chin and upper lip black with stubble. His eyes flickered oddly.

'Have you any food?' Bruccoli asked.

'Yeah, that bag's stacked full. Stopped at a supermart.' He pointed to a knapsack lying on the floor. Benjy moved in his arms, and he quite tenderly tucked the collar of the jacket under his chin. Maybe he wouldn't have harmed him. Bruccoli sensed the two policemen were getting restless. He didn't want them to make any sudden movement.

'You weren't proposing to set up house here with Benjy?' he asked. He was alert.

'Listen to him, you guys!' Laskins's eyes were moving about his head now. 'Trying to get round me. Miss Gottleib had the same tricks.' He raised his voice. 'I know my rights! You're on private property and you haven't a warrant.'

Bruccoli was deadpan. 'What was your plan, Paul? Because you know you can't stay here indefinitely. It's too cold for one thing. Think of the kid.' Laskins didn't reply. He was bent over Benjy, who was making occasional puppy-like movements in his sleep. He spoke, still with his head down.

280

'I was going to give Bobbie another chance. Thought she would change her mind when she thought about it. It's what she wanted. And this one's past the diaper stage. Nearly.' He wrinkled his nose.

'She hasn't changed her mind.'

'How do you know?' He still didn't raise his head.

'She's turned you in. Informed on you. Remember, she *said* she would.' He watched Laskins, who nodded slowly, head still down, as if cogitating. His voice was flat when he spoke.

'I'm not surprised. Women are bitches. Shouldn't get mixed up with them.' He didn't speak for a moment, his head moving, looking around the boathouse. 'Do you know the only time I've been happy?'

'You tell me.'

'Coming down here, to my own bay, taking the boat out, going crabbing, soft-shells, Mom and Dad like them, just the birds for company. Dad understood that. Said I could come back any time to the farm, even if I didn't help him with those goddam heifers, clumsy bitches with their great slavering mouths.' He made an undulating movement with one hand. 'Now, ospreys, they're elegant, with that wing spread of theirs, snow-white underneath, and then the plunge, feet first, scored every time. Never got tired watching. Yeah, Dad said we couldn't all be the same, that I could come back any time.'

'He's still saying that. When we get this kid back to his parents we'll see how it works out. Maybe in your case there will be extenuating circumstances.'

'Like I'm crazy?' He smiled slyly. 'That Miss Gottleib! She deserved a bit of a fright. Couldn't make up her mind about me. She knew I was intelligent, so she couldn't see why I wouldn't go to the clinic. Why waste their time?' He included the two policemen. 'Eh, Brisby?

Meer? *You* know what they all said about me.' His eyes narrowed. 'And Kathleen, that bitch of a sister of mine, filled up Gottleib's mind with lies about me, that I was . . .' Benjy suddenly woke, struggled out of Laskins's arms and sat up. He looked round, rubbing his eyes, and then began to cry. It rose from a whimper to a piercing ululating sound which drowned everything, putting Bruccoli's teeth on edge.

'I'll take him,' he said, bending down and lifting the child out of Laskins's arms. 'I'm good with kids. You go along with the two officers.'

'Okay.' Laskins was docile as he got to his feet. He let Bruccoli take the child. 'Wouldn't you know it? Nothing works. You try to please a bitch of a woman by getting her what she wants and then you're under arrest.'

'Just so as we'll get you in without trouble, Paul,' the younger of the two policemen said, snapping handcuffs on Laskins's wrists. Desperate to be in on the action, Bruccoli thought.

'Your Mom and Dad are standing by you,' he said. 'You'll be able to talk with them.'

'Who the hell cares?' Laskins shrugged. 'It's over.'

The journey back over the marshes took only ten minutes. Getting there had seemed to take hours. Brisby carried the child, saying it would be safer that way, seeing as how he knew the route and he was a family man.

At the local station Bruccoli picked up a policewoman and set off with Benjy for the children's unit of the nearest hospital. He had telephoned the Laidlaws, who were driving all night to get there. He was pleased to see that policewoman Marge Shields was cuddling Benjy against her substantial bosom as to the manner born.

Thirty-one

Anna and Ritchie paid a visit to Kirkcudbright when
she could face the thought. So soon after Jean's suicide
there had been the dreadful anxiety of Benjy's disappearance, and it was only when a hysterical Mish
had telephoned them with the good news – Ritchie said
he hadn't recognized his usually calm son in the incoherent voice which had nearly burst his eardrums –
'We've got Benjy back, Dad! We've got him back!' –
that Anna said, 'Thank God. Now we'll drive to Kirkcudbright. I promised Sarah.' She had been only too
well aware that Sarah was bereft too, first of her father
then so quickly afterwards, her mother. No husband,
however caring, could fill that gap.

They found her wan; the busy mother and wife had
gone temporarily. She clung to Anna when she arrived,
and they wept together for a long time. Alastair and
Ritchie had left them alone. Later, when the children
were settled in bed and the four of them had a late
supper, they went to Jean's house and down the garden
path to the studio where the paintings were stacked.

'We'd like the one Mum did of the garden and her
studio,' Sarah said. 'You don't mind that, do you?'

'Of course not. She would want that. Are there any
others you'd like?'

'No, we aren't painters. Besides, they were left to you.

283

And they wouldn't be properly looked after here. You must take them with you.'

'If you'd like the idea, we could hang them at Clevedon Crescent where they could be safe, and where the family, or others, could see them. The room I shared with Jean has been used as a guest room.' Anna's voice wavered. 'I think she would like them there.'

'It would help her to rest in peace,' Alastair said, surprising her.

She didn't, or couldn't, talk about the Wigtoun Bay one yet. Sometimes she felt as if she had been mutilated inside. She had tried to explain this to Ritchie in the first terrible days of trying to come to terms with the fact that her beloved sister had taken her own life, and in so doing, had taken part of hers. 'A physical pain, deep inside me, as if there had been a wrenching, a tearing apart, which is going to make me incomplete for ever, unable to cope.'

'You mustn't think that.' He had held her close. 'We need you, especially now. You have to be there for Karin and Mish in their despair, for Hal and Van in their coming happiness.' And looking down on her as she had lain supine in bed, hands over her face, he had said, 'And I need you. I always will.'

But now that Benjy had been found safe and well they had gone to Kirkcudbright to see Sarah who had a heavy cross to bear, and to bring back the paintings to Clevedon Crescent. Jean had left her house to Van. It would be good for Sarah to have her cousin coming there with a young family which would match their own.

'I don't want to make the room a shrine,' Anna said, her eyes widening to hold back the tears – she was becoming weary of those incessant tears which were ruining her make-up, she joked. 'Jean was too lovely for a shrine, but it's fitting that they should be in the room we shared.' They were back home again.

'Full circle,' Ritchie said. 'I can face now my own mortality.' Anna looked at him. It was a remark totally unlike him. She went to him and put her cheek against his. 'It comes to everybody,' he said, 'as well as, in my case, a sagging belly and creaking joints.'

'We'll go on a health programme when we get back to work. Evening walks. Along to Anniesland Cross and back. Sunday strolls in the Botanic Gardens.'

'I'll even try morning swims.' He was looking at one of Jean's paintings as he spoke. The canvas was three-quarters turbulent sky, one quarter angry sea. 'That one's boiling with rage,' he said, 'boiling with life. Jean will never die.'

They hung the painting of Wigtoun Bay on the upstairs landing outside the drawing-room door where the light from the stained glass window on the staircase flooded through it. 'We'll see it every time we go out and in, up and down,' Anna said, 'and it will vary with the light from that great window. Visitors and family will be struck by it when they pass. They will see Jean. And we'll call it "Jean's room" where we've hung her paintings. The family can make their choice, but they haven't to be taken away until we join her.'

'When you want to be quiet with her you can go and sit there.'

'And think of us as girls, of chattering and laughing as we dressed and undressed, brushed our hair, all the time knowing what the other was keeping to herself but respecting that, because eventually it would come out. She knew I was in love with you before I knew it myself.'

'You should have looked in the mirror. Your eyes were full of it.'

'And I knew she was in love with Frederick Kleiber, but so did she. She was tortured by it. She knew there was nothing but sorrow for her at the end.'

When the hanging was finally finished, they went to bed. Anna knew a terrible tiredness, a weariness of the soul, but she remembered that Jean had been lovely in her gaiety and would not have liked Ritchie to have a glum wife on her account. 'Soul mates,' she had said of them often.

And so, when he turned to her with a vigour which surprised her, and no doubt surprised himself, she felt the old sweet stab through her body, and bonded it to his. How good it was, she thought, how everlastingly good, as she was swept by the great tide of feeling. 'You're the lucky one.' She heard Jean's voice when they were at the height of their passion. But it was true. She was mouthing the words when they came together.

There was no annual get-together at Clevedon Crescent that Christmas. Anna hadn't the energy for it. She discovered that one of the results of intense grief was fatigue, a fatigue so deep and penetrating that her very bones ached with it. She doggedly went to her studio each morning, but ideas would not come – the first time in her life that she had experienced any block.

Ritchie was patient and loving, but preoccupied. His new painting had received much acclaim in Barcelona, and there was to be an official ceremony when it would be handed over by the City Council there for hanging in the Miró Foundation on the hill of Montjuïc. The Spanish press made much of this Scottish painter, one newspaper even saying that he was following closely in the footsteps of the great Picasso. Ritchie and Anna had been invited, but at the last moment she could not summon up the energy to go.

Hal took her place when Ritchie said he could do with some moral support. Van, now happily pregnant, urged him to go. When she and Sam had their Christmas holidays they would go to Glasgow, and Hal and Ritchie would join them there after the ceremony.

She telephoned Anna. 'We'll talk about Jean together, Mum,' she said. 'You'll tell me how you miss her, and all the things you did when you were girls. You need to talk. And Sam will cheer you up. He might even let you listen to his little brother. He's sure it will be a brother.'

But in fact it was Nancy who saved Anna's sanity before that. She was sitting in her studio one morning staring at a brooch she had designed but which didn't please her. For the past few years she had concentrated on smaller objects, due to what she called 'a spot of arthritis' in her right wrist, and had hit on the idea of making a jewellery tray of small pieces, all done in the same idiom, this time not Spanish but Celtic. It enabled her to use silver and wire, and the meticulous work suited her always present craving for perfection. She wanted to incorporate her personal motif, a woman's head with a thin white face enclosed on either side by two triangular blocks of black hair. It was, of course, Jean.

When would this feeling of having been butchered go, an ugly word, but it fitted. 'Joined at the hip', they used to say of each other. There was a brief knock at the door, and when she looked up, startled, she saw it was Nancy, dressed up to the nines as usual, and puffing slightly. 'You'll have to give up having your studio in the attics,' she protested, 'that climb's fair killed me.' She collapsed into a chair, stripping off her grey suede gloves from her beringed fingers, and slipping her feet out of her high-heeled court shoes. Her ankles were thick. Anna flexed her own slim ones subconsciously.

'You should have shouted up and I would have come downstairs. Besides, going up and down keeps me thin.'

'It doesn't keep Ritchie thin. He's got a fine belly for a watch-chain.'

'It's all these rich dinners he eats. Especially in Barcelona.'

'You should have gone with him, Anna. On all important occasions in your husband's life, you should be at his side. I never missed any of James's RIBA dinners. It was a chance for a new frock!' Her eyes glistened.

'You must have dozens of those elaborate things in your wardrobe.'

'I wear them when we go on our cruises. That's what you need, Anna, a good cruise with nothing to do but rest and eat and dress up three times a day. And go to the hairdresser, and the masseur, and maybe do a wee bit of Keep-Fit, ready for the next meal. And the officers dance with you. James is past it, poor lamb. And . . .' She saw the tears running down Anna's cheeks. 'What have I said now?'

'It's not you, Nancy, it's Jean. She's with me, morning, noon and night. She's asking why didn't I help her when she needed me . . .'

Nancy got up and put her arms round her sister, cradling her head against her pink Angora bosom. Her pearls pressed into Anna's cheek. 'You can't blame yourself,' she said. 'And another thing. You can't go on being selfish. You've made that man of yours miserable, sending him off to Barcelona without you. You know you had trouble in that department before.' Anna pulled back in surprise. She sneezed in Nancy's face.

'Sorry! It's the Angora. Fancy you bringing up that business about Maria Roig after all that time! That was

288

only one episode. It was in nineteen hundred and sixty-two for goodness' sake! And besides, he's got Hal with him.'

Nancy was unrepentant. 'He's another of the same kind. He's got those eyes. What Wendy calls sexy eyes. But don't start me off about Wendy! That's quite another story.'

'Van likes her.'

'I'm sure she does. Van's past leaves a lot to be desired, if you cast your mind back.'

Anna's tears came afresh. She felt them hot and scalding on her cheeks. 'If you've come here to pick holes in my family you would have been better to have stayed away. You're just like Jean. She used to quarrel with me like mad, hurling insults.'

Nancy went back to her chair, produced a minute handkerchief edged with lace and dabbed at her eyes. 'I don't allow myself to cry like you.' She put the handkerchief away. 'But don't you think *I* miss Jean? She was my sister too, though sometimes you wouldn't have thought it. You were like a double act, leaving me out. I know how you feel, losing her. But when you said to me just now, that I was just like her, my heart gave a wee jump, I don't mind telling you.'

'A wee jump?' Anna repeated the words. She dried her eyes with a much bigger handkerchief. Her head ached, but not so badly as before. The despair was not so profound.

'That's what I said.' Nancy raised her chin. 'I was always jealous of what was between you. You left me out. Oh, I know you didn't mean to, but that closeness; well, I couldn't compete. That was why I grabbed James when he proposed to me, even although he was a lot older. I wanted that closeness. But maybe if you and I, Anna, well, even row together, just sometimes, it might make you miss her a wee bit less, and gradually, just gradually, mind you, I could – not take her place, I know it will never be like that – but maybe kind of . . . fill the gap for you.'

'Oh, Nancy.' She was bereft of words, searched around. 'You know I've always thought you were so . . . dainty, and . . . nice, and I've always admired you, how you give those big dinners and how you . . . organize James, now that he's older.'

'He's ill as well as old,' Nancy confessed. 'I don't talk about it much, but I want to make his life as happy as I can.'

'You've always done that.'

'I try.' She nodded her head decisively. 'Would you like to go down town with me for a wee change? We could have a spot of lunch at Fullers?'

'You know I hate Fullers – all those chattering women with their fancy hats,' and, seeing her sister's face fall, 'I could drive you out to Drymen, to the hotel. We could have a drink as well.'

'I'm not so keen on drinking during the day.'

'Neither am I. But this time maybe. What do you say?'

'Well, we've had our wee quarrel.' She smiled at Anna and looked delightful, pink and perfumed, as she shuffled her feet into her high heels and stood up, wobbling a little. Her silver fox cape was too heavy for her, but if it had been made of lead she would have worn it since it had cost the earth.

'Yes,' Anna said, smiling back at her, 'it's done me a power of good.'

She drove Nancy swiftly out of Glasgow to Loch Lomond and on to Drymen, listening to her rambling on about Gordon's children and their prowess in everything mental and physical. 'I'm sure Gordon's faithful, but he's a good-looking young man although I say it as shouldn't, and with the position of importance he has in the city, there will be plenty of women angling after his favours. I've told Wendy she should stop him choosing such good-looking typists, but she goes off on those jaunts on her own leaving him to organize everything, run the house, with adequate help, I know, and even take the children to Arran! It's not good enough.'

'They say it's good for married couples to spend some time apart,' Anna volunteered, 'keeps them from becoming stale.'

'We were all taught to put husbands first.' Jean hadn't. Was it remorse which had made her walk into Wigtoun Bay? 'He's always wanted her to go to the golf club with him at Lamlash, like the other wives.' Like the obedient ones. 'He doesn't like being teased about Wendy not being there.'

'Wait till she writes her first travel book and then he'll be able to boast about her.'

'I'm sure he'd rather she played golf with him. It's not suitable for the wife of a prominent city architect to take the limelight. She should know her place.'

'She takes after her father. Didn't he go off on his yacht to France, leaving Mrs Armour?'

'Yes, but he's a man! And he had a crew. She hikes! And sometimes she hires a guide, a native, half-naked, judging by her snaps. Water-colours is one thing, and I gave that up years ago, but traipsing about the world in shorts is another!'

Anna laughed, the first time she had laughed since Jean died. 'You sound like Mother! Remember the lectures she used to give us when Daddy was driving us to see great-aunt Jessie at Kirkcudbright? "Watch how you sit on your pleats, *gerls*!" Our camel coats neatly folded in the boot?' How happy, how carefree the past seemed.

'And that time they took us to Portpatrick Hotel, and Daddy had to dance with us each in turn because nobody else asked us? And the Christmas dinner we had in the Selkirk Arms to spare Aunt Jessie?'

'So cosy, looking back, the waitresses in their black and white, the starched tablecloths, Burns's poem on the wall, Daddy, beaming on his brood . . .' They stared at the past together. 'And now they've all gone, Mother, Father and great-aunt Jessie. And Jean.' She could say that, just.

'She enjoyed that house of great-aunt's. Even before she married John.'

'Yes, she craved solitude. She's left it to Van.'

'I know. She and Wendy get on well. Maybe she'll invite them all in the summer. And maybe she'll persuade Wendy to give up this nonsense.'

'Maybe she'll encourage her to go on with it. You know Van.'

'Yes, she gave you a time of it too.'

'Yes, she did,' Anna agreed meekly. One wee quarrel was enough for the time being. And there was no doubt about it, Nancy was the only one left to quarrel with, now that Jean was gone. 'I'm glad you came to see me today,' she said. 'We must do this more often.'

'Wait till you see what the lunch is like. I heard that place has gone off lately. We might have done better in Fullers.'

'Yes, we might.'

Family.

Thirty-two

They were watching television about eight o'clock when Van said, 'I think it's started.' Anna had arrived a week ago for the event, as they called it, and one glance at Van made her get to her feet. Her practicality had returned. It was eight months since Jean's death, and the approaching birth had helped her to come to terms with it. A new life to replace her.

'You help her to get ready, Hal,' she said. He was bending over Van. 'I'll tell Sam. He's in his room.' She went swiftly upstairs, relieved that at last things were happening. But not half so relieved as Van must be, she thought. She remembered how interminable the last few days always seemed. Sam looked up from the floor where he was sprawled when he saw his grandmother.

'You ought to be in bed, young man,' she said. And then, 'Guess what? The baby's coming. Daddy's taking Mummy to the hospital.' She saw the fear in his eyes.

'Will she get there in time? One of the boys at school told me he was born in a taxi!'

'Fame at last,' Anna said. 'Yes, she'll be there in time, and she's going in Daddy's car. Run down and wish her luck.'

Anna had taken like a duck to water to the regime in the Purvis household, utter frankness. When she thought of her mother's coyness about birth, and how

293

it was a taboo subject in the Clevedon Crescent household, she was only relieved that she hadn't had to resort to subterfuge with Sam. He was quite knowledgeable for nine years of age, more so than she had been when Mish, her first-born, had arrived. And Ritchie had been like a quivering jelly that night in Kirkcudbright, unlike Hal who had all the air of a gynaecologist at times.

Each generation is edged forward by its children, she thought, we are eternally having to adapt, to shift our sights. She remembered when Van had rung her from London over nine years ago and said, 'Mum, I'm pregnant.' That hadn't been an edging forward, that had been a leap. She was proud of the fact that it had only taken her a few seconds to make it. And I must hand it to my mother, she thought. She took it on the chin too. She might have criticized Wendy and Gordon's shotgun wedding, but Van's baby out of wedlock had been sacrosanct.

She heard Hal's voice from the hall. 'We're off, Anna.' She ran downstairs and found a bulky Van with Hal's arm round her. Sam was beside them, struggling with her case. Anna kissed her.

'It's not as if it's the first time, Van. You're a seasoned performer.'

'As long as I don't forget my lines.' Her smile was cut off while they waited for the contraction to pass.

Anna shut the door when she and Sam had waved them off in the car. 'What do you say if you and I have a little kitchen feast?' she suggested.

'Good idea.' His smile wavered, but he followed her eagerly enough to the kitchen. Anything which delayed his bedtime was a bonus. He sat at the table while Anna made cocoa and toasted teacakes. 'The contractions were coming regularly,' he said. 'Daddy said he was sure she'd be all right.' At what stage had he eased himself into calling Hal 'Daddy'? she wondered. Perhaps it was peer pressure, or was it to assert his rights before the new arrival?

'Of course she will. They're good in hospitals, and besides Mummy works in the one she's going to. She'll get special attention.'

'I would like to work in a hospital,' he said, when Anna had put his mug and plate in front of him. 'It's in the family.' He attacked his teacake, putting it down again to lick his fingers covered with oozing butter.

'Do you mean as a nurse?'

He laughed uproariously. 'Grandma! I don't want to wear a fancy hat! Or an apron! That's for ladies. I mean, as a doctor!'

'Well, that would be pretty good,' she said consideringly. 'A change from painters and architects. And then when Grandpa and I got old and doddery we could call in Dr Purvis who would prescribe some wonderful medicine which would make us feel all right again. Where do you intend to set up practice? Kirkcudbright? There's Sarah's Alastair, Dr Campbell.'

'And there's Uncle John, the one who died. He was a doctor.'

'Yes, your great-uncle. Alastair would probably take you into the practice. Have another teacake. It's home-made strawberry jam.'

'Thanks.' He was so grown-up, poor lamb, she thought. She refrained from cuddling him. 'No, it would be Glasgow, without a doubt. I'm going to study there. Grandpa showed me the University once, up on the hill. He said it was handy for your house.' His face was earnest, and jammy round the mouth. 'Do you think Mummy will be all right?' He put down his teacake. Then she did cuddle him.

'Of course she will. She's been well all the time. Before

you know it you'll have a little sister or a little brother.'

'It'll take an awful lot of looking after.' His voice trembled.

'Only when it's a baby. What about going upstairs now and getting into bed. We'll skip bath tonight. A cat's lick will do.'

'Oh, Grandma, you and Grandpa say such funny things! A cat's lick!' His tongue came out and rapidly cleaned up the home-made strawberry jam round his mouth.

Anna sat up when she had tucked Sam in. She wanted to sit and think and wish her daughter well. She seemed to be prescient because she was tired. She saw into the future, Sam, a strapping young man of eighteen arriving at Clevedon Crescent to live with them and attend the University. She saw him lighting their lives with his youth and laughter.

Mish, too, had boarded with Granny Rose when he went to the Art School there. And Mother and Bessie had been charmed by him. 'A man in the house,' they had said.

What a source of strength he must have been to Karin when Benjy had been abducted by that patient of hers. Always calm. Karin, as a mother, career woman or not, would need his support. And he had never criticized her working, nor leaving Benjy in the care of that kindly girl, Ruth, who was, nevertheless, not too bright in the upper storey.

Both children settled in their married lives, looking to the future. Gave Ritchie and herself a future too. Because there was no doubt about it, something had happened to her when Jean died. She would never be the same Anna . . .

But life went on, as everybody assured her, with its patterns, always patterns.

She saw Mish and Karin arriving at Christmases with their children, Hal and Van with theirs, Nancy with James, or in ten years' time would Nancy be alone? Gordon with his children, with or without Wendy. Wendy was an enigma, a free spirit. And she and Ritchie, beaming and welcoming them all in the oak-panelled hall of the house she loved so much.

'God,' she prayed, because she was at low ebb at four o'clock in the morning. 'Don't take Ritchie away from me. You have had your dues with Jean.'

At half-past four the telephone rang and it was Hal without a trace of weariness in his voice because of the joy. 'She's fine, Anna. A little girl. They both look beautiful. And Van says I've to tell you, we're calling her Jean.'